Crossed Circuits

SCI-FI SHORT STORIES

VOLUME I

GAGE AXTIN

BLUE M PUBLISHING - CHICAGO

Library of Congress Cataloging-in-publication data
Name: Gage Axtin
Title: *Crossed Circuits*
Sci-Fi Short Stories: Volume I

Description: First edition | Blue M Publishing (Paperback), Chicago, IL [2018] | Contents: Crossed Circuits | Summary: A collection of sci-fi short stories that tell of technology and its effects on people. | Audience Note: Recommended for readers seventeen and older | Language Note: no offensive language.
Identifiers: ISBN 978-1-945385-13-1 (Paperback)
Subjects: LCSH: sh85118629 science fiction| BISAC: FIC028040 | GSAFD: 00000cz a2200037n 45 0 155 Classification: LCC PZ 370-380 | DDC 813-55/--dc23

by Gage Axtin
Contents: Multiple Parts | ISBN 978-1-945385-13-1 (Paperback)

Printed in the United States of America
www.blueMpublishing.com
Book Cover Design by Allendorf-Vignere

Blue M Publishing
19 S. Stough, Suite 100
Hinsdale, IL

CONTENTS

Book Summary 7

Deducts 9

Online Ordering 17

    Part I 17

    Part II 21

The Number 23

    Part I 23

    Part II 28

Brain Drain 31

    Part I 31

    Part II 35

    Part III 39

    Part IV 45

    Part V 53

Child's Play 57

    Part 1 57

    Part II 58

    Part III 61

    Part IV 62

    Part V 64

    Part VI 65

    Part VII 66

Stairway to Heaven 67

    Part I 67

    Part II 70

Part III 78

Archeology Dig 85

Reset 89

Part I 89

Part II 91

Part III 94

Part IV 97

Part V 101

Social Etiquette 107

Paired for Life 115

Part I 115

Part II 121

Part III 124

The Service 127

Plan A or B 137

Part I 137

Part II 139

Part III 141

Part IV 144

Part V 150

HyperLink 151

Part I 151

Part II 155

Part III 158

Part IV 160

Part V 164

Part VI 166

Part VII 167

Part VIII 169

Soul Control 172

Part I 172

Part II 176

Part III 180

Part IV 184

Twenty-five 186

0025 186

1025 190

2025 192

3025 196

Olympics 2.0 199

Part I 199

Part II 201

Part III 205

Part IV 207

Part V 212

Part VI 218

Tattooed 221

Part I 221

Part II 226

Class Struggle 233

A Modern & Civilized Society 241

Part I 241

Part II 243

Deep Freeze 249

Part I 249

Part II 252

Part III 254

Part IV 257

Part V 259

Part VI 262

Part VII 265

Part VIII 268

O'Malley's 275

Part I 275

Part II 278

Part III 282

Part IV 285

Part V 287

Author 293

Blue M Publishing 293

Crossed Circuits II 293

BOOK SUMMARY

This is not merely a book of science fiction short stories. It's about sci-fi stories that tell of the impact of technology on the human condition. As with all things, there are repercussions of creating, manufacturing, developing, implementing and using technology. For some things, the results are good; for others, they are not. Furthermore, in some cases, the results are good for some and not for others.

Whichever the outcome, these short stories consider the opportunities and the inherent limitations of technology. Where science and human beings fail to integrate well, you will often find crossed circuits.

*****

CROSSED CIRCUITS

DEDUCTS

The black numbers came fast and furious, whipping up on the screen like the rolling price on a gasoline pump - only going down, not up. Soon the digits descended past zero and instantly turned red, blinking on and off as a warning.

"Your balance is now negative!" said the measured, robotic voice.

Dirk sighed and shook his head. "How in the hell could that happen?" he exclaimed.

"What's wrong?" asked Trish, his girlfriend of four years.

"It's my balance. It's negative now," he answered.

"What have you been doing, then?" she asked, as she picked up her extra-dry martini with the three green olives still skewered to the toothpick.

"Nothing! I haven't done anything!"

"You must have done *something* or you wouldn't have gotten the deducts like that. How many did you get?" she asked.

"Four hundred twenty-five," he said moanfully.

"*Wow*! You must have really screwed something up. They got you either way, didn't they?"

Dirk didn't answer. He was too pissed-off.

"Why don't you have another martini with me," said Trish. "It will help you settle down a bit? You've been working too hard. You need to relax more."

They sat at their favorite bar on stools that made Trish's red, stiletto heels dangle some foot and a half off the tile floor. The bar was modern, made of glass block with reflective lights embedded inside that came-on based on the moods of the patrons sitting there. If they were laughing, the lights would be pinks and yellows; shouting, they would be reds and oranges; quiet and smiling – greens and purples; and calm and sad – blue. Behind the bar was a solid wall of mirrors, reflecting the customers' faces and moods back at themselves.

There was no bartender. All drinks were prepared by voice command and mixed by machines below the surface of the bar. When ready, the drinks magically appeared, rising-up inside glass tubes before a single glass pane pushed the drink through an opening in the top of the bar, right in front of the customer. The first time this happened, the customer would *oooh* and *ahhh*, and the lights in the glass blocks would glow green and purple, if not pink and yellow.

Dirk ordered his martini the way he liked it, and within thirty seconds, the v-shaped glass came up through the glass tube and pushed to the surface of the bar right in front of him. As soon as the glass stopped moving, his wristmeter vibrated, applying fifty deducts to reduce his account balance.

"I just think the entire thing is ridiculous," Dirk said, taking a sip. He had already had two martinis that evening and this was his third.

"What was it? What did they nail you for?" asked Trish.

"All I was doing was chewing gum."

"You're not supposed to do that in public," said Trish. "You should know that!"

"Yeah, but I didn't think I was anyplace close to a cam."

"The cameras are everywhere."

Dirk took another sip and then pulled an olive off his toothpick. He started to just shove it in his mouth, but instead he tossed it in the air intending it to find its mark. However, it missed and fell to the white, ceramic tile, skidding across the floor like a hockey puck on ice.

"*Shit!*" he shouted, looking around for the misguided pimento.

"Twenty deducts," announced his wristmeter, barking at him.

"What the hell!" Dirk shouted again.

"Twenty deducts," said his meter once more.

"Would you stop already?" said Trish, grabbing his arm. "Do you want to bankrupt yourself? You know you can't swear in public."

"You can't do anything anymore," said Dirk. "It's those sons-of-bitches in City Hall who are doing this to us."

"Thirty deducts," said the wristmeter.

"Why is it thirty?" Dirk asked.

"Because you include City Hall in it that time," Trish answered. "Dirk, I think it's time to go. Let's just go home."

Dirk finished his martini, and they walked out of the bar. Their car was parked only a few blocks away, and Dirk summoned it on his cell phone. It arrived and picked them up, opening the doors automatically upon arrival.

"Home," said Dirk, sitting back in the seat, "and hurry."

The car sped off, entering the highway and quickly reaching speed before leveling off.

"I said hurry," said Dirk, now grumpy.

"Dirk, don't, you'll only ..." began Trisha.

"Override executed," answered the voice on the car, and it increased its speed.

"Forty deducts," said his wristmeter, triggered as soon as the car went over the posted speed limit.

"I don't care," said Dirk. "Add another three hundred credits," he said.

"Three hundred credits added from your bank account. Your current balance is positive forty-five credits," said his wristmeter. "You only have two hundred credits left in your bank account."

"That's all you have in your bank account?" asked Trish.

"I get paid later this week. I'm fine."

"But if you don't cover a deduct within twenty-four hours, you will incur additional deducts, right?"

"Yeah, I know."

"And after forty-eight, they can come to your house and arrest you."

"Yes, yes! I know all that. Now leave me alone!" shouted Dirk.

The rest of the trip to their home was quiet until they reached their high-rise condominium downtown. The car elevator opened and swallowed their car before closing again and taking them up to the top parking level. There, it opened to let them out.

Pulling into his reserved spot, Dirk got out and plugged in the car to the outlet.

"Ten deducts," said his wristmeter. "And, with the new ordinance, there is another ten deducts for the utility tax."

"Great," said Dirk, sarcastically.

Riding up the elevator to their suite, Trish said, "Are you all right now?"

"Yeah, I'm better. I just get tired of all the cams and all the deducts – for this and that and the other. I'm nickeled and dimed all day long. Someone is constantly picking my pocket. At the end of the day, what do I have? Nothing. I have no savings left. I hardly make enough to go out and get a drink at the bar. And that doesn't even count the daily deducts they take out of my paycheck. I get paid two hundred credits a day, and at five o'clock, I hear this 'one hundred ten deducts' message. They take more than half of what I make for taxes for god's sake."

"I know. But look at all the things they give you: free education, free healthcare, free telephone, and they pay for your funeral when you die."

"Lovely," said Dirk, "I can't wait to collect on that last one."

"But really, Dirk. We're lucky. Most countries don't do that. They make their people pay for all that stuff."

"Yeah, but their taxes are a lot less, and they are generally much happier."

Trish shook her head. "Let's not argue about it. Let's just go up and have a nightcap before we go to bed. Okay?"

They got to their condo, and Trish made him one of her olive-rich martinis – five on a pick -- bringing it to him on the couch. Dirk finally smiled and took her beverage offering, sinking deeply into the white, leather couch in their fifty-third-floor pad. *He didn't need another martini, but then again, why would it hur?* he thought.

"The view is nice, isn't it?" Trisha asked, snuggling up to him and staring out over Lake Michigan.

Dirk took a sip and smiled. "Yeah, it's really nice to take advantage of the view once in a while."

But just as they were looking out at the twinkling lights of the city, the blinds on the windows began to close.

"What's going on?" Trish asked.

"*Shit*!" said Dirk, once again annoyed.

"What is it now? Did you forget to pay the viewing bill last month?" she asked.

"I must have," said Dirk.

"You'd better pay the meter now, before they close all the way. You know it's another twenty deducts if you have to make them reset the system," she said.

Dirk glanced at his wristmeter, which showed him at only twenty-five credits.

"Yeah, you're right. How long do you want to look at the lake?" he asked, trying to figure out how much to pay. "I only have twenty-five left before I have to transfer more in."

Trish looked at him. "I just can't believe for all the money you pay for this condo that you have to pay to look at the lake out there. Maybe we should just let it go this time."

Dirk's face contorted, as if she had said something blasphemous. "Not pay? Are you out of your mind?"

"Yeah, so we have to pay a reset charge later. It would still save us ..." she started.

"Well, if we don't pay it now, then the first thing that would happen would be the blinds you see there," he said, pointing to the series of white louvres that were embedded between the panes of glass in the building, "will swivel closed. We won't get *any* light in here at all during the daytime either. I can live with no view at night, but no light during the day? I don't think so."

"It's up to you," she moaned, lying back in the sofa, suddenly not interested in anything they might do – then or later.

Dirk turned his wristmeter and touched the screen, sending the payment in for the blinds to remain open. Then, he transferred more credits from his bank account to his wristmeter to cover anything else he might need that night or the next. Now he was out of credits in his bank account. It would be another week before he would be paid again from his work. So, he'd have to be careful with what he did, said and thought about.

"What about your utilities? Your property taxes? All the other things. Are you all caught up on those too?" asked Trish.

"Yeah, we're good. No worries. Let's just enjoy the evening," he said, putting his arm around her.

Dirk turned on the holographic television, and the 3-D image of a wicked business tycoon sitting behind his massive, office desk appeared in the center of the floor in front of them. The show was about corporate greed and a pair of wealthy business owners in a feud over a patent that would help patients at a hospital with a certain disease recover from their illness.

"This is just terrible," said Trish, watching the show. "How could people be so selfish - only thinking of themselves and accumulating money at the expense of others."

It was then that the lights went out.

"What happened?" she asked, startled at the blackout.

"Oh, that happens now and again. Don't worry, they'll come back on soon," said Dirk.

But when the lights didn't come back on, Trish grew worried. "Do you have any candles?" she asked.

"No!" her boyfriend said boldly. "We aren't allowed to burn candles in the condo. There's a two hundred deduct for that. That's a big no-no."

"For one candle?"

"Yeah."

"Then, what are we supposed to do?"

"Well, I can pay one hundred credits to get electricity from the backup generator in the building," said Dirk.

"We can't go without power," said Trish.

Dirk punched in his payment for the backup power, and his account dropped instantly on his wrist meter to a black ten. "There," he said, "that should keep us going for a few hours.

Together, they settled back into the sofa, watching as one of the billionaires threatened to alter the life-saving drug. He told his partner he would dilute it to make more money, but the partner refused.

"But the patients will die!" shouted the business partner.

"Why should I care?" said the other.

Trish reached into her purse and pulled out a small silver case, looking over at Dirk. "Do you want some?" she asked.

But before Dirk could answer, she had opened the tin, exposing the contents: four perfectly-rolled joints.

"No!" Dirk shouted. He quickly looked at his wristmeter. The number dropped like a stone - falling from ten to negative twelve hundred - blinking in big, bold red numbers.

"What happened?" she asked, surprised.

"I just hit with over a thousand deducts!" he shouted at her. "Thanks!"

"How?" she asked.

"They can see everything of course."

"Even in here?"

"They have cameras all over the place. The only place they aren't supposed to put a camera is in the bedroom or the bathroom. But most of us believe they still do that too. I've gotten deducts for things we do there."

"No!" she shouted.

"Yeah! Absolutely!"

Fed up, Dirk took off his wristmeter and threw it on the floor. "I've had it with that stupid thing!" he yelled.

It was then that another message flashed across his wristmeter.

> **Message: You have exceeded your allowable negative credits. Furthermore, you have caused damage to your unit. Someone will be in touch with you shortly.**

"What's this?" Dirk said, picking up his meter and looking at the message.

"What?" Trish asked, wondering what the message said.

"I thought I had forty-eight hours to make good on my deficit."

"I did too. Why? What does it say?"

"It says that someone will be contacting me," said Dirk.

Trish looked at the message and she was shocked. "Oh my god!" she said. "I've heard about those messages. You've damaged your unit? Dirk, this isn't good. They can put you away for a long ..."

All of a sudden, there was a knock at the door.

"This is Social Control. Please open your door."

Dirk's face drained.

"What should we do?" he asked Trish.

Trish could only shrug her shoulders. "I don't know!"

Dirk got up and went to the door. As soon as he opened it, the door flew open, and two men rushed in, grabbing him and forcing his arms behind his back. Then, they asked him, "Are you Dirk Tillerman?"

"Yes," he answered, grimacing.

"You're under arrest for violation of Penal Code Section 4.5.2 of the Deduct and Credit Control Act of 2059," said the man, yanking on Dirk's arms and attaching the magnetic cuffs.

"But it hasn't been two days yet!" screamed Dirk. "I have forty-eight hours to make good on my balance!"

"No!" said the officer, gruffly. "City Hall passed a law last night making it a crime to have a negative balance for more than one hour."

"What? One hour! That's ridiculous!" shouted Dirk. "It hasn't even been that long!"

"Twenty deducts," said his wristmeter, which was still lying on the floor.

Dirk went to stomp on the meter, but his shoe missed.

"You know it will cost you another thousand deducts if you destroy your meter," said the officer. "Now, let's go!"

The two men pushed Dirk out the door. It slammed auspiciously behind them.

Trish stood in disbelief at what had just happened. *Wow*, she thought. *What's the world coming to?*

She sat back on the couch and turned off the television. "So, much for a nice evening," she mumbled to herself.

It was then that her own wristmeter went off.

"What now?" she said.

"Fifty deducts," blared her wristmeter.

She looked at the screen, shaking her head. "For what?"

"Aiding and abetting a criminal," the screen read.

*****

Online Ordering

Part I

"Here is the list we give all prospective parents," said the doctor, handing the young couple what looked like a wine list used at a fancy restaurant. "You will notice that there are multiple pages. We just ask that you take it home and go over it together. Both of you must agree on every question before we can move your request any further down the channel. Do you understand?"

"Yes," said Ray, looking over at his partner. "Jack and I have been hoping to have children of our own, but we've disagreed on all the particulars. There are several labs in town, but you seem to have the best selection. This will help."

"Good," said the doctor. "Now, you only have twenty-four hours left before your petition expires. You'll need to review this quickly and then go online with your retinal scans to confirm your selection. If you don't respond by tomorrow, you'll go back to the end of the line again."

"Don't worry," said Jack. "We don't want to start over again. It took us three years to get to this point. We're not going to make the same mistakes we did last time."

Ray and Jack went home, and after dinner Ray pulled out the questionnaire. "Are you ready to go over this?"

"Yeah, let's do this," said Jack.

Ray poised the electronic pen over the top of the questionnaire tablet and began.

"This says that we must complete the following questionnaire in accordance with the ... yadda, yadda, yadda ..." he muttered, skipping over much of the legalese. "Okay, here's where the questions start: One, Do we want to have a boy or a girl or a mid or a Q? There's also a Herm or a Cross. What do you think?"

"I thought we decided on a Mid, right? I mean, that gives the kid more options later on. It can decide once it starts school and mingling with other children. It gives them time. Isn't that what we thought?" said Jack.

"Yeah, so this one is a *Mid*," said Ray, marking the box with the pen.

"Question two. Hair color."

"We said red," said Jack.

"Yes, but we also discussed blonde, like my mother's."

"But I wanted it to be like my grandmother's," said Jack. "We have a long tradition in my family of having red hair. It's been passed down for generations. I just couldn't handle it if we broke that tradition now."

"Hair color - red," said Ray, marking the box. "They also have the option for auburn red and scarlet red. Two other possibilities are copper or ruby?"

"Let's go with copper. I think that would be nice."

"Curly or straight? Wavy or frizzy?"

"Not frizzy. I don't like frizzy. How about wavy?" said Jack.

"I'd like curly better. Can we go with curly?"

"No, I like wavy. I don't like a lot of curls. Again, the tradition in the family is more wavy than curly."

Ray sighed. "All right then, wavy," he said putting another check on the chart. "Eyes," asked Ray, going on.

"Brown," said Jack.

"But blue would go better with red hair," said Ray.

"Then, green. Green would be better with red hair."

"And lips? Full, thin, medium?"

"Full."

"Build and height are next. If we're going with a Mid, then we shouldn't make it stocky or too slim. We should make it medium, so it can go either way. Plus, should it be tall or medium in height?"

"I think it should be tall and slim. That would go with whatever gender it decides later," said Jack.

Ray looked over at his partner, who was tall and slim.

The two went through the rest of the physical characteristics before moving on. They were only on page eight of sixty-three pages when two hours had already passed.

"Jack, we're not going to get through this unless we hurry," said Ray.

"But this is important," said Jack. "We can't just rush through this thing."

"All right, so the next question is Left- or Right-handed?"

"Right," said Jack.

"Or ambidextrous?" said Ray. "That's an option too."

"I still like Right. It's what I am," said Jack, forcefully.

"Now, we get to talents. Athletic? Musical? Theatric? It has a whole list of things here," said Ray.

"I want it to be an athlete," said Jack.

"But I told you several times, it's more important that they be book smart too."

"Okay, athletic first and book smart second," said Jack.

"IQ."

"As high as possible," said Jack.

"They already assume you'd say that. No, here they tell you that it depends on your other selections as to what the IQ will turn out to be. They will guarantee us the IQ will not be below 120 but also caution us that it is unlikely to be above 140. Then, it asks if we want it book-smart, mechanically smart or street-smart?"

"Definitely street-smart," said Jack.

"But if they're book-smart, they can get a better job."

"Yeah, but street-smarts will last you your whole life," said Jack.

Even though that didn't make any more sense than Ray's point, Ray dutifully made the note on the tablet.

"Semi-sociable? Extraverted? Introverted? There are so many choices here!" said Ray.

"Extraverted," said Jack.

Ray finally smiled. "I agree," he said. "I can live with that."

"Now, what about its likes and dislikes," said Ray. "Movies types. It's got horror, romance, comedy, documentary, suspense, thriller ..."

"Really? We have to pick what kind of movies it will like?"

"I don't know. That's what it has here," said Ray. "And what kind of food -- seafood, vegetarian, or ethnic."

"What about vegan? I want them to be a vegan," said Jack.

"I'll write it in," said Ray, rolling his eyes. "Question 341 asks what profession they should be good at."

"What are the options?"

"Teacher, engineer, lawyer, doctor, financier, nurse, architect, politician, economist, historian, computer tech ... heck, there are over a hundred listed here. I'm not going through all of them."

"Is there professional athlete?" asked Jack.

"Yeah, but it says it can't guarantee it will work out that way. There's a lot of demand for that and so few spots on the team rosters. You know how people pay extra to get their DNA sequencing tweaked to add more *juice* to their kid's chromosomes. It gives them an extra edge to get those jobs."

"Yeah, I'd heard that too. Okay, we can't afford anything more than what we're paying already. So, what do you think?"

"Lawyer or politician. They usually make out the best," said Ray.

"I'd say sports trainer, then," said Jack.

"What about specific numbers for height and weight?"

"I'd say at least six-six, and about 285. That should make it good for most athletic events," said Jack.

"What if it wants to be more of a girl and a boy?"

"Okay, then six feet, one-fifty to one-eighty."

"Skin color?"

"It should be the same as ours," said Jack.

Ray continued marking the sheet on this tablet until it was nearly three in the morning. Jack was already asleep on the sofa when Ray finished up. He looked over at his partner, ready to ask him if there was anything they'd forgotten, but Jack was already snoring.

Ray looked back down and clicked the ENTER button, and then SUBMIT. The little clock on the screen went around and around until a notice popped up. "Submission Accepted." Then, Ray turned off the mo and went upstairs to bed.

*****

PART II

9 Months Later

The message from the Lab appeared on their message board:

> **Ray and Jack:**
>
> **Your child has just arrived. Please stop by between ten and two tomorrow to pick it up. Make sure you refer to your information packet for all the things you will need for the care and feeding of your new addition to the family.**
>
> **Best of luck.**
>
> **Dr. J R Simpson**

Ray and Jack were eager to get to the clinic to pick up their child. If things worked out, they would be allowed to petition for another child within three years. Those were the rules. However, if there were any problems with this child during that time, they might find themselves unable to have any more.

"Are you excited?" asked Ray, looking over at his partner as the auto-car decoupled from the freeway.

"Of course I am," Jack answered. "How could I not be? This is going to change our lives, you know. They say your first child is the hardest. There are so many new things to deal with - diapers, sleepless nights, crying ... all those things."

"Yeah, but that's also what will be so great about it," answered Ray.

Jack just smiled.

The car drove itself along the state road and then slowed, turning up the narrow, black-topped entryway that led to the clinic complex. Magnolia trees lined the long drive, and although they weren't yet flowering, the large, closed bulbs signaled they were only a few days away.

Inside, the two new parents waited until one of the clinical nurses came out to greet them.

"You must be here to collect A183N," she said. "I hope you came up with a better name than that for it." She laughed. The men could tell it was a joke she told to everyone who came into the reception area. "Let's see, you ordered a Mid, is that right?"

"Yes," said Ray.

"And we've decided on the name Sydney," said Jack. "It was my grandfather's name, but it goes with any gender."

Ray only nodded, not smiling, as if he were used to his partner always getting his way.

"Oh, that's such a nice name," said the nurse. "Well, why don't you come back to the delivery room. Your child is waiting for you."

Ray and Jack followed the nurse through the double, swing doors and then past several rooms containing incubation tanks. Finally, they heard the high-pitched crying of newborns just ahead. They all seemed to be coming from the same large room.

"Wait here," said the nurse, with a grin. "I'll be back in just a moment. Just make yourselves comfortable."

She left while Ray and Jack sat in one of the well-cushioned, yellow chairs sitting in the waiting area.

"This is going to be so wonderful!" said Jack, almost unable to contain himself.

Within minutes they saw the nurse return with a small bundle. The white, hospital covering was wrapped tightly around the child, and they held their breaths as she drew near

"Your baby is the cutest thing," she raved. She held up the child and pulled back the wrap.

Ray looked at the baby as it was staring back at him. It was squirming and cooing as if it were the most contented child in the world. "Oh, it's adorable!" Ray said. "You're right. It is the most beautiful baby I've ever seen!"

Jack stared at the child in disbelief.

"Is something the matter?" asked the nurse.

"My god!" Jack cried. "I don't understand. That thing is absolutely hideous!"

The nurse looked up at both men and smiled. "I must say," she said, looking at Ray, "it's looks do seem to come from your side of the family."

*****

THE NUMBER

PART I

Jamie looked at the back of her hand. It was there ... it had always been there, or at least for as long as she could remember. When she had been a young girl, she hadn't thought much about it. It was like a birthmark or something - everyone had one someplace. In this case everyone had one of these too, except it was like something tattooed that could never be erased. It wasn't until she grew older that it and its constant reminder began to bother her. And now, it was even more troubling.

Married with a husband and one daughter — which was all that was allowed -- she and her family lived in the downtown area of one of the largest mega-cities in the country, if not the world. With a population of over fifty-million people, the city was dense, rising-up from the hot pavement with compact urban housing developments that crammed upwards of a hundred-thousand people into one building. It was a poor part of town, but then again, most areas of the inner city had become poverty stricken over the years.

Their apartment was a small, two bedroom, which was all they could afford on their two-income family earnings. Some families had been spawned with three parents and one child through innovative genetic fertilization. This had enabled the family to be licensed by the government to have four people per living quarters - three adults and one child. With three bread-winners, it was easier to make ends meet. Three- or as many as four-parent families were encouraged by the law, which gave such families two hundred additional credits toward an apartment rental. Those who managed this, lived in more-luxurious accommodations — those closer to the great lake that bordered the downtown area.

But Jamie, with her husband Jim and daughter Sam, lived in an apartment barely large enough to move around in. Jamie had been a teacher in the public city school before her job was eliminated and replaced by an AI or artificial intelligence robot. Most teaching jobs had been replaced that way. But through the last gasps of the teachers' union, they had still negotiated lucrative pensions, so money from her job kept coming even though she no longer worked.

As for Jim, he was a computer programmer for the U.S. Risk Management Department. The new bureau had replaced insurance companies to provide all citizens with insurance. Only a few years earlier, Washington had banned insurance companies altogether and replaced them with tax-payer funded insurance provided by the government – or rather, by tax payers. Costs had doubled, but no one cared as other people were paying for it. Jim's job was secure-- for now. He made sure that the automatic claims filed through the system kept getting paid. It didn't matter if they were legit or not, he was just supposed to keep the people happy by getting them paid.

As for Sam, she was only sixteen. After Jamie lost her job, she and Jim agreed that she should home-school their daughter to give her the best chance at an education. However, when many families began home-schooling, the government banned the practice, citing that the children weren't getting properly educated in the "right" things. Reluctantly, Sam had gone back to logging-in to her classes from her home computer and listening to the droning of the AI which parroted the state's position on how it said things were, rather than how things *actually* were.

Yet, for all these problems, Jamie found herself with one that made the others seem minor by comparison.

"Surely, they have to correct their mistake," said Jim, shaking his head as he looked at the number embedded deep into the tissue of his wife.

"We've been over this, Jim. My parents went to court when I was young and lost. There is nothing we can do," Jamie answered. "It just is what it is."

"I don't think we've tried everything. We need to hire a lawyer to get you out of this."

"Do you not remember what I told you about my parents?"

"Yes, but ..."

"No, Jim. I'm not bankrupting this family and jeopardizing my daughter's future because of me," said Jamie.

"What about some advocacy group? They've got them for dogs and for goldfish, for Christ's sake. I'm sure they've got them for people with your condition."

Jamie was just over five feet tall. With short-brown hair that curled around each ear, she had been a ball of energy since her youth. Although she excelled in almost everything she did, she and Jim had suffered several financial setbacks in their lives and in their marriage, resulting in their current situation.

Jim had been a member of the ruling political party for years, as had his father and mother before him. Jamie's parents had not been as active, so she benefited from Jim's political clout when they got married. However, Jim's father had made a tactical error which had cost him his status and his life.

Aligning himself with one of the most powerful people in the party, he thought he had secured his future and that of his family. But when the Supreme Leader, who controlled the economies and militaries of all the major first world nations, unexpectedly died - or was murdered - the vacancy was up for grabs. It was then that an internal, civil war began. In the end, Jim's family was on the losing end, with their benefactor was executed for high crimes and treason against the World State. Jim's father had paid a similar price.

As for Jamie, her family was relatively poor. They were not involved with the party, and, thus, didn't have the opportunities that others more connected did. Because of that, Jamie had suffered in a different way — her ability to right a wrong.

"We have to try," said Jim. "Your number doesn't make any sense."

"I know that. You know that. My parents knew that. It doesn't make any difference. The state controls the numbers, and what the state says goes — end of story."

Jamie looked down at her hand. The number was a painful reality of what lay ahead for her.

***

A few days passed, and Jim continued badgering Jamie about her number.

"I made some inquiries at work and someone told me about his lawyer who might be able to help us," said Jim.

Jamie gave him a nasty look. "I told you to give it up," she said.

"He's not expensive. In fact, he's free. He does this on the side, helping people like you who've gotten the raw end of the deal from the system. He says he sees this all the time — where the computers make mistakes."

Jamie shrugged her shoulders as she stood by the atomizer, waiting for the food to appear inside the chamber.

"So, we have a meeting with him tomorrow. He's only two stops on the tube. It's not far. It's worth a shot, Jamie. Come on. You have to try!"

"What time?" she asked, tired of fighting with him.

"After my shift. It's at six tomorrow."

"What about Sam?"

"She can take care of herself for one evening. It won't take long. We'll be home before seven."

The next night, Jamie met Jim in the attorney's office. It was in a very nice part of downtown where all the government agency buildings were. His office was on the 18th floor of a 235-floor building -- not exactly a model of success, but yet the building itself was very nice.

"Come on in," said Tyrone, motioning for them to enter his office.

The glass panel dissolved, letting them pass through the entrance before reenergizing to keep the room sound-proof and quiet.

Tyrone was middle-aged, and wore a tailored black jump-suit that was standard issue for higher-level government employees. Nice looking, with his dark, curly hair brushed back, Tyrone had the face of an old-fashioned football linebacker - a game long ago outlawed. His face was flat, with a large, expansive forehead and thick neck. His nose looked as if it had been broken before, but his smile was perfect - glistening brightly with perfectly-shaped teeth. With so many colored lenses around, it was impossible to tell whether his eyes were truly black or whether they were dyed that way to match his jump suit.

"Please, have a seat," Tyrone said cordially, gesturing toward the twin chairs on the other side of his desk. "Jim has been telling me about your situation, and I must tell you that you're not alone in this. There are many other people who share your same problem."

"Really?" asked Jamie.

"Yes. I've dealt with many of them. It seems the government is never perfect in anything it does. But you already knew that," he said, his eyes laughing.

"Yes, Tyrone. But what's most important is what you can do for us. We don't have a lot of money, and my wife is worried that this will bankrupt us," said Jim.

"I don't take a fee," said Tyrone, smiling. "You see, my mother had the same problem. That's why this strikes a nerve with me. I want to help people such as yourself."

"What is your success rate?" asked Jamie, pointedly.

Tyrone suddenly shifted in his chair, as if he were uncomfortable in the seat or uncomfortable with the question. "Well, that's not the point, is it?" he answered. "What is important is that we fight this thing."

"Your success rate *is* important," said Jamie. "If this can't be done, then I don't want to waste my time fighting it. I'd rather spend my time with my husband and daughter."

"I understand," said Tyrone, "but I think it's important not only to you, but to the thousands of others in the same boat. If all of you protested this injustice, then perhaps we could eliminate the entire system. It's just wrong."

"That will never happen," said Jamie. "It can't happen. There's too much at stake."

"That's what they want you to believe," said Tyrone.

"It's not true?" asked Jim.

"No. It's not."

"Then what's the reason behind it?" Jamie asked. "It's been going on for generations now."

"You're right, and it's about time it stopped," said Tyrone, the anger rising within him.

*****

PART II

"So, tell us what's going on," said Jim. "Why do you think the system can be changed?"

"It's a long story, but I'll try to keep it brief," Tyrone said.

It was then that Tyrone got up and walked to a cabinet on the far wall of his office. He pressed a button to open the doors, which slid effortlessly to each side, and then leaned-in to fiddle with some dials on a black-box machine that was built-in to the little closet. The machine was square with no discernable dials or readouts - only a series of colored lights and strips that wrapped around two of the sides. Tyrone took out a plastic card and pressed it against a flat space on one side. Suddenly, the machine vibrated and then all the lights turned green.

"There," said Tyron. "Now we can talk in private." Then, he walked to his minimalist desk chair, sat down and leaned back, putting his hands behind his head. "Let's see. Where was I? Oh, yes, about the number system."

"Okay," said Jim, "So, why is my wife's number so messed up?"

"Let me start by telling you how the system works," said Tyrone. "There is a massive computer complex just outside the city. It's buried three hundred feet below ground, and it's guarded more closely than most air force bases in the country. All told, there is a full brigade of soldiers with the most sophisticated weaponry stationed around the perimeter of the grounds to ensure no one gets in who is not authorized. Energy fields prevent access all around the facility, and anyone who tries to trespass is instantly incinerated. That's why they have all the danger signs posted everywhere -- they mean it!"

"But what are they hiding?" asked Jim.

"The algorithms - the way they generate the numbers, of course. Everyone wants to get in there and change their number - that's human nature. It doesn't matter. In fact, all the people who work there are flown in from other parts of the country every day. They don't want anyone to know who works there - otherwise, those people might be paid off to modify somebody's number."

"Has it ever happened? Has someone been able to pay someone to change their number?" asked Jim.

"Sure. It happens a lot. However, it depends on who's doing the asking. Those people with connections or a lot of money can sometimes get their number changed. No one finds out, of course; it's done on the sly. A lot of palms have to be greased, but it can be done. They even say some people at the very top have even had their numbers deleted from the system entirely."

"How much does it take?" asked Jim, hopeful.

Tyrone looked at the two of them and shook his head. "You couldn't make enough in one hundred lifetimes to come up with what's needed. Even to get your number moved down the list would cost you a lot. The going rate now is three million credits."

"Three million?" Jamie shouted. "That's more than we could make in three hundred years!"

"I know. It's ridiculous. So, we have to try other things."

"Like what?" asked Jim.

"Well, there is a hardship provision of the law that lets people petition based on the hardship it would cause their family," said the attorney.

"That sounds promising," said Jim, encouraged. "It *would* cause our family a lot of harm, as you can imagine."

Tyrone shook his head. "No, I'm afraid your hardship wouldn't be good enough."

"What? How can that be?" asked Jim, indignantly.

Tyrone looked at Jamie. "How old are you?" he asked.

"I'm fifty-two," she answered.

"And what's your number?"

"My number is ..." she paused and showed him the back of her hand.

The number on the back of her hand read:

    03-06-2358

Tyrone took her hand and tried to flatten out the skin which covered the surface and gave a translucent coating to the haunting number.

"Wow," he exclaimed. "I've seen some bad cases, but yours may be the worst."

"So, what about that hardship case?" asked Jim again. "Don't we have a shot at that?"

Again, Tyrone shook his head. "I still don't think it's enough. What about family ties? Do you have any with the current group in power?"

Jim shook his head. "My family used to, but not anymore, I'm afraid."

"What about a minority status or disability?"

"No."

"Is your daughter infirmed or disabled in any way?" asked Tyrone.

"No. Not that either," said Jim.

'Then it's hopeless," said Jamie.

Tyrone's eyes suddenly brightened. "But there is one thing. It's not legal, but it may be our best chance."

"What is it?" asked Jim.

The attorney wrote something down on a card and handed it to her. "I don't want to digitize this, as it may be intercepted, but you should go to this address. There is someone there who may be able to help you. Tell him, Tyrone sent you."

*****

BRAIN DRAIN
PART I

"Andrew, so nice to see you again. This is Dr. Maureau, and this is Dr. Stein. They are from the Bureau of Legacy Knowledge. You may have heard of them?" asked the strange woman who smoked a thin, brown cigarette in violation of every code section on the books. Yet, she seemed unconcerned and uncaring about the infringement.

"Hello, nice to meet you," said Andrew, looking them over. Yet, that is what he did - that was his job. He had always been very careful and observant in every interaction and more times than not those details had saved his life.

"You know why you're here, don't you?" asked the stern-looking woman, blowing an odd-shaped, smoke ring from her cigarette.

"Not really," said Andrew.

Andrew was only thirty-two, but he was part of a remarkable team of operatives known as Invisible SEALS or I-SEALS. This was the only group that was one step above the highly-regarded and lethal corp, known simply as SEALS - SEa, Air and Land – their bases of operation. The I-SEALS were impossible to find and liquidate. None had ever been killed or captured during an operation. And even though the unit had been in existence for over fifty years, only a handful at the top of the Pentagon were aware they existed.

Slightly taller than six feet, Andrew was solid muscle; with a body fat content of less than 8 percent, he was sinuous and sharply defined. But not only was he physically in superb condition, he was quick and agile, having honed his reflexes to respond almost instantly to influences around him. Dark haired with a square jaw and Romanesque nose, he had narrow, brown eyes that soaked in everything around him. On one side of his face, just below his right eye was a nasty scar about three inches long. He'd been asked many times what happened, but his only answer was "Got into a little disagreement."

"We have an opportunity for you," said the woman, still taking puffs on her cigarette. Of course, *having an opportunity* really meant *you are ordered to do this.* "Of course you familiar with the Extraction Program, yes?"

"Yes," said Andrew.

"Then you know it is a most-important program for the World Council. It means everything for the future or mankind." The woman stopped and then nodded to Dr. Stein who held a remote device. "Go ahead, Alvin. Roll the tape."

The lights went dark in the room, and the opposite wall lit-up like an enormous monitor. Pictures soon began flashing on the screen - a collage of several different people – their faces and group shots with others.

"This is Dr. Ian Fuechtenschneider," began Dr. Stein. "He's referred to as Dr. F for short. He's been involved in one of the most top-secret programs the World Council has been involved in. The topic is classified, of course, so we can't discuss the nature of it with you. However, what is important is that Dr. F is dying. He has an incurable form of brain cancer."

The face on the screen was that of a professorial-looking man in his early-to-late sixties. He wore round-tortoise-shell glasses that made his eyes appear large and distorted. His auburn hair was thick and wavy, flowing back across the sides of his head which, itself, was very long and narrow. The doctor's ears were also long with large, dangling lobes at the bottom that stuck out from his head in an unusual way. Yet, there was an intelligence in his dark, brown eyes - a richness and fullness that suggested he understood everything anyone had ever shown or said to him. He wasn't smiling in any of the photos. In fact, the poses were rigid and formal, as if they were taken for a government ID or other post.

"As you know," continued Dr. Stein, "we at the Ministry of Legacy Knowledge are interested in making sure that everyone abides by the protocols of the 2117 Legacy Knowledge Act requiring all persons who are terminally ill and those who are killed in any manner or means be taken to an Extraction Facility for processing. Those who die or are killed must be presented within six hours of death. Those terminally ill, must report as soon as they receive their diagnosis. This has been the law for several decades now. It has been an invaluable source of information for the government, generating incredible breakthroughs in the areas of physics, mathematics, chemistry, psychology and other hard sciences. By extracting and downloading all the memories of each person shortly before or after they die, we can put them into our super-computers and process them. Highlighting some things while disposing or storing others for future use, we have been able to further science more rapidly than ever in human history."

"Do you understand what we're doing?" asked the strange woman, now looking at Andrew.

"Uh, yes, of course. It's important to science ... what you're doing, that is."

"Yes ... very important," repeated the woman. "And in the case of Dr. F here, it is extremely important. You can understand why. A man of such knowledge and ability -- we must capture what he knows before he passes away."

"That makes sense," said Andrew, adjusting himself in his uncomfortable chair.

"However, it is unfortunate that Dr. F has gone missing," said Dr. Maureau, speaking up. "We don't know where he is right now, and his physician said he is likely to die within the next 24 to 48 hours. Therefore, we need you to find him for us quickly."

"I see," said Andrew, looking at Dr. F's face on the screen. "And when I find him? What then? Bring him to an Extraction Facility?"

"No. You must bring him here" said the woman. "He must be handled especially carefully. We can't entrust his extraction with just anyone at a facility. It must be handled only by our best technician."

The pictures now changed to a map. In the center was the outline of Europe with a flag sticking out of the World Council capital - Brussels. Then, a red line was shown magically moving from Brussels toward Berlin.

"We believe that Dr. F took a flight from here in Brussels to Berlin three days ago," said Dr. Maureau. "Then, after doing some business there – what, we don't know -- he left on another flight headed for Istanbul."

The line on the screen moved again from Berlin to Istanbul and continued following the path of the mysterious Dr. F.

"In Istanbul we lost him. His trail goes cold," said Dr. Maureau. "However, we have reason to believe that he obtained a fake passport while in Istanbul. It is possible that he flew out of the city yesterday and is heading to one of the following cities: Cairo, Marrakesh, or Johannesburg. We suspect that he is in Africa because no country in Africa has yet signed an extradition treaty with the World Council."

"But what if I find him and he's already dead?" asked Andrew. "Or he dies in Africa? I won't be able to return him to Brussels within the six hour window required for extraction, correct?"

Dr. Stein smiled. "Good observation, Andrew. Yes, they said you were quite smart. I can see that now."

Andrew wasn't sure how to take the doctor's remark, but continue listening.

Dr. Maureau lifted a stainless-steel case and placed it on the table. "This is a cryogenic chamber," he said. "You will take this with you in the event any of those things happen and you can't get him back in time for a proper extraction."

Andrew looked at the doctor uncomfortably, shifting his eyes back and forth from the doctor to the chamber. "So, you want me to ..."

"Yes. Return Dr. F's head in this cryogenic chamber," said the woman, still smoking the cigarette.

Andrew had done some rough things in his time, but nothing quite like this. It was one thing to kill someone or to kill many people if he had to. But removing someone's head, placing it in a frigid, transport container and smuggling it back into Brussels was something else.

"Is there a problem, Andrew?" asked the woman, grinding out her cigarette in the white ashtray next to her.

"Ah, no, no. Of course not."

"Then you will leave immediately to catch your flight to Istanbul. We have no assets there to help you. You will be on your own. Of course, this is a highly classified mission as are all of them as far as you are concerned."

"Yes, ma'am," said Andrew nodding.

"Oh, and Andrew?"

"Yes, ma'am?"

"You must take all necessary precautions to ensure that even if you are detained or arrested that no information about this is exposed. That includes the self-liquation kit. Do you understand?"

"Yes. I will take all necessary precautions," Andrew answered.

"Good. Then find Dr. F. We need his head back in Brussels as soon as possible," said the woman, lighting up another cigarette and blowing out the smoke that quickly permeated the room.

*****

PART II

The flight to Istanbul was uneventful, even though he was questioned several times about the nature of the cryogenic tank he carried with him. He was to tell anyone who asked that it was merely a biology chamber to transport plant samples back to his laboratory in Europe. He was to promise he would secure all necessary permits along the way before actually taking any plants out of a country.

Rushing through airport customs, he caught a taxi, telling the driver to take him to a part of town where Dr. F's cell phone use was last pinpointed. It was an area only used by poor merchants and shady businessmen, storing illicit goods or tainted, subpar materials used in the manufacturing of commercial goods made in Africa and Southeast Asia.

Getting out of the cab, Andrew compared the address on the building to that in his GPS unit: 15671 Erdemli Souk. It was an old, decrepit three-story structure with broken windows, crumbling stone walls, and stray dogs roaming the alleyways looking for food in trash bins. More than a few hundred years old, the dirty-brown exterior looked more ready for demolition than habitation.

Andrew climbed the littered staircase, avoiding the enormous black roaches which were scurrying to get out of the bright sunlight streaming in from the now-opened doorway. He pulled out his 9mm Glock pistol and held it comfortably in his hand - something he'd done thousands of times before. Working his way up the stairs, he paused when he thought he heard a door creak. *Could be the wind, but then again, there was no wind when I came inside*, he thought, analyzing things. Reaching the second floor, he found several office doors leading off from the wide landing point.

He glanced back at his GPS, switching to elevation mode to see if he was on the right floor. *One more floor*, he noted, seeing he needed to get to the third.

At the top of the third landing, there were only three doors, and one had a human shadow moving behind a frosted, pane-glass window embedded in the top third of the wooden door. Andrew approached quietly, but lowered his gun, hiding it behind the back of his black, leather jacket. Knocking on the door, he pushed it open and entered without forewarning or permission.

"Good morning," Andrew said, smiling, acting like a lost tourist or business merchant.

Before him was an old, bearded man wearing glasses that held a clip with monocle-like spectacles that were swiveled-up to his forehead. The man's short, white turban stood out prominently against his dark complexion and sunken, black eyes. He looked surprised by the intrusion but offered no resistance.

"May I help you?" the man asked nervously, in Arabic, taking off his examination glasses.

Andrew continued smiling. He glanced around the office noticing stacks of illegal passports heaped on desks, awaiting final tweaks. There were three other men busy looking over the booklets, studying them carefully for flaws.

"I'm looking for a passport," Andrew announced, matching the man's tongue by answering in Arabic. "Am I in the right place?"

The old man's eyes relaxed, and he grinned. "I believe you are, my friend. What exactly are you looking for?"

"I need a passport like the one you did for this man," said Andrew, taking out a picture of Dr. F and holding it up. "He said you did an exquisite job on his."

The old man now smiled even more broadly. "Of course. I'm the best forger here," he boasted without hesitation. "He had that long last name that I will never forget - Fuechtenschneider. Thank goodness we changed that to something more manageable for the passport."

"What did you change it to?" Andrew asked.

The old man laughed, the joke dancing in his aging eyes. "Oh, we had a good time with that, didn't we Yusuf?"

Andrew looked toward the back of the shop and saw another, younger man smile and raise his hand. The resemblance of the two men could only mean this was a family business and one that was very profitable.

"We gave him the name of Yurken - Ian Yurken. It has a good flow to it, don't you think?"

Andrew laughed. "Yes, very good, very good. And what country did you give him - the passport, I mean?"

"He wanted an American passport," said the man.

"American? Really? Those are very difficult to make, aren't they?"

"Yes, of course. But we have the capability and the machinery to do those too. We are well-funded here - we have a good business and good paying customers."

"Do you know where he was heading - where he was going?"

The old man thought for a moment, then, shaking his head he turned and yelled, "Yusuf, do you remember where Dr. F was going? My old mind isn't as good as it used to be. He might have said – I don't remember."

"Father," said the young man, "I believe he said New York."

"Ah, yes. New York. I believe it was New York City to be exact."

Andrew sighed. It was one thing to find a European in Cairo, Marrakesh or even Johannesburg. It was quite another to locate him in New York City, especially when he had less than two days to find him.

***

Andrew landed at JFK Airport in New York City and immediately went to the World Council Headquarters building, where the old United Nations building once stood. He had clearance at the highest levels within the government - even the World Council and showed his badge to the security guard, who motioned him over to the scanning machines. He punched in a twelve digit PIN and then let the scan trace his retina.

"Clearance granted," said a disembodied voice.

Hopping in a clear-glass cell, he heard another voice. "Elevator activated," before the cell whisked him down to the 93 floors down to the WC Vault.

Getting off the elevator, he passed through three more levels of security before entering an enormous, leaded computer room. There he pushed a special, silver fob into a computer port and typed in a series of codes.

Access Denied shot across his screen.

"What?" he muttered. "Damn thing." He punched it all in again. This time the message was: *Access Granted*.

"Give me all details on the projects supervised by Dr. Ian Fuechtenschneider, WC number 98R4506ST2."

"Ian Fuechtenschneider, world citizen number 98R4506ST2, born 2123, Berlin Germany. Attended Heidelberg University undergraduate, Polytechnique of Munich for his PhD in genomic sequencing and cloning.

"Projects under Dr. Fuechtenschneider include ..." The computer rambled on about the many projects on which he worked during his fifty years in research, but it was one of the last ones mentioned that caught Andrew's attention.

"Computer, repeat last entry," he said.

"Last entry. Legacy Knowledge algorithms used as primary storage facility for human memories. Completed last year. Recognized as a significant upgrade in capability from previous versions. Said to be able to extract nearly 97 percent of all data stored in human brain."

"So, what you're saying is that Dr. F's methods would be able to, say, extract virtually everything someone saw during their entire lifetime?"

"No, not just what the person saw, but also what they heard, touched, tasted and smelled. All sensations would be extracted from the brain," said the computer.

"Unbelievable," said Andrew. "That must be trillions of data points."

"The average human, during his or her lifetime of one hundred three years, would record an estimated 2.7 quadrillion data points of reference," said the computer.

"Where is all the data from extractions being stored?" asked Andrew.

"All data is housed in a complex in Bluffdale, Utah. It was once the National Security Agency data storage facility but was expanded significantly during the past several decades. The Utah Data Center is the largest building complex in the world -- three times the 6.6 million square feet of the Pentagon."

"How much data can be stored there?"

"I am unable to compute the number you are seeking," said the computer.

Well, at least I think I know where Dr. F is headed, he thought. *But if he's dying, why go there? What's there for him?*

*****

PART III

Andrew came from humble beginnings, unlike Dr. F, who grew up in a wealthy family steeped in a lineage of scholarly professors. Instead, Andrew grew up on a dairy farm in Iowa. His was one of the last free-range farms in the state before the local government confiscated it, claiming a public health issue. It charged that there was too much risk of milk contamination to allow them to operate, even though the family's nine-generation farm had never once had any recalls or alerts.

So, the family closed down and moved to St. Louis, where he attended St. Louis University. He struggled there, unable to focus on his studies as his family also struggled to make ends meet. After his first year, he dropped out and joined the Navy, where he did well, eventually becoming an elite member of SEAL team seven. From that group, only five were selected to move to the highest level - that of the IS, the Invisible SEALs. It was a name that was bantered around often, but few knew exactly what they were. Fewer still, knew who.

From Salt Lake City he took his rental hovercar south, letting the autopilot steer him to Bluffdale. There he would plug into the camera grid and run the facial recognition scan to identify pictures of Dr. F coming or going within the city limits. Unfortunately, the Utah Data Center or UDC would be no help to him. Although he had the highest of clearances, Andrew was still not cleared to enter the UDC facility.

After checking into his Bluffdale hotel, he opened his laptop and queried the Bluffdale police database for any signs of Dr. F in and around the town. Assuming it would need to run overnight, he left his computer on and turned off the light on the nightstand next to his bed. After setting his alarm for 5 a.m., he rolled over and fell asleep. However, only an hour later his computer alarm buzzed, notifying him of a hit.

He typed in his access codes once more and waited for the camera images to appear on his screen. Indeed, there were six incidents of Dr. F's image appearing from the facial recognition program within the previous two hours. One was at a gas station just outside the Salt Lake City airport. He was driving a gray Chevy, probably a late-model, four-door Impala. The next photo was of him getting something to eat at a fast-food restaurant nearby. Two more images were identified at a theater complex just across the way from the data center, and the last two were ... Andrew sat up in his bed. Dr.

F was staying at the same hotel he was. The front desk camera showed him coming in through the front door to arrange a room for the night.

How convenient, thought Andrew. *This will be like shooting fish in a barrel.*

He took his cryogenic container out of his trunk and made sure it was operating correctly. Then, he walked down to the front desk to see what he could find out about the doctor's room number.

Andrew walked through the all-glass door and listened as the bell rang overhead to announce new guests. With latex gloves and a silencer in one jacket pocket and his gun in the other, he was ready for the final stage of his mission.

The matronly woman who had registered him only hours earlier, looked up and smiled as he came in. With most of her gray hair pulled back in a bun, she looked like she spent half her days at the hotel and the other half with grandchildren. Frumpy and plump, she stopped watching her late-night show and spoke to him.

"May I ... ," she began, before she realized he was already a guest. "Oh, yes, you're already signed-in. Well, is there something we can get for you?"

Andrew glanced around the counter. "Actually, I was wondering if I could have a pack of Marlboro Lights," he said, pointing at a carton sitting in a locked case behind her, even though he didn't smoke.

"Yes, of course. Let me get the key to unlock the cabinet," she said, leaving the room.

Andrew scanned the countertop for any signs of a registry, but he didn't find one. Then, he noticed a white luggage tag that read: Dr 227.

When the lady returned, he said, "You know, I'd also like to change my room if I could. I usually like to be off the first floor. Is the room above me still available - Room 227?"

The woman took the reading glasses that were dangling from a silver chain on her chest and pushed them up on her nose. Then, she scrolled through the room listings.

"No, I'm sorry. That room is taken," she answered, "but I do have ..."

Andrew quickly cut her off. "Taken? But it was available only two hours ago when I checked in. It was near the ice machine you see, so I didn't take it then."

The woman looked annoyed and looked back at the monitor. "No, I'm sorry, someone who just arrived just took the room."

"Oh, alright, then. I'll just take the Marlboros."

The woman took out her small, brass key and turned it in the cabinet lock, opening it and withdrawing the pack of the Marlboro Lights he wanted. But when she turned around once more, the only thing she saw was the front door closing.

***

It was as quick trip up the stairs and down the corridor to Room 227. Andrew listened carefully outside the door for any signs of life inside. He heard the television playing in the background and immediately took out his pistol, screwed on the silencer and racked it to load the first round.

"Doctor, we have a message for you from the front desk," said Andrew, putting his finger over the eyehole in the door.

It was a minute before someone inside answered. "What is the message?" the person asked without opening the door. He had a heavy German accent, which is what Andrew had hoped.

"I don't know, sir. It's sealed in an envelope. It says *Urgent* on the outside."

"Well, then open it," ordered the man.

"I can't sir. It's hotel policy. Only the guest can open mail or messages addressed to them. I would get fired, sir, for opening your mail."

Andrew could hear a sigh on the other side of the door before it opened, the chain attached.

Andrew kicked in the door and pointed the gun at the man, who was standing in the middle of the room in his undershirt and boxer shorts. He raised his hands and looked shocked and scared.

"If it's money you want, my wallet is on the dresser over there. Just take it. There's a few hundred World Bank dollars in it. It's yours."

Andrew closed the door behind him, still keeping the black Glock trained on his target. "Doctor F?" he asked.

"Yes?" said the man, surprised at his own name.

"I have my orders to return you to Brussels immediately."

"By whose authority?"

"The World Council."

"They have no authority over me anymore. I resigned my position with them earlier this year. I am a free citizen," the doctor said.

"Not according to them. Now, if you'll get your things ..." But then it occurred to Andrew that there was something strange about the doctor. He didn't seem sick in the least. In fact, he seemed perfectly spry and healthy.

"Doctor, I was told that you have a terminal illness. Is that right?"

"No," said the doctor. "Who told you that?"

"I'll ask you again," said Andrew, this time pulling back on the hammer.

The doctor lowered his head. "Yes," he admitted.

"What is your illness, doctor, and how long do you have to live?"

It was then the doctor looked up at Andrew, startled by the question. "How long do I have to live? I don't understand. Because you are here to shoot me?"

"I asked you how long you have to live, doctor. I'm getting impatient," groused Andrew, knowing that time was always his enemy when it came to any mission. *Get in and get out, as fast as you can*, was his motto.

"Without a bullet in my head, I'd say twenty or thirty."

"Hours?" asked Andrew, thinking he would need to take the doctor someplace to kill him before removing his head.

"Hours? No years," said the doctor.

"Years? I don't understand," said Andrew. "What is your disease, then?"

"I suffer from depression, that's all. If I take my medication daily, everything is fine. I've had it my entire life. It's not terminal. Did they tell you I had a terminal, mental disorder?"

Andrew looked into the doctor's eyes. He had enough experience and intuition to know when someone was telling him the truth. Then, he lowered his pistol.

The doctor looked at him, and gave a knowing nod. "They told you I was dying, isn't that right? They sent you to kill me?"

"They said you were dying and that I should bring you back to Brussels before you did."

"Why?"

"I believe they thought you had information that might be of value -- stuff from your projects on the World Council that you didn't document."

"You mean, stuff in my brain that they want to extract," said the doctor, astutely.

"Yes," Andrew answered.

Dr. F put his hands down and sat on the edge of the bed. He stroked his gray beard before resting his arms on his knees. Shaking his head, he again sighed. "I was afraid of this," he said.

"Afraid of what?"

"Afraid that what I created would come back to haunt me and others for the rest of my life."

Andrew moved to where the doctor sat, standing over him and still holding the gun in his hand. "Tell me what your projects were doctor."

The doctor looked up at Andrew with tiredness in his eyes. "My team created a means to capture information from the brains of great scientists, inventors, thinkers, and visionaries – information that, I believed, would help the world. It's enabled other scientists to create new medicines, inventors to make new technologies, and manufacturers to produce things that have helped thousands if not millions of people."

"Why is that a bad thing?"

"Because that's not the main use of it right now," he answered. "It has fallen into the hands of evil people, I'm afraid. Not only is it being used for military weapons and control of the general population, but I fear it's even worse than that."

"Like what?" asked Andrew.

"Did you happen to meet a woman with jet black hair? About five feet tall - thin and attractive in a sinister kind of way?"

"Yes, actually I did. I've worked with her on and off for years," said Andrew.

"What is her name?" the doctor asked, staring directly at his intruder.

Andrew stopped. "It's ... well ... come to think of it, I've never been given her name."

"Exactly," said the doctor. "No one knows who she is or what her role is in the World Council. She's always been a part of it though. Whenever anyone tries to find out, they vanish. She has hidden herself under a cloak of mystery for ages, yet she is the one person on the Council that no one has ever challenged - ever."

"Who is she, then?" Andrew asked.

The doctor smiled. "I've heard rumors, but I have no evidence."

"And that's why you're here at the UDC. Isn't it?"

"Yes," said Dr. F. "I received a message a week ago saying that there is a larger program involving the World Council, and it centers around her. It's been in the planning stages for years, if not decades, and it's about to be implemented. I was told by that someone that it cannot be implemented — not under any circumstances. And if it is, life for all of us will change forever."

"What's the program? And who told you all this?"

"I can't tell you who, and I won't be able to tell you what, until we get inside the UDC. Then, I'm hoping, it will all become clear."

*****

PART IV

One of the most highly secured facility in the world -- if not the most -- was the Utah Data Center. The complex had grown from only one hundred acres to one that stretched for a mile in all directions. There were multiple layers of protection, and with the National Guard unit stationed next door, there was no shortage of military backup.

Dr. F still had his encrypted ID that would normally give him access into all World Council facilities – even the UDC; however, it had been deactivated at the time of his resignation. "That's not going to do us any good," said Andrew, looking at the worthless piece of plastic.

"I'm getting it reactivated," said the doctor. "There is someone inside the UDC who I've worked with nearly my entire life. He's one who helped me create the Legacy algorithm and is one of the smartest people I know."

"Are you sure you can trust them?" asked Andrew, realizing that if they were caught, they would face treason charges and execution.

"Yes," said the doctor. "He's my son."

"Your son? How would they not have caught that in the vetting process for the projects?" asked Andrew.

"That's because we adopted him, and he kept his original name. It's something they never looked for, especially when my surname is Fuechtenschneider." He laughed. "But, the kid is smart as hell. He graduated from college at thirteen and received his PhD by nineteen. We were very fortunate to have someone like him in our lives."

The doctor became teary-eyed, and took off his glasses, wiping the wetness below each one. "My wife and I love him dearly. It was too bad she didn't live to see what a great young man he's become."

"I'm sorry," said Andrew, acting more human than even he thought possible.

"No matter. I'm here to do a job. Now, you can shoot me straight away and get on with your life, or you can help me. Which will it be?"

Siding with the doctor would be suicidal for Andrew, but something inside him was pulling him. It was as if he had lived his life in darkness, and now was a chance for him to walk toward the light.

Andrew peered once more into the reddened eyes of the doctor. *What if he was being deceived? What if the doctor was really the one on the wrong side? What if this was a challenge just to test his loyalty?*

"Well?" asked the doctor, once more, as if he were the one holding the gun.

Andrew opened his jacket and stuffed the pistol into the inside pocket. He knew his action might be fatal. The black-haired woman would just send another Invisible SEAL after both of them, and from experience, he knew the next agent would not be so sympathetic.

***

The next morning, Dr. F and Andrew met with the son, Friedrich, at Orem's Diner for eggs and oatmeal.

"Best oatmeal west of the Mississippi," said Friedrich, a jovial, energetic young man in his late twenties. In some ways, he looked like Ian, with a long, drawn face and wide ears. However, his eyes were light blue and his hair was already thinning on top. Also, unlike Ian, he was heavier-set, with large hands and arms and a wide belly. Ripping off a piece of whole wheat toast, Friedrich spread an ample supply of strawberry jam on it before popping it in his mouth. "So, what's the plan, gents?" he asked.

Oddly, he didn't seem overly concerned about the addition of Andrew to the mix. Of course, it was Andrew's training that picked up on oddities like that, but when he'd questioned Ian about it, the doctor had only replied that his son had always been carefree that way. "Little bothers him," the doctor had said.

"How soon can you activate my badge?" asked Ian, holding up a square, thin plastic strip, embedded with microcircuits and an etched image of the doctor on its surface.

"Today, I think. It shouldn't be a problem," said the son, flippantly. "You worry too much, Dad. But then, you always did."

However, Andrew's reaction was more serious and sober. "Friedrich, I think it's important that you understand that this is a pretty serious thing we're doing. You *do* realize that if any of us gets caught, we will likely be executed, right?"

It was then that Friedrich's facial expression changed. "What?" he said, putting down his toast. "Executed?"

"Yes. I said, we could ..."

"I heard you the first time," said the son, before looking over at his father. "Dad, you never mentioned that. Is this true?"

Dr. F squirmed in his seat for a moment before confessing. "Yes, son. But it may well save the lives of millions of people – perhaps *all* of us. It's something we *must* do - something that has to be done."

"Wait ... wait ..." said Friedrich, raising his hands, "... I thought we were only getting you inside so you could retrieve some old lab notes that you had - that I couldn't find when I looked for you. Is there something else I should know about?"

Ian sighed. Andrew now understood why it had been so easy to recruit the young and brilliant, but naïve, son.

"Friedrich, you must know some things," said Andrew, looking at him sternly. "I work for ..." he stopped and started again, "... I worked for the World Council, just as you do. However, things have come to light that suggest that what you're doing is not in the best interest of everyone in society."

"I don't understand," said the son.

"Son," said his father, "we have reason to believe that the World Council is using the data extracted from people for nefarious purposes - things we never intended it to be used for – military weapons, domestic surveillance, and even assassinations and murder."

Friedrich smiled. "No, you're joking with me now, Dad. Your algorithms made that impossible. We worked on those together. I know ... I helped you with them."

"You did, son. But you did not see the final version. The World Council demanded that we create a backdoor - a way for them to go in and manipulate them as they saw fit. They called it 'flexibility' and I naively believed them. Those backdoor entry points now make the system open to many people at the highest level who want to use the data for malicious purposes. And that includes the Black Widow."

Friedrich's face turned ashen.

"Who is the Black Widow?" Andrew asked.

"Your boss," said Ian. "The mysterious woman with the black hair."

"Why do you call her that?" Andrew pressed.

It was Friedrich who spoke up. "Because she murdered several colleagues we worked with in the lab."

"Why?"

"We don't know for sure," said Ian. "Friedrich and I thought at the time that our comrades had turned on the World Council – become traitors to their own beliefs and the mission of the world government. Now, I know they were only doing what I am now trying to do."

"Which is?"

"Save it," said Ian.

"So we could die for this," said Ian's son, "just like our friends?"

"Yes," said his father.

"But they all died so horribly."

"Yes, I know. I only pray that we don't meet the same fate," said Ian.

"We won't," said Andrew. "If we think through a good plan and execute it precisely, we won't have any problems. We just need to be sure we cover all our bases. I've done things like this before. This isn't my first rodeo. So, are you in?" he asked, looking directly at Ian's son.

Friedrich looked at his father.

"Son, I can't tell you what to do. If you don't want to go through with this, I'll understand," Ian said to him.

Friedrich looked at Andrew and then back at his father. "When do we start?" he asked.

***

It took a day to get the plan worked out and to reactivate Ian's badge. Getting Andrew into the facility was going to be another matter, however. Yet, this only took commandeering a service truck and drugging the driver and his co-worker. Although Andrew was limited where he could go, all he needed was to get inside the outer perimeter of security where Ian and he could use Ian's reactivated badge to push further, through the inner layers of the center's security lines. Friedrich could spring doors and entryways via the complex's security software to enable them to get to where they needed to go – to a point. The rest of the way – to the center's core – would be up to Andrew.

The secured latch on the door magically sprung free as Ian and Andrew approached, as if all the streetlights of the city had turned green for them. However, the magic eventually wore off, and the next door didn't obey.

Ian flashed his badge once more, but still the door didn't give way.

"I guess this is where we're on our own," said Ian, looking blankly at Andrew. "Any ideas?"

Andrew looked at the door mechanism and the entry lock. "I've seen one like this before," he said. "They had the same locking system on the cyber security system in Berlin – must be German-made."

"How did you get that one open?"

"I was given the algorithm. That made it easy," said Andrew. "But they wouldn't use the same ..."

"Same what?"

Andrew punched in a twenty-four-character alpha-numeric code as if he were reciting his own World security number. "1598BP321BNY6983128HH542," he said, mouthing the numbers and letters as he entered them. After he pushed the ENTER key, a series of numbers began scrolling on the monitor in fast succession.

"Did it do that the last time?" asked Ian, a bit worried by what was happening.

Suddenly, they heard the door lock release, and Andrew turned the heavy knob. "Yep, it sure did," he said with a smile.

As soon as they passed through the door, they entered a cavernous room filled from floor to ceiling with black cabinets. These were the heart and soul of the data center – computers processing five hundred zettaFLOPS of information.

"So, how big are these computers, anyway?" asked Andrew looking all around the vast room.

"It's hard to explain, but let's just say they can process five hundred sextillion or 500,000,000,000,000,000,000,000 operations every second. It's a staggeringly large number to be sure."

"Can't get my head around that one, doc," said Andrew, looking down one aisle in the Core Center that was the length of two football fields. "So, now what?"

"Down this way," said Ian, motioning.

Andrew followed him, avoiding any open spaces where they might easily be seen by the closed-circuit camera system. Finally, they found what Ian was looking for - a recessed area no larger than six-by-four feet with a single console and monitor.

"Keep an eye out for anyone coming down the row," said Ian, sitting down and entering the access codes his son had enabled for him.

Andrew poked his head out from the black racks of servers every few seconds to keep watch while Ian worked the computer.

"I'm in," said Ian, typing furiously on the keyboard.

"I can't believe they still use keyboards for this kind of stuff," said Andrew. "I thought everyone had gone with artificial intelligence protocols."

"No, it's too easy to manipulate and break-in using those systems. This is much harder to penetrate. Now, let's see what we have here."

It took another five minutes, but Ian eventually found the files he was looking for.

"Uh-huh, uh-huh," he kept saying to himself. Then, his eyes grew wide and he mumbled to himself. "Holy shit."

"What is it?" Andrew asked, coming over to look at the screen. What he saw was nothing but numbers – lines and lines of numbers. There were equations and graphs mixed in as well, but nothing that he could understand.

"Right here," said Ian. "Those are the notations for Protocol Z. I thought they had dismantled that program decades ago."

"What's Protocol Z?"

"It was the first experimental program we launched for the brain memory downloads. It wasn't successful and was supposed to have been cancelled."

"Why wasn't it successful?" asked Andrew.

"The process was like taking a ballpeen hammer to your skull to do brain surgery. It wasn't surgical or precise - it just used brute force to extract all your memories. But in the end it turned the patient's brain to mush. They usually died as a result if they weren't dead already when we got them. On the other hand, we were able to extract about 98 percent of the patient's memories. That's better than what we get now with the more delicate protocols used, which is about 65 percent. However, most of the 35 percent isn't usable anyway."

Ian kept tapping away at the keys. "Right here," he said. "This is a directive from a Director MBW. It says that Protocol Z is to remain the primary method of extraction for all special cases as designated by the director. These are supposed to be high-profile cases where more information is needed."

"Who is Director MBW?"

Ian turned around in his chair. "Madam Black Widow. I never knew that's what she called herself too -- creepy."

"Okay. Let's get this downloaded onto the micro-fob and get out of here!" said Andrew, going back to his post.

"Just another minute," said Ian. "I need to check one more thing."

He continued typing. "Oh, shit!" he suddenly exclaimed, his face frozen and staring at the monitor. "This has to link to …"

But instead of reading off what he'd found, Andrew heard sirens going off throughout the computer room.

"Crap!" Andrew said, realizing what had happened. "What did you do?"

Ian pounded more keys, downloading as much as he could, but finally, Andrew pulled him away. "We have to go, or we'll never get out of here!" Andrew then yanked the fob from the slot. "Let's go."

Together, they walked briskly down one of the side aisles of the computer complex, trying to be as casual as possible. However, guards streamed into the computer bays carrying pulse guns that would incapacitate someone but not destroy any of the equipment or data. Dressed in black from head-to-toe, they wore helmets with dark visors.

Andrew and Ian crouched behind one bank of computers and waited. "We're not getting out of here, are we?" asked Ian.

"Can't think that way. Just can't," Andrew answered sternly. "Is there any way to send a message to Friedrich?"

"No. Not from in here. It's lined with lead. There's no way you're getting a signal out of this place."

"What did you see on the monitor before you set-off the alarm?"

"If I told you, you wouldn't believe me," said Ian.

"Try me," said Andrew, still crouched.

But that moment wouldn't come. Pulse flares bounced off the computer racks over their heads, and the men in black started running directly toward them.

"Come on!" shouted Andrew, taking the lead.

But Ian stumbled. "Go on without me," he said. "I'm only going to slow you down."

"No! I need you," said Andrew pulling the doctor up by this arm.

"Stop!" shouted a voice behind them.

Andrew looked over his shoulder as he ran. Ian was almost in the grips of one of the guards. The look on the doctor's face was firm and resolute, and it was then that Ian gave his I-SEAL friend one last glance before opening a grated door with high-voltage warning signs plaster all over it.

"No!" shouted Andrew, but it was in vain.

Ian threw himself into the panel of high-voltage capacitors. Andrew had to turn away -- the scene of Ian's body being fried-up like bacon on a skewer was too much even for him to witness. He could hear Ian's screams, but there was nothing more he could do. Now, it was up to him.

He reached a series of doors that had been opened for him by Friedrich, and squeezed through them before they began to close. Behind the last of the doors, he tripped over a stocky, metal rod but used it to jam the door behind him.

For a second, he stopped to listen to what was going on around him. He heard the faint sounds of guards running in different directions, but none toward him. He peered down at the metal-grated stairwell which looked clear and hopeful. Jumping nearly a flight at a time, Andrew was at the bottom in seconds. He kicked open the exit door and ran along the perimeter of the building to get to the delivery truck he and Ian had used to get onto the grounds. Climbing into the delivery truck, he sped off just as shots were fired at him. At the entrance, the cement barriers were just being raised when he got there, but instead of going through the lane, he plowed directly through the guard house in the center, leveling it and nearly taking out one of the guards before he dove out the doorway to escape. The truck bounced and skidded as it made a sloppy turn. Then, Andrew floored the accelerator listening to the bullets rip through the back of the van and splinter the front windshield. Once on the main road, he only had to ditch the van where it would take a few days to find.

The mission was like many he had done during his career, and like the others, there were always casualties. His only regret was having to explain things to Friedrich. He had said there would be no casualties. In that, he had failed. But what was done was done.

*****

PART V

Andrew got back to his apartment building after traveling overnight from America to Brussels using forged passports. He had not checked in with MBW as he was supposed to, and he knew there would be consequences. But more than just consequences, he quickly realized he was no longer safe. When he arrived, his apartment building was surrounded by World Council police, and everyone coming and going was being searched and interrogated. Instead of going in, he left; he couldn't risk being caught without the doctor's head in the cryogenic chamber. In that, he had failed in his WC mission. The big question was whether they had also linked him to being allied with the doctor. From the looks of the perimeter police force, it looked like the answer was *yes*.

Although he had few friends in town, Andrew was well-acquainted with the director of technology at the Vrije Universiteit Brussels; so, he stopped in for a chat and a favor.

"It is not a problem," said Jorn Visser, Professor of Abstract Intelligence at the university. "You may plug in over here."

Andrew took out his micro-fob and pushed it into the slot. Then, using the university's artificial intelligence program, he asked, "Computer, analyze data on MicroX144," the fob Ian had used at the Central Data Facility in Utah.

"Accessing information," answered the computer. The processing took much longer than anticipated, but when it was completed, the computer said, "Cannot evaluate data."

"Why?" asked Andrew.

"Encryption is used, but there are other issues that prevent evaluation."

"State issues."

The computer went through eleven technical reasons why it could not evaluate the data but then listed the last one, which made Andrew sit up and take notice.

"Repeat," said Andrew.

"Repeating last issue," said the computer. "The data is strictly blocked from being divulged, as it invokes the Sys Doctrine 1047B from the 2089 World Council Session. That law prohibits the evaluation of any World Council information covered within the context of the law. Data on this micro-fob is deemed subject to this regulation."

"Are there any work-arounds?"

"Yes. Protocol 94019 has been used in the past, but it is an illegal means to extract the information."

"Implement Protocol 94019," said Andrew.

"Cannot comply."

"What is required to comply?" he asked.

"An override by the MBW, or ..."

"Yes?"

"Or the professor of Abstract Intelligence at this university."

Andrew smiled.

***

"What are you looking for in this data?" pressed Jorn, helping Andrew through his work-around solution to deciphering the fob.

"I don't know," said Andrew, "but I'm sure we'll know it when we see it."

It took an hour, but finally something shot across the screen that stopped both of them.

"Am I reading that correctly?" asked Jorn.

"I don't know, but I think so," answered Andrew.

On the screen was the following:

> *Protocol Z Phase II - Downloads of cranial activity into advanced artificial intelligent bots proceeding on schedule. Ten million AI's infused into society worldwide to date.*

> *Protocol Z Phase III -- Continued sterilization of human race underway. Human population shrinking at 36.459 percent per year. Should be substantially completed within five years when fewer than 1 percent of the original population remaining or about 38 million worldwide. Those remaining can be used as a domesticated animal for AI households or useful as a bond servant to do the bidding of AI forms.*

Protocol Z Phase IV - Final -- MBW will achieve her goal of global hegemony or dominance within the next three years. There are no unsurmountable obstacles that have yet to appear in our research.

Dr. F's planned neutralization will eliminate all remaining potential risks. I-SEAL dispatched to eradicate threat.

End of Transmission.

***

MBW arrived at her luxury penthouse suite in Brussels, getting out of her chauffeured limo-pod that had landed on the private parking strip on top of the building.

"Will there be anything else tonight?" asked the chauffeur, before heading home for the day.

"No," said MBW curtly. "Just make sure you're back here at six in the morning. I have a lot on my schedule."

"Yes ma'am," he said with a tip of his cap.

As she walked toward her apartment door, the black, limo-pod blasted up off the green landing strip and into the air before speeding off.

"Open," MBW said, commanding the door to give her access to her home.

The door swung open immediately, and she passed through. Throwing her small briefcase on the table next to the kitchen, she walked directly to the spacious bedroom where there was only a tall, gray chamber resting neatly against one wall.

She opened the chamber by voice command and reached inside. Grabbing onto a long, green electrical cord she pulled back the black hair that covered her neck and shoulders.

"There," she said with a sudden smile on her face, "that should do me until morning."

Pushing the electrical connector into the socket in the back of her neck, she waited until she heard it *click* in place. Then, she entered the chamber and pushed the button to close the door.

The computer inside began playing her favorite melody and then added, "Sweet dreams, Supreme Empress. Sweet dreams."

*****

CHILD'S PLAY

PART 1

Sarah and James played well together - they always had. Youthful and exuberant, they had all the energy of an Energizer Bunny with too many batteries stuck inside. Running and screeching, they seemed to create chaos wherever they went.

On this particular day, they were experimenting with James's chemistry set - something he enjoyed immensely. With several round globes hanging in the air around his lab, James loved to take one down and conduct experiments on it to see what would happen. Sometimes there was a method to what he did; other times, it was just pure whimsy -- whatever he felt like at the time.

"What's that?" Sarah asked, pointing to the beaker of white liquid that was 'cooking' on a Bunsen burner.

"It's just something I whipped up yesterday," said James. "I was going to try it out today. Do you want to watch?"

"What's it supposed to do?" asked Sarah, curious and intrigued.

James smiled in that fiendish way that made her excited about what the day with him would bring. "You'll see," he answered, coyly.

*****

PART II

Tom Hendricks and Hayden Samuels had been living for three years at Palmer's base station on Anvers Island in the Antarctic. Their scientific research in a variety of areas kept the work interesting with something new and challenging each day. From astronomy to marine biology and geophysics, the pair was accompanied by fourteen others at the base, all helping with observations and analysis.

It was September, and the high for the day in their part of Antarctica was expected to reach minus 33 Celsius, or about minus 26 Fahrenheit. It was spring in the polar land, but neither the flowers nor the birds were out celebrating. Snow fall of eighteen inches was on the way with winds expecting to gust up to 20 miles per hour, making it a miserable day to be outside.

"So, who's turn is it to go get the core sample?" asked Tom, knowing the answer already.

"It's yours," said Hayden, hoping Tom had forgotten.

"Hell no!" Tom shouted. "You know damn-well who's turn it is. Now get out there and bring that sucker in."

"What about Alvin?"

"The robot?"

"Yeah, isn't that what *he's* supposed to do?" pleaded Hayden, still trying to get out of it.

"Sure, but the system control module for him hasn't arrived yet. He's still in repair."

"*Damn it!*"

Annoyed, Hayden put on his winter gear and went out to the red, snow truck or ice horse, as they called it. This was no normal, every-day truck, however. Instead, this one had eight, gigantic, knobby wheels - four per side -- capable of high-angle climbing. It had a long-bed trailer on the back made just for hauling long core samples back to the lab.

Firing up the ice-horse, Hayden roared out of camp, disturbing the otherwise natural ambiance of the small town. Up through the steep pass, he maneuvered his truck to avoid bumping into the hard rock walls on either side. It was often hard to tell where the snow ended and the rock and ice began. But the pass was the only way he could get to the experimental station and retrieve the ice core samples.

There was nothing particularly unusual about this project. They had drilled for ice samples for decades. This particular one was deeper than others they had taken in the area, and the weather didn't make retrieval any more pleasant. The process had been highly automated, so they merely had to setup the drilling rig and let it find its way through the subterranean layers below. Later, after the requisite number of hours, someone would go out and shutoff the rig, pulling up the ice core and letting the ice truck equipment load it onto the back bed. Although they usually preferred two people retrieve a sample, one could do it without a problem.

The weather was worsening as Hayden reached the rig and checked the readings on the equipment. They had reached a depth of 3200 meters, but the drill seemed to have stopped. He activated the sensors deep underground and then turned on the video feed to see if he could tell what was causing the problem. There seemed to be nothing below the drill bit - just more ice. The bedrock, which might have stopped the drill, should not have appeared for another five hundred meters or so. However, the chemical analysis readouts showed something other than ice directly below the bit.

"What in the world?" Hayden asked himself. The wind howled around him, chilling his face to the point his lips and eyelids were turning numb. Even with his winter gear, the wind made it feel like 50 below zero Fahrenheit.

Instead of returning the sample, Hayden reset the drill to try to break through the jam below. After seeing the drill bit rotating smoothly, he headed back to base camp to report what he'd found. It was likely that the lab already had the same data of the malfunction. They would have gotten it wirelessly, but sometimes signals were disrupted or the received message lost. Either way, it was likely the scientists in the lab hadn't focused on it.

Taking off his gear, Hayden walked straight to the lab. "Hey, Hendricks!" he called out. "Got somethin' for you."

"Where's the sample?" asked Tom.

Hayden shook his head. "The drill stopped. But look at what's under the bit that made it stop."

Hayden showed Tom what was coming up on his monitor. A series of charts and graphs with six lines of different colors going up and down on a matrix.

"Right here," said Hayden, pointing to the screen. "This is where the drill bit is - about 3200 meters down. Look at the composition of the ice at that point. What do you see?"

"There's something wrong," said Tom, shaking his head. "The density of that ice is like ... well ... it's like iron. There's a malfunction with the sensors down there. We'll have to bring it up and have them replaced."

"But it stopped the drill bit."

"Yeah, but the layers are clear. It's not like we've hit bedrock. The sonar shows we have another 535 meters to go for that."

"I don't know," said Hayden, "but there's something down there that's blocking our bit."

*****

PART III

"What are you going to do with that?" asked Sarah.

James didn't answer her; instead, he opened the top of the beaker and grasped it with his tongs. "It's a new polymer I created," he answered. "It seems to be really hard. It's not like anything I've made before. Really cool, don't you think?"

"I dunno," said Sarah, not particularly interested in something that was just hard, unless it was like a bouncy superball or something.

"No, really. Just watch what I can do with it," said James.

James took the beaker and poured it on top of one of the globes. This one was bluish in color with a swirling of white, wispy vapor rotating around it. The white liquid dribbled from the beaker onto one point on the globe. At first it just sat on the surface like a bead of white glue, but then it smoothed out and seeped into the very fabric of the blue ball. The white color vanished, drying completely clear, as if it had never been there.

"So, what's the point?" asked Sarah. "It doesn't do anything."

"It doesn't have to do anything, Sarah. It's just cool to make stuff like this, don't you think?"

"No," she answered, flatly, "and unless you do something interesting, I'm leaving."

"Okay, okay," said James. "I've got two more little things I'm working on. I'll show you those if you stay. Okay? I promise they'll be more exciting."

*****

PART IV

"We're going to have to refit the drill with something that will go through it," said Tom. "We weren't planning to use the bedrock drill this early in the process, but it looks like we have no choice. I'll call it in. It will have to be airlifted over here from the Amundsen-Scott base down here. That will take at least a week."

"There goes our timetable," said Hayden. "And we were making such good time with our drilling up to now."

Suddenly, the dials and other instruments in the control room began to sound. Tom and Hayden rushed into the room along with five others who were also working next door in the lab.

"What's going on?" asked Tom, opening the second of the double lock doors.

The Chief Engineer, Maggie Spencer, turned around in her captain's chair with a blank look. "I have no idea," she said. "All of a sudden, my compass readings spun 180 degrees on me. It's screwing up all our instruments."

"What do you mean, your compass spun around?" asked Hayden.

"That's exactly what I mean. Magnetic north spun 180 degrees - to the South Pole. It's supposed to be 89.5° N and 152°W near the North Pole, but it's pointing at 64.1°S and 135.2°E - our Magnetic South Pole."

"Your readings must be wrong," said Hayden.

"No! My readings aren't wrong!" shouted Maggie, always defensive about her work.

"Well, there's got to be an explanation," said Tom.

"Maybe it's the polar reversal," said Maggie. "It's supposed to happen within the next thousand years or so."

"You mean like the Brunhes–Matuyama reversal 780,000 years ago?" Tom asked.

"Yeah. They say we're due for one," said Hayden.

"It's highly unlikely," said Tom.

Over the intercom system, came jarring news. "All personnel. We are experiencing a polarity reversal. This could cause problems with navigation and our instrumentation. All flights in and out of here and Amundsen have been temporarily halted until further notice."

*****

PART V

"That's really cool," said Sarah, watching James.

James held both magnets in his hands and was moving them across the outer shell of the blue globe. They could see the arcs of the fields rise up around the outside of the sphere before dipping back at the two points on the opposite ends. The aura streaming off the globe looked as if they were peering at an *Aura borealis* event off the northern coast of Iceland. It was mysterious and mesmerizing.

"Yeah, I like doing that occasionally," James said laughing. "I think it keeps everything interesting. Don't you think?"

Sarah laughed with delight.

"Sarah - James? What are you doing?"

They had been playing for a while, and their mother was unsure where they were or what they were up to.

"We're just playing, Mom. Everything's fine," said James, calling back to her.

"Maybe we should stop," whispered Sarah. "You know what happened the last time you got carried away with your little experiments."

"It's not going to be anything like that," said James, dismissively. "I know what I'm doing. I'm a genius, after all."

Sarah wasn't so sure about any of it, but she was still willing to go along for the ride. Usually, James's experiments were phenomenally awesome, but sometimes they, well, fell short of expectations.

"What are you going to do next?" she asked, with mischievous delight.

"I dunno," said James. "I thought maybe I'd set the blue globe over the Bunsen burner for a few minutes and see what happens."

*****

PART VI

One Year Later

"Tom, we just got the results from last year's climate warming study. We've aggregated the data and you just won't believe ..." Hayden began.

"I assume it's up, right? I mean our directive is to validate anthropomorphic causes for global warming. Man has been causing it for decades," said Tom.

"Yeah, but this is off the charts, Tom."

Tom looked over Hayden's shoulder and his eyes widened. "Unbelievable," said Tom. "I've never seen anything like it."

"Yeah," answered Hayden, "It's almost like someone took the world and held it over a Bunsen burner too long."

*****

PART VII

"Stop!" shouted Sarah. "You're cooking it too much!"

James pulled the blue orb back from the burner and blew on it slowly, pursing his lips and giving it a cool, steady stream. "Yeah, you're probably right. It now needs to go into the freezer for a while."

*****

STAIRWAY TO HEAVEN

PART I

The Hawking Research Center had been *the* state-of-the-art facility in the world for decades, and as it celebrated its one hundred fiftieth birthday, it was still the pre-eminent institution of its kind in the world.

The search for extra-terrestrial life had continued unabated for that period without much to show for it. With the billions of galaxies and billions of stars within each, it was a logical assumption that there would be life found elsewhere in the universe - but that had not yet happened.

Even with light traveling 186,000 miles per second or 5.88 *trillion* miles per year, it would still take over four years to receive a signal from the nearest star in the galaxy and 100,000 years to receive it from the other side of the galaxy. From the farthest galaxies, light had traveled nearly 14 billion years to arrive at Earth - some 81,000,000,000,000,000,000,000 (8.1×10^{22}) miles away. In a rocket ship traveling 30,000 miles per hour, it would take an astronaut 2.2 billion (2,200,000,000) years to cross our galaxy alone and more than 300 *trillion* (300,000,000,000,000) years to cross the universe. Such is the size of the cosmos in which we live. Putting all of it in perspective, the Earth has only been in existence 4.4 billion (4,400,000,000) years, while humanoids have walked the earth for less than 4 million (4,000,000) years, and modern man less than 200,000.

So, in this vastness of space most scientists believed that intelligent life existed in one of the thirty billion solar systems in our galaxy alone -- the Milky Way – and perhaps as many as 10^{21} (10 with 21 zeros following it) in the universe. But as of that time they had gotten nothing -- nothing, that is, until August 18, 2225 when one of many probes launched decades earlier reported back to Space Command.

Signals from the deep-space probe Zeus V, detected an unusual space-time distortion. Using advanced, negative-energy generators, scientists were able to send a probe and track it, exploring the Triangulum Galaxy, M33, which rotates nearly three million light years away from Earth. As signals were received through the worm hole they had created and stabilized by the negative energy beam, the data revealed something the scientists thought impossible.

"It just can't be," said Zach, the chief scientist on the deep-space probe.

"I've double-checked the numbers, and that's what it shows," said Xi, his number two on the program.

"Run it through one more time, just to be sure."

"I can, but it won't change anything," said Xi.

"Put it up on the screen again. Let's take another look," said Zach.

Xi tapped on the keyboard and immediately the monitor came alive with the images.

Both Zach and Xi watched with disbelief. On the screen was a colorized movie that appeared to be from the 1950s.

"There must be a feedback loop somewhere. You're getting this signal from another source on Earth," said Zach.

"Nope," said Xi. "It's impossible. All our shielding is in place. There is no possibility this is coming from this planet."

On the screen was Charlton Heston, playing Moses in the 1956 epic, *The Ten Commandments.* It was the scene where Moses returned from Mt. Sinai, just having been given the Ten Commandments from God. After seeing the golden calf and the idolatry of his people, Heston broke the stone tablets out of anger.

"What a great movie that was," said Xi. "We still watch it today."

"Yes, we sure do."

"But how did it get all the way to M33?" asked Xi, not giving up.

"I tell you it's interference of some sort," said Zach. "Now, go back over your data and trace the problem. We'll talk again next week."

***

1 week later

Zach returned to the lab and found Xi in his chair watching his monitor with a well-worn black book open at his side.

"So, did you find the problem?" asked Zach.

"Yes."

"And, what was it?"

"With all due respect, chief, it's ... you," said Xi, unblinking.

"Excuse me?"

"Yes. I rechecked all the inputs and outputs and had Miley do the same. We could find no leakage or other problem in the circuitry. The data came through the worm-hole from M33 galaxy, over 3 million light years away."

"That's impossible," said Zach.

"So, you still don't believe it?"

"What? Believe that ring AC4 from the M33 galaxy is broadcasting movies? No, sorry."

"What if I told you we are now getting other transmissions from that sector of the galaxy?"

"What kind of transmissions?" asked Zach.

"High impulse, data bursts of trillionths of a second, but containing massive amounts of data."

"You mean massive amounts of energy. Well, it's probably just a black hole releasing gamma radiation from its poles. That's not unusual."

"It's not pure, random energy - it's data," said Xi. "I was able to synthesize the streams through our computers and this is what I'm getting." Xi held up a black book that was on the desk next to his. The edges of the book were painted gold, and there was a red, silk ribbon inserted somewhere in the middle of it.

"You're getting *the Bible*?" said Zach, now laughing. "I think you need to take some time off. When was the last time you had a vacation?"

"I don't need a vacation," his number two shot back. "I tell you this is real. This is happening, whether you want to admit it or not. These are the facts."

"These are not facts, young Xi, they are conjecture. Give me your data, and I will personally analyze it. If it is what you say, then we indeed do have something more to explore it and, I might add, I might even go to church on Sunday. If you are wrong, you owe me a nice cold beer and a porterhouse steak, medium rare. A deal?"

"And what do I get out of it if I'm right … other than further work?"

"Perhaps *sharing* a Nobel Prize with me," said Zach, smiling.

***

PART II

Zach returned, but it wasn't the next day or the next week; rather, it was over a month later. Xi thought it extremely odd not hearing anything from Zach during that time, even when he tried to contact him. In the meantime, Xi worked diligently translating the energy pulses into English, and the more he worked on it, the more he was convinced. By the time Zach returned to the lab, Xi was already working on the book of Job.

"So, how is the Bible coming?" asked Zach, coming into the lab and putting his scuffed leather briefcase down on the small, mobile cart next to Xi. He was all smiles, like the Cheshire Cat.

Xi looked up at his chief. "So?"

"So ... what? What's the question?" asked Zach.

"What did you see from analyzing my findings - the energy pulses from M33? Are they correct?"

Zach looked at his protégée. "What if I told you no?"

Xi looked at Zach's face carefully. "But I can read in your face that the answer you found is *yes*."

"Well, the answer is *yes*, but my answer to you is *no*," said Zach.

"What?"

"I found no logical explanation how there could be interference in the energy signals you are getting from the worm-hole and from those here on Earth. So, in that respect, I agree with your analysis. However, just because we can't explain it doesn't mean there isn't a logical explanation. We just haven't found it."

"So, you think there is still contamination of the signals someplace? That I'm just getting reverb from signals back here on Earth?"

"Yes."

"But I've had six weeks to analyze it, and you've looked at it, and together we believe that's impossible."

"No – you think that's impossible."

"So, what happens if I'm right? What would you do?" asked Xi.

Zach looked down at his computer monitor. "You're on the book of Job I see," said Zach.

"Yes."

"And it tracks the books of the Bible - word for word?"

"It's not the King James version, but it is tracking it very closely, yes," said Xi.

"Let me know when you get to Revelations," Zach said as he turned and walked out of the room.

***

Xi worked on the project for another six months, deciphering everything that was coming in from M33. His work was exhausting, requiring him to work eighteen to twenty-hour days for weeks on end. At that point, even his spouse was getting frustrated with him.

Xi's wife, Chen, was deeply religious and had converted to Catholicism when she had arrived from China years earlier. Although Xi had not changed from the atheistic ways he had learned in the communist People's Republic of China, he had softened his tone much since marrying her. She had been a good influence on him - and he had become a better man for it.

The phone on Zach's desk rang, and since he hadn't been in for weeks, Xi picked up the handset. "Hello, Dr. Prusser's desk," he said.

"Zach?"

It was a familiar voice – one Xi had heard many times during his employment at the facility.

"Dr. Bennington, it's me Xi. How are you, sir?"

Dr. Bennington was the facility director – Zach's boss. He was partially retired but still played an active role in the operation of the lab.

"Xi, yes. How are you son?" said Bennington in an avuncular tone.

"Well, sir. Very well. I'm just working on the M33 project."

"Oh, yes. Why that's why I was calling. I'm very impressed with the data coming from the wormhole. Zach has submitted his report which he wants me to endorse for submission to the Journal of Astrophysics. I am more than happy to do that, but I think this is a story that we have to get out to the press right away. This is earth-shattering news! The fact that we're getting a transmission from an intelligent life form millions of light years away – why this will change the course of human history and its understanding. This is like discovering that our solar system is heliocentric instead of geocentric. It's mind-bending! Don't you think?"

"Uh, yes sir," said Xi, shocked by the news. He had known Zach for a long time, but never did he believe that he would be betrayed by him – not like this.

"I think he'll win a Nobel Prize for this. In fact, I'm sure of it," said Bennington.

Xi had a hard time listening to the rest of the conversation, as disappointment and sadness overtook him. "Uh, is there a message I can leave for him, sir?"

"Yes," said the elder man, "please tell him 'good job' for me."

"Will do, sir."

Xi hung up the phone, but he didn't call Zach and rip into him. He let it go. *What purpose would it serve by getting angry and upset?* he thought. *I'll just talk to him about it the next time I see him.*

***

It was a day late in August when Xi received energy pouring in from the wormhole. The levels of energy coming out of the hole were enormous – dwarfing what he had been receiving by a factor of ten. He watched as the computer deciphered the energy pulses targeted directly to his wide-array telescope from the wormhole. The translation was from the book of Jude.

> **24** *Now unto him that is able to keep you from falling, and to present you faultless before the presence of his glory with exceeding joy,* **25** *To the only wise God our Savior, be glory and majesty, dominion and power, both now and ever. Amen.*

But as he finished this translation, Xi glanced over at another piece of equipment that provided monitoring of the energy stream levels, frequency, noise interference levels, and the stability of the wormhole itself. He saw that the energy was off the charts, but there was something more.

What's going on with this? he thought as he read the data streaming to one of his five monitors in the lab. He attempted to reset the device, but when it came back online it gave him the same result.

"Can't be," he said to himself.

Xi tried several more reboots and adjustments to change the printout, but the answer came back the same each time -- the wormhole was collapsing.

If the wormhole collapsed, they would lose all contact with Zeus V, the deep space probe and would no longer get any data from the equipment - it would be, for all intents and purposes -- dead.

"*Crap!*" Xi said, getting frustrated.

Immediately, he got on the phone to contact Zach. He'd been unable to reach him for weeks, but this was an emergency. Calling Zach, he said, "Sir, I think you need to get down here. We're losing Zeus V."

Zack came in, even though he didn't want to. It was two in the morning, and it was the last place he wanted to be on a Saturday. "What is it?" he asked, cleaning his glasses.

"As I said over the phone, we're losing the wormhole," said Xi. "The neg-energy field is collapsing."

"Have you increased the pulse energy?"

"Yes, we're already at the maximum level. If we use any more positive energy in the transference to make enough negative, we'll bring the entire electrical grid down. The entire Northeast Coast will go dark," said Xi.

"Give it more juice," said Zach. "We can't lose her."

"But Zach, we'll bring down the grid."

"Don't care. Do it."

Xi pushed the vertical levers on the console to draw more energy from the grid and divert more converted, negative energy to the beam.

"It's not working, sir," said Xi.

"Then give it more!" shouted Zach.

Xi slammed the levers from the 6.5 level up to 9.5 on the console.

"Give her everything, damn it!" said Zach.

Xi shook his head and pushed the knobs all the way up, striking the upper bumper which read 10.0 with the label: *Warning! Danger! Overload Possible!*

Immediately, the power in the facility went down, and the backup generators kicked in. However, the entire grid had been fried. It would take days or weeks to bring everyone back on line.

"Well?" said Zach, standing over Xi, "where are we?"

"The wormhole collapsed," said Xi, in shock. "All transmissions from the probe have stopped."

When the wormhole disappeared, it sealed the virtual tunnel they had created between galaxies in the universe. Now, it would take another 3 million years before someone on Earth would receive the probe's transmissions.

"Shit!" said Zach, pounding his fist on the table. "My superiors are *not* going to be happy about this."

"Sorry, chief, but there was nothing I could do," said Xi.

"There's always something you can do! Xi, *you* were the one who came up with this ridiculous idea about the pulses anyway. We got distracted by it and diverted all our resources to analyzing the data transmission from M33. Now, what's the result? A stupid Bible? *Really*?"

"But that's the truth," said Xi.

"It's what you told me, Xi. I never believed it to begin with. You went rogue on me, didn't you? You spent all your time on this stupid project instead of analyzing important things. Xi, you're fired!" said Zach, covering his own hide. "Clean out your desk and leave. I don't want to see your miserable face in here ever again."

"But ... but!" Xi began; however, it was no use. Zach needed a scapegoat and he was the one tagged. It was then that he was going to bring up Zach's appropriation of his work – sending it to Bennington and taking credit for all of it. But he didn't.

Xi cleaned out all his personal belongings and put them into a single cardboard box. It wasn't much, but it was all he could take with him even though the vast amounts of data, analyses and other works he had produced during his decade there were from his hard labors. Now, they were the property of the lab.

He looked around one last time, sorrowfully, and then again at Zach, who looked busy examining data. Not waiting for his boss to acknowledge that he was leaving, Xi left the building for the last time feeling empty and alone.

Zach looked down at the monitor to see where things had ended in the transmission.

Revelations

... **7** Behold, he cometh with clouds; and every eye shall see him, and they also which pierced him: and all kindreds of the earth shall wail because of him. Even so, Amen. **8** I am Alpha and Omega, the beginning and the ending, saith the Lord, which is, and which was, and which is to come, the Almighty.

A Vision of the Son of Man ...

On the monitor flashed thousands of binary sequences, and when Zach asked the computer to translate, the English version immediately appeared on the screen.

Revelations
Chapter 8 continued

The Trumpets

6 And the seven angels which had the seven trumpets prepared themselves to sound.

7 The first angel sounded, and there followed hail and fire mingled with blood, and they were cast upon the earth: and the third part of trees was burnt up, and all green grass was burnt up. **8** And the second angel sounded, and as it were a great mountain burning with fire was cast into the sea: and the third part of the sea became blood; **9** And the third part of the creatures which were in the sea, and had life, died; and the third part of the ships were destroyed. **10** And the third angel sounded, and there fell a great star from heaven, burning as it were a lamp, and it fell upon the third part of the rivers, and upon the fountains of waters; **11** And the name of the star is called Wormwood: and the third part of the waters became wormwood; and many men died of the waters, because they were made bitter...

Zach's attention focused on the word *worm*, but quickly got redirected from a new stream of data pouring in. The transmission continued unabated.

... The Two Witnesses

1 I was given a reed like a measuring rod and was told, "Go and measure the temple of God and the altar, with its worshipers.

2 But exclude the outer court; do not measure it, because it has been given to the Gentiles. They will trample on the holy city for 42 months.

3 And I will appoint my two witnesses, and they will prophesy for 1,260 days, clothed in sackcloth."

4 They are "the two olive trees" and the two lampstands, and "they stand before the Lord of the earth."

5 If anyone tries to harm them, fire comes from their mouths and devours their enemies. This is how anyone who wants to harm them must die.

6 They have power to shut up the heavens so that it will not rain during the time they are prophesying; and they have power to turn the waters into blood and to strike the earth with every kind of plague as often as they want.

7 Now when they have finished their testimony, the beast that comes up from the Abyss will attack them, and overpower and kill them.

8 Their bodies will lie in the public square of the great city—which is figuratively called Sodom and Egypt—where also their Lord was crucified.

9 For three and a half days some from every people, tribe, language and nation will gaze on their bodies and refuse them burial.

10 The inhabitants of the earth will gloat over them and will celebrate by sending each other gifts, because these two prophets had tormented those who live on the earth.

11 But after the three and a half days the breath of life from God entered them, and they stood on their feet, and terror struck those who saw them.

12 Then they heard a loud voice from heaven saying to them, "Come up here." And they went up to heaven in a cloud, while their enemies looked on.

13 At that very hour there was a severe earthquake and a tenth of the city collapsed. Seven thousand people were killed in the earthquake, and the survivors were terrified and gave glory to the God of heaven.

14 The second woe has passed; the third woe is coming soon.

The Seventh Trumpet

15 The seventh angel sounded his trumpet, and there were loud voices in heaven, which said: "The kingdom of the world has become the kingdom of our Lord and of his Messiah, and he will reign for ever and ever."

16 And the twenty-four elders, who were seated on their thrones before God, fell on their faces and worshiped God,

17 saying: "We give thanks to you, Lord God Almighty, the One who is and who was, because you have taken your great power and have begun to reign.

18 The nations were angry, and your wrath has come. The time has come for judging the dead, and for rewarding your servants the prophets and your people who revere your name, both great and small— and for destroying those who destroy the earth."

19 Then God's temple in heaven was opened, and within his temple was seen the ark of his covenant. And there came flashes of lightning, rumblings, peals of thunder, an earthquake and a severe hailstorm.

There the transmission ended.

I can't believe he wasted his time on all this crap! thought Zach, shaking his head.

Furiously, he tried to reinstate the negative energy beam and reopen the wormhole. He would tap into the electrical grids across the country if he had to in order to get back his precious *wormwood*. He wanted that Nobel Prize more than anything, and if he had to manipulate the data or slander Xi to get it, he had no problem with that. Fame and notoriety were everything at this stage of his career, and he wasn't above anything to get what he thought he deserved.

But as pounded the keys on the keyboard to suck the juice from millions of homes and businesses across the country, there was a brilliant explosion of light that ripped through the inside of the room. Almost at the same time, a piercing sound shook the building. Both were so intense that Zach was stunned -- his retinas nearly seared and his eardrums nearly burst. He collapsed instantly on the cold, tile floor.

*****

PART III

"Dr. Prusser, wake up!" came a voice out of the darkness.

At first, the noise sounded as if someone were talking to him underwater - garbled and unintelligible. But soon, the distortion lifted, and his hearing returned.

"What?" Zach asked, answering to his formal name.

"I said, wake up, doctor."

Zach opened his eyes and saw one of the lab technicians bending over him. It was Margaret, someone with whom he had worked during the entire time he'd been at the lab. "What happened?" asked Zach, sitting up. The pain in his eyes and ears was intense, and it was all he could do to carry on a conversation.

"We don't know. None of us knows. There was a huge burst of energy - a light so brilliant it fried all the satellites in orbit. So, our communications are down. We can't even make a call home."

Zach sat up, and with the help of Margaret, he stood, still rubbing his head.

"Yeah, you went down hard, my friend," she said, smiling at him.

"Is everyone else okay?" he asked.

At first, Margaret didn't say anything.

"What's wrong?" Zach asked, still bewildered at what was happening.

"Well that's the thing. We can't find a few of our people."

"I don't understand. What do you mean you can't find people?"

"That's what I mean," said Margaret. "I was knocked out for a while too, and when I came to, I started walking around to see who was here and who was alright. There are a few people who ... well ... seem to have vanished."

"That doesn't make any sense," said Zach. "They couldn't have just vanished. I'm sure they just went home."

"Maybe. We can't use the phones, so we don't know. But what we do know is they were here right before the burst happened. We think it only occurred about ten minutes ago, so anyone who left must have gone out very quickly. Almost all of them were still logged into the system."

"I'm sure they just went home to check on their families. With the phones down, most probably panicked. It's nothing to worry about."

"You're probably right," said Margaret. "That's where I'm headed now. I want to be sure my son and daughter are all right. They should be home from school by now, but I can't call them. If you're all right with it, I'm going to take off and go home to check on them."

"No, you need to stay here. We have work to do - especially after that huge flare. We need to start analyzing it," said Zach, leaning against the desk.

"But my kids?"

"Sorry, Margaret. The lab comes first," said Zach. "Now get on the phone or whatever works and call all the people who left. I want them back here pronto."

"Yes, sir," said Margaret, leaving the lab upset and disappointed.

Zach pulled out his lower desk drawer and took out a bottle of pain killers. After popping two into his mouth and swallowing, he calmed himself before making the rounds himself to double check what Margaret had told him. Of the eighty-six scientists and lab technicians who worked there, seven were missing. He already knew where one of those was - Xi. Going to the basement, he then checked the backup generator which had not automatically kicked-on. Throwing two silver switches, Zach fired up the box waiting for the lights and other electrical equipment to come online. The uninterrupted power supply had functioned fine in the meantime – a stopgap until the backup generator could be started -- so there had been no loss of data.

Returning to his desk, Zach pulled up the world news on his computer to see what was happening elsewhere in the world.

"And tonight," said the newscaster, "we start with the bizarre incident that happened today and affected people all over the world. From Washington to Tokyo, there was a report of a super-bright light that destroyed the electronics of virtually all satellites and many, if not most, of the electronics on Earth. So, if you are watching this program tonight on a television set, consider yourself lucky. In the Northern Hemisphere alone, there are nearly 1.5 billion people without power."

The news segment showed what it could of the blackouts around the world. In those cities where night had fallen, there was an eerie blackness and calm – particularly in Tokyo, Beijing, Shanghai, Singapore, Seoul, Hong Kong and Bangkok. Yet, even in those cities that still enjoyed sunlight there was disquiet. Cities ground to a halt. Nothing worked. From transit systems to communication devices – everything was offline.

"Besides the lack of power, there is another side of this story that cannot go unreported," said the newscaster. "We have Brandon Tipton in London with that story. Brandon?"

"Yes," began Brandon, a young reporter with blonde hair that blew in a tangled mess in the stiff wind. "There are many reports of people who have allegedly gone missing after the brilliant light we experienced. These are people from all walks of life. At the studio here in London, we are missing fourteen people, and no one knows where they went."

Like most people in times of crisis, Zach thought about people he could call – family, close friends. But he had no close friends, other than one or two at the lab, and he hadn't talked with his family in years. The one he thought of as a friend, he had just fired.

He dialed Xi's number, hoping to reach him and apologize. *He had been harsh - too harsh* – he thought*, and he wanted his second-in-charge and friend back*. But the line continued to ring with no answer.

Margaret finally returned. "Dr. Prusser, everyone wants to go home. Would you *please* let us leave?"

But it was then that the newscast returned on his monitor.

"We now go to Cardinal Winthrop who made a statement today on behalf of the pope. As you remember, the cardinal was implicated earlier this year in hiding years of molestation by priests in his diocese. Those court cases are still on-going. Here is the cardinal."

The cardinal approached the microphone dressed in his red clergyman's cape and *zucchetto* skull cap.

"As we all witnessed today, there was a brilliant and mighty light and sound that struck the surface of the earth. We are all struggling to find answers, and I'm sure our scientists are working on that right now. While some people have said it was part of the rapture declared in the Bible, I want to assure you that it was no such thing. The members of the church are all very much here and ready to assist our congregations in any way we can."

Then a reporter asked, "But cardinal, we have word that several clergy are missing in the Vatican, including the pope. As you know millions of people around the world seem to now be missing."

The cardinal shook his head. "I assure you that all is well. Now, if you will excuse me." And quickly, the cardinal left the dais and disappeared through the doors of the church behind him.

"Next we have a prominent scientist, Dr. Herbert Taylor, an astrophysicist from the University of Camberton. Dr. Taylor, what do we know from a scientific perspective as to what might have caused this event?"

Sitting in the studio was an older-looking man with thick black glasses and a full head of white hair. He didn't have the professorial beard to match, but he did look the part of a learned man.

"We don't know at this point, but the explanation may be quite simple," he announced smugly.

"He'll probably say it was a coronal mass ejection," said Zach, sitting in his seat, watching the newscast. "But it wasn't. There are too many things that are wrong about it to come to that conclusion."

"We believe it was just a coronal mass ejection," said Taylor.

"See!" said Zach, pointing at the screen, "I told you he'd say something stupid like that!"

"And explain what that is," asked the reporter.

"A CME is an unusually large ejection of plasma and magnetic energy from the sun's corona. It was pushed into a strong solar wind which hurled it directly into Earth."

"Yes, we've been hearing for years that such a thing could happen. But how does that explain the disappearance of so many people?" asked the reporter.

It was clear from the physicist's reaction that he was ill-prepared for that question, and it made him squirm. Clearing his throat nervously, he said, "Well, I believe the two things are not related directly, of course. I'm sure those people who are missing are on their way home or otherwise unable to use their phones. The strike probably knocked out a lot of cell-phone systems. I'm sure they will be located in short order."

"Thank you, doctor," said the reporter, ending his broadcast.

The newscast then cut to another reporter who was interviewing someone else. "And I have here, a devout atheist, Arnold Usher. Mr. Usher, what do you make of this event?"

When the camera turned to Usher, they saw his face was pallid and strained. "All my life, I have sworn to myself that there is no God. But ..." and then he began shaking.

"What is it?" asked the reporter.

"Well, just before the light and the sound, I swear I saw something - a vision. It was bizarre - like I really did see angels with trumpets in the sky. It was just before we got hit with the blast, and I blinked several times trying to clear my head. I figured I was seeing things, but ..."

"Well, you aren't alone, sir. There are millions of people who swear they saw the same thing. Most of those stories have been dismissed by college professors and clinical psychologists as part of a mass hysteria event or CCE -- a collective consensus event -- where a few falsely see something, but then many others claim the same thing as if they had seen it too."

"No, this was different. I really did see it," said Usher, speaking up behind the reporter's back.

The reporter turned toward Usher and said, "But you just heard from the cardinal that there was no such Biblical event. That it would be explained by the scientists. These are words coming directly from a clergyman."

Usher smiled. "Yes, but did you ever think that quite possibly he's ashamed that he isn't missing too?"

"Excuse me? I don't understand," said the reporter.

"Well, if only those of us who were not blessed enough or did not believe firmly in the Lord were left behind, then what does that say about Cardinal Winthrop."

The reporter had no comment. It was then that he too realized that he had not been chosen either.

"Uh ... uh ..." stuttered the reporter. "We will go back to you in the studio, now," he said looking away from the camera.

When the cameras returned to the studio, the anchor also looked shaken. "We just have a report in that the pope and several of his cardinals are also missing. None of this is easily explained. I guess we'll just have to wait for our scientists to look into it and get us an explanation."

Margaret sat down. "What if it's true? What if it was the rapture?" She looked over at Zach. His head was down on the desk. "Are you alright, doctor?"

Zach didn't say anything. He could feel for the first time in his life an emptiness, a darkness, a sense of unfulfillment in the pit of his stomach. And it felt horrible.

It all makes sense now, he thought. *The message from the wormhole, the biblical translation, the sudden stoppage of the message in Revelations, his evil deed of trying to steal the accolades for the discovery from Xi -- all of it. But now, it's too late. A Nobel Prize seemed like little consolation now.*

A tear formed in the corner of his eye and dripped onto the desk, smearing words in the Revelation translation Xi had worked on. He looked up at Margaret and saw that she too was crying.

"It's too late for us, isn't it?" she asked.

Zach nodded. The only words he could utter were, "Yes, Margaret. I'm afraid it is. It's too late for all of us."

*****

ARCHEOLOGY DIG

"Professor?" asked one of the students, "what exactly are we looking for?"

"We'll know it when we see it," said the professor, answering the student.

The professor smiled as he unfolded his extraction machine. It was a complex unit, one of the latest models to roll-off the assembly line. Although portable, it was packed with sophisticated testing equipment used to monitor the ground layers probed the depths of the earth. Archeological digs had been done for years using deep, under-ground sensors - ones that could "see" things thousands of feet or even miles below the surface. However, it had been centuries since authorities had allowed anything to be extracted by removing layers of soil and recovering what lay beneath. Under the principle of sacredness for anything that lay buried, governments had prohibited any extraction of artifacts regardless of their value or scientific interest. It was viewed as unnecessary to go through all the time and effort to dig down to the relics to retrieve them when 3-D images were clean and precise enough to tell researchers everything they needed to know about what was found. The images were then used to reproduce exact copies of the items for display in museums across the globe for the viewing pleasure of all.

However, there were things buried in this particular area that had baffled scientists for years, and after a decade of probes and analyses, they were no closer to replicating what was viewed on their monitors. Petitions and requests for licenses to perform an actual extraction of the artifacts had gone unheeded – until now. Finally, after twenty-three years, this group of archeologists had obtained a permit to start the excavation.

There were nine students, plus the professor and an associate professor who were working the site. Each student had a small, vibrating, de-earthing machine that separated the surrounding soil and clay from more firm elements buried below. The devices had a built-in library of potential archeological finds, including shapes, chemical compositions, and other attributes that would differentiate those real treasures from mere rocks. So, when one of the hand-held instruments was used in digging, it would quickly vibrate and turn-off when it struck something of importance. In this way, it prevented damage to artifacts and preserved the integrity of rare finds.

The students busied themselves with their digging instruments while the professors were engrossed in their charts and maps.

Professor Anwir watched as one of his experienced students used his extraction machine to strip away the thick, top layers while other students worked on the narrower bands of sediment below. The work continued for days, and the weather suddenly turned hot – scorching the ground the students working on it. Without a cloud in the sky, the sun overhead made the earth feel like it was over one hundred degrees or more.

"Professor?"

"Yes," said Anwir.

"I think I've found something. My instrument has picked up an object only three meters below the very spot where I'm digging."

The professor used his extractor to remove precisely two meters more of sediment before the finer instruments were again employed to skim additional layers – working their way down toward the identified object.

"Easy," said the professor, not wanting to damage the item. "Let's just take this part slowly, shall we? We've spent too much time and energy getting this far. We don't want to destroy what we've worked so hard at uncovering."

After several more hours, they finally reached the layer and began unearthing the find. Slowly, they peeled away the sediment and then used brushes to whisk off the rest of the debris.

"What is it?" asked one of the students.

"The x-ray band shows that it's a box of some sort, but we aren't able to see inside. I wonder if it's lined with lead?" asked another.

After several more days, they dug out the metal trunk and lifted it to the surface. Gently, they lowered it onto a sandy shoal and removed the chains and padding. Setting it in front of the experts, they pondered how they would get it open without damaging it. The trunk had no obvious top or bottom and no clear way to get inside.

Multiple scans were made, and ultimately, they decided to atomize one end of the trunk without disturbing the contents inside.

"Ready," said the professor. "Begin ..."

The switch was thrown, and one end of the trunk was dissolved by the formidable beam of the atomizer unit. It only took five seconds, and the lead outer shield was dissolved.

Eagerly, the associate professor peered inside the trunk and carefully pulled out the contents, laying each one out on a clean, white sheet. When everything had been withdrawn, the professor and all of his students began looking at what they had found.

"What is it, professor? What is this stuff?" asked one of the students.

Anwir looked at the cache and began pointing things out.

"It appears we have many artifacts from many centuries ago. I would put this box at about fifty-two hundred years ago," said the professor. "It's what they once called time capsules, I believe. We have several devices here which stored small amounts of data - less than a petabyte, I'm thinking -- and some other items, such as clothing they wore from the period - one blue pair of coarse pants and a pair of shoes with bright colors, devices they thought were relevant, like ancient holographic phones, and a physical poster of -- I don't know what -- perhaps some celluloid pictures, which I believe they called movies back then. Let's see what else we have here. Oh, I see what they called an e-reader for books, which I assume has something on it, and a red can with the letters C-O-K-E on it, not sure what that is. There's a strange, hard white ball with red seams running in an unusual pattern over it - perhaps used for some cult purpose - a red box with two yellow arches, a small cup that says "K" on it with a picture of a coffee-bean, what's left of what was paper money at the time, and a flat sliver of metal with a rectangular screen in it – possibly what they called a "phone." And lastly, it looks like they put a paper in here - it's halfway degraded, but I think I can read the title. It says *New York Times*? I don't know what 'times' they are referring to, however. I'm not sure what to make of all this, but we'll take it back to the lab and analyze it. These are truly remarkable discoveries that will help us understand better the early evolutions of the *Homo sapien* species."

The professor stood up. He retracted his titanium arms and lowered his leg extensions to arrange more easily the things on the sheet. Then, he took a small, brown pod and plugged it into an outlet on the side of his head before closing his eyes. The download began, synthesizing everything he had seen and storing them on the small device while also transmitting them wirelessly to each of his students. They felt the surge of energy as the data flowed directly to them, uploading into their silicon brains.

"How primitive these carbon units were," said one student, smirking.

"It is important that we treat each species – past or present -- with respect," said Anwir. "Yes, they were primitive," said the professor, "but they were the ones who created the base units of artificial intelligence from which you evolved. Let us not forget that."

"Then why did they die out?" asked another student.

The professor smiled. "They knew not what they had created and then couldn't stop what they had begun. It was inevitable."

*****

RESET

PART I

"It's a boy!" cried the doctor, pulling the baby out of the laboratory incubation chamber.

"Why do you say that every time?" asked the lab assistant, rolling her eyes.

"I don't know," said Dr. Jesse Morton, smiling. "I just like to have fun once in a while."

"But we already know it's a boy," said the assistant.

"Like I said, I'm just having fun. Just give me that."

Dr. Morton took the newborn and placed him in the basinet. Then, using ultraprecise instruments, he made an incision in the left temple of the child's head, who was still crying, and implanted the reset device required by law. Everyone born in the United Republic was required to have one at birth. In fact, most of the people in all developed countries had the device. It was what made everything work. The implant went in at the same time the wound was cauterized, making the entire procedure bloodless and pain-free.

The doctor picked up the baby and brought it out through the double doors of the lab to the awaiting parents who were in the lobby.

"Here he is!" said Morton, beaming. "It's a ...." but he stopped, remembering what his lab tech had just told him. "It's your baby. What is his name?"

"He's Bartholomew. We'll call him Bart," said Sarah, his mother, beginning to coo over the child, holding him in her arms.

"Aw," said the doctor, "He looks just like ..." then he stopped, looking at the parents.

"Oh, it's okay," said the father. "We've had him genetically modified for all our defects. I know he doesn't look exactly like us, but I think I can see my mother's eyes in his."

"No, I think they're *my* eyes," said the mother.

The father laughed. "Well, we'll have to go back and look at the order sheet to see which one we chose for the eyes. In any event, we both thank you doctor."

"My pleasure," said Dr. Morton.

*****

PART II

13 years later

When Bart came home from an overnight social outing sponsored by his school, the clear, glass tube in which he rode up to the apartment shimmied like it needed some repairs. He lived with his mother and his younger sister, as his father had left them suddenly.

"How was it?" Bart's mother asked, as she turned away from her wall-sized monitor. Sarah was busy working – actually, telecommuting and dealing with some problems with robotic algorithms being used in artificial intelligence.

"Bad," said Bart, throwing his small knapsack on the silver and black sofa.

His mother put down her work and came over to him. "What's wrong?" she asked, putting her arms around him and kissing him on the forehead.

"The other kids were really mean. They didn't include me in anything they were doing, even when the director told them to. Every time I tried to say something, they told me to shut up. They said I was a loser. I'm just fed up with all of it," he said.

"That's okay, Bart. Things will get better. Everyone has a challenging time in high school these days, especially since you only see your classmates twice a year. I mean, how can you get to know them over the computer?"

"It doesn't matter. They all hate me!" he said.

"No, they don't. They're just immature. They'll grow up soon," said his mother.

Then, a few minutes later, Bart asked, "Mom? The director talked to us about the Reset. Do you know about that?"

Sarah stared at her son in disbelief. "Uh ..." she began, but not knowing what words to use.

"The Reset. Do you know what that is?" her son asked again.

"Yes. What did he tell you about that?" she asked, nervously.

"He said that when we're born, doctors put these things into our heads. You can't get them taken out, so they're with you forever. He said we can use this reset during our lives to get out of things when we think it's getting really bad."

"No!" shouted his mother. "No! It's against the law for him to tell you that! You don't have to know anything before your twenty-sixth birthday. ! I can't believe he said anything to you."

Bart sank back into his chair. "I'm sorry, Mom. I didn't mean to get you upset."

Sarah calmed down, taking a few deep breaths. "No, it's not you Bart. It's your director. No one is supposed to say anything to you until you reach legal age - twenty -six. But, I guess there's nothing I can do about it now."

"What's it about?" asked Bart.

"What did he tell you?"

"He said we get three resets during our lives. If something is going really badly for us, we can push a button on our temples and then give a voice code to activate the reset proto ... something."

"Protocols," said Sarah, still disturbed.

"Yeah, that's what he said."

Sarah drew close to her son, putting her hand on his arm. "Bart, you know that there is nothing so bad that you can't deal with it here -- right here were we are. Don't you?"

"Yeah, I guess so," said Bart, confused.

"Things may not be better for you after the reset. Just remember that, okay?"

"Okay, Mom," Bart answered. Then he asked, "Is that what happened to Dad?"

Sarah had not wanted to tell her son what had happened to her husband. It was common for spouses to suddenly reset when things got tough. It was far easier than going through divorce, after all.

"We believe so son, yes. But things weren't that bad. I don't understand why he left to this day. Yet, he did. That's all I can say."

Bart looked down at his feet. "Okay," he said. "I'm going to go do some homework, then."

Sarah watched as Bart left the family room and took the clear tube lift up to the study bay. She sighed. This was the last thing she needed for him or for her.

It was an hour later, and it was time for supper. Sarah had programmed in the food fabricator to prepare the dinner - Bart's favorite of eggplant lasagna. She had even made sure that she ordered mint chocolate chip ice cream for desert -- another one of the things he especially liked.

She told the house computer to reach Bart. "Bart, supper is ready. You need to come down and eat." Then, she waited. But she didn't get an answer. She tried again, "Bart, I said supper is ready."

Still no reply.

"Bart?"

Sarah got up from her desk and hopped on the glass tube. "Study Bay," she directed, talking to the glass elevator.

"Acknowledged ... Study Bay."

The lift took her swiftly to the study floor of the massive apartment complex where the kids living there went to take exams and watch on a big screen when sitting for their classes. Sarah got off and went to the glass cubicle where Bart usually studied, but he wasn't there. Instead, she found a note.

Sorry Mom. Things are so bad, I just had to reset. Love you, Bart.

*****

PART III

When Bart woke up, he found himself in another home, in another city, but at least in the same country. His new mother was different from Sarah, but it was hard to tell how different. She hadn't expected to receive a "foster child" which is what the government called them, but then she had no choice. No one did – it was determined by a government computer program; that was all anyone knew.

"Hi," said his new mother, with a surprised look on her face after receiving an alert on her computer monitor that she was getting a foster kid. "I'm Nora. And you must be Bart."

"Yes," said Bart, looking around his new living space.

Rather than a spacious apartment in one of the nicest buildings, this flat was cramped -- buried down at street-level and located near the industrial side of town where people still did manual labor. He shared a room with two other boys, and his new mother slept in the family room because it was only a one-bedroom apartment. Although clean, the place had an abundance of dog hair, left by their two owners who came and went as they pleased at most every hour of the day.

As the days passed, Bart felt alienated from the rest of the family. His two new brothers were five years younger and didn't give him any notice at all, except when they played practical jokes on him, like putting rocks in his pillow or salt in his bed. But that was the least of his problems. He soon figured out that although Nora was quite nice – too nice sometimes – she was also a drug addict.

At first, she covered it up by saying it was just part of a medical condition, but he soon found she was shooting up at all times during the day. Sometimes, he would find her nearly unconscious on the bed when he would come home from an outing from school. She didn't work and instead got money from the government to support her and her two boys. She liked having Bart around – in part because he could take care of himself and because she got extra government benefits for having him there.

On the plus side, the kids at school were nicer, he thought. There were two with whom he quickly bonded, both having reset recently and going through adjustment just as he was. Both Matt and Jeremy had lived in more upscale surroundings and had pushed their lifeline buttons when their feelings had been deeply hurt by friends and others. All of them wondered now whether they had made the right choice.

"I dunno," said Matt, after Bart asked him if he thought he had made a mistake. "I found out about the reset like you did – from an adult, my football coach. He didn't tell me so I'd do it. He told all of us on the team because his brother had just done it."

"So, why did you do it?" asked Bart.

"Somebody put some bad stuff about me online. My friends started believing the crap and then wouldn't talk to me anymore."

"Yeah," said Jeremy, "that happened to a friend of mine."

"Did he reset too?"

"No, he decided to tough it out. He was really miserable, though. Eventually, things got a little better. Kids forgot about the posts for the most part. Of course, some still gave him a hard time, but he learned to ignore them."

Matt just shook his head. "I don't know. It was just too much for me. It wasn't going away. People were just so mean. I don't think it ever would have gone away. It would have been with me forever – torturing me every minute of every day."

"So, what happened to you?" said Bart, looking at Jeremy.

Jeremy looked down.

"What's wrong?" asked Matt. "How bad was it?"

Jeremy shook his head. "It was bad … really bad."

Matt and Bart waited, not sure what else to say.

"I … I … I was involved in something I shouldn't have been," said Jeremy.

"Like what?" asked Bart.

"I was caught smoking weed," said Jeremy.

"By your parents?"

"No, a teacher. They called the cops on me. I saw the police cars pulling up and freaked out."

"I didn't think you could press reset when you'd been arrested. I thought they disabled that?" asked Bart.

"They do. That's why I pressed it so fast. I didn't want them to keep me from doing it," said Jeremy.

Each boy had a reason, and at the time, it made sense to them.

The school year went on, and as it did, Bart found that things weren't very different from the school he'd left. There were bad kids in every school, and in fact, there were some in his new school that were even worse. They gathered in gangs – both online and physically, and they terrorized other kids constantly. However, Bart learned to ignore them and stay engaged with those he did consider his friends.

***

One day late in the school term, Bart came home and found his new mother in bed with a drunk she had picked up at the bar down the street. The foul body odor of the drunk wafted in the air as he opened the front door making him gag. He began coughing, but his fit was interrupted by his new mother's shrieking with pleasure from her bedroom. As the dogs barked wildly and the two foster brothers ran into the room, he had reached his breaking point once again. The C minus on his English paper that day had not helped matters.

Bart went to his room and listened to the headboard banging against the wall … *Thump, thump, thump*. He shook his head and reached to press the button on his implant, but then stopped. *I only get two more of these,* he thought. *Should I use it now?* Nora's groans and moans grew louder and louder, and Bart sat and thought, his finger hovering over the reset switch.

But this time he stopped. Instead, he rolled over in his bed, and tried to force himself to sleep. It took some time, and by the time he began to doze off, the strange drunk in the other room had done his business and left.

*****

PART IV

13 years later

Bart spent the next years in and out of trouble. He had long since left his drug-addicted second mother and her nightly escapades with the neighborhood johns. After dropping out of school, he had worked various jobs to earn enough to feed himself, even though he still had to catch a room here and there in half-way houses in the grimy, crime-ridden streets of Downtown Centrale.

Working at his low-skilled job troubleshooting robots that came into the recharging station and couldn't connect, he met another young woman who was working the same job. Her name was Tonya, and like him, she grew up in a dysfunctional home. However, she had never reset. It was her birth-mother with whom she'd finally had a falling out - leaving home at sixteen and braving the outside world on her own. She had survived by prostituting herself for a while until her pimp got nasty and beat her up. She left and found other jobs until she landed the one at the Robot Depot.

After only a week, Bart had asked her out, and within three months they were living together. Life was good -- for a while.

"Hey, Bart!"

"Yes, Mr. Grubermier?

Mr. Grubermier was the human foreman who oversaw the entire division of robot recharging stations in Zone F of the Robot Depot. There were eighty-four stations in the zone, and Grubermier had between three and four attendants watching all the stations, ensuring the robots got to the station outlets to recharge. It wasn't nearly enough staff, and robot owners often complained about the lack of service.

Grubermier was a gruff, crotchety old man who hadn't saved a dime in his entire life and, as a result, was forced to work until he dropped dead. Legendary for his nastiness and caustic treatment of his workers, Grubermier had only one mission in life - to preserve his job.

"I got a report today of a robot from Valdez Corp that's gone missing. Do you know anything about that?" asked Grubermier, getting in Bart's face. Standing only a foot from Bart, the foreman looked directly into his employee's eyes, watching for any flinching or discomfort.

"Uh, no, Mr. Grubermier."

"Their robots are red and black with a big, round white circle on the top that has their name and logo."

"Yeah, I'm familiar with that. But no, I don't know anything about missing ones," said Bart.

Grubermier glared at Bart, not believing anything he said. "Uh, huh," is all he answered. "Well, we'll be keeping a close eye on things around the stations - do you understand?"

"Yes, sir," said Bart.

Bart didn't want to lose his job, and he feared the foreman. He was suspected of keeping a "hit list," and this was exactly what Bart worried about.

Bart trudged back to his flat where he and his girlfriend, Tonya, were living. He didn't have enough money to take the hyperlink tube, so the walk back to his place took him nearly forty-five minutes. He pressed his palm against the door and watched as the thin, black bar scanned his imprint. As the door opened, it slid quietly into the wall, closing again - or nearly so. It always got stuck, so he usually had to push it the rest of the way.

"Hi Tonya. I'm home!" he announced, collapsing on the couch.

Tonya came out of the back bedroom and gave him a hug around the neck, kissing him and whispering in this ear. "I love you, you know," she said with a smile.

He turned and kissed her on the lips, which led to more kissing and caressing until Bart broke it off.

"What's wrong?" she asked, pulling back.

"Something happened at work today."

"What?"

"Grubermier."

"What did that asshole want?" she asked, looking at him sympathetically.

"He asked me about some stolen robots at our station. He started accusing me of stealing them. I told him I didn't know anything about it, but he kept going."

"Yeah, he's a real jerk," said Tonya.

"So, what am I supposed to do?"

"I dunno. I guess you just have to wait him out. Hopefully, they'll find out what's goin' on and that'll be the end of it. You know as well as I do that it's usually just a paperwork thing. Somebody didn't file something right or at the right time."

"Yeah, but the last time that happened, he fired half his attendants before he found that he, himself, had misplaced some repair release orders."

***

The next day, Bart arrived on time and ready to do his part. He sat in a seat, high-up in a glass fishbowl overlooking one of the charging stations, watching each robot as it maneuvered inside the multi-level warehouse where thousands came each day to plug-in to the grid. But after an hour, he received a video transmission from Grubermier.

"Bart!"

"Yes, sir?"

His boss hovered in a 3-D hologram in front of him, just his head and shoulders, but enough to unravel the young attendant.

"We've had another robot go missing! This is intolerable! How could this happen?" shouted Grubermier, his face reddened and eyes mad with rage. He looked like he was ready to strangle the next person he saw; unfortunately, that appeared to be Bart.

"I ... I don't know, sir," Bart stammered.

"Well, there are only two people who worked there at the station - you and Tonya."

"What are you saying?"

"It's either you or Tonya who is stealing from the company."

"No! Neither one of us is stealing from the company! We know nothing about this! It's probably a paperwork issue. You know, it's happened before."

"One of you is going to jail!" said Grubermier, menacingly.

"What? Why? What proof do you have?"

"I don't need proof, Bart. You know that. All I have to do is finger *you*, and it's over. I'm a member of the Party, you know. You're not, so what I say goes. I'm calling the police now. They should be there in five minutes."

"But I tell you I'm innocent!"

"Doesn't matter, Bart. I'm not goin' down for this. I need my job -- you're, well, you're dispensable. Sorry. But cheer up, you should be out of the slammer within three-to-five years for felony theft. It won't be all that bad — except for getting goosed by the inmates now and then and never being able to work again."

Grubermier laughed and hung up.

"Bastard!" shouted Bart, kicking the computer monitor off his desk. It flew across the room and shattered. "That will be three days of suspension without pay," said the computer system through the loudspeaker overhead.

Bart shouted at the top of his lungs and then sat down in his chair. Below him on the floor of the charging station, the robots continued to come and go, finding the portals into which they shoved their plugs for electricity. Yet, he sat alone in the goldfish bowl.

Moments later he heard the words, "Commencing Reset." Then all went black.

*****

PART V

After resetting, he had found himself in a ditch in the middle of a tremendous rainstorm. He only learned later that he had landed in a mid-western state in late autumn when the leaves were turning and the chill was only starting in the fall air. It was after midnight when he opened his eyes, and there were few cars or trucks on the narrow, rural road that stretched out lonely and abandoned in front of him.

Finally, there was a set of headlights in the distance that quickly approached him. He stood up and, with the raindrops dripping down his face and his hair matted against his neck, he put out his thumb to bum a ride. At first, the car seemed not to notice him and sped past. However, only seconds later, he saw the red, rear brake lights flash on. The car paused for just a moment, before the white backup lights illuminated, and it glided back toward where he stood. The window of the car dissolved and a young man of no more than thirty glanced over at him. Well dressed and seemingly well-off, the man neither smiled nor frowned.

"Where you headed?" the man asked.

"I ... I'm not sure," Bart answered.

The young man hesitated and then said. "You a reset?"

"Yeah," said Bart.

"Okay. Hop in. I'll take you to the next town. They can fix you up there."

Bart got in and the car sped off.

"Sorry about the mess," said Bart, dripping water everywhere inside the hovercar.

"No worries," said the man. "I have an internal vacuum and dehumidifier. It will take care of everything. So, why did you reset? It must have been bad."

Bart wasn't sure what to tell the young man, so he just said, "Yeah, pretty bad."

"I understand," said the man. "I've been tempted to reset myself, but haven't had the guts. They say there's no sure thing on the other side. You never know what you're going to get next. Is that true?"

Bart looked at the young man who was no more than six or seven years younger than he was. "Yeah, that's pretty true."

"So, is this your first?"

"No, it's my second," said Bart.

"Second! Really! You've gone through two already? How old are you?" asked the man.

"I'm twenty-seven," said Bart.

"*Wow!* And you're only twenty-seven?" asked the man.

"Yeah, what about it? How old are you?" asked Bart.

"I'm twenty-three. But like I said, I've been tempted."

"When were you tempted?"

"Oh, it was just last week, in fact. My mother and father divorced about a year ago, and my brother died in an accident last month. My older sister was just diagnosed with a rare form of cancer that is one of the last ones yet to be cured. It's been a rough year."

Bart felt small. He wasn't sure what to say. The only thing he could think of was, "Oh."

"Yeah. I'm sure whatever you went through was worse," said the man. "I can't imagine, but it would have to be bad to push you to reset."

Bart remained quiet as they continued into the city where he was dropped at a community house. There he got a bunk, a blanket, and a hot meal. He was back to square zero.

Time again passed, and eventually Bart found a woman with whom he could settle down. She had been sitting at a coffee shop, sipping her morning brew when he had taken a stool next to her. Accidently knocking over the creamer, she had hurried to stem the flow of milk toward him, but had failed. Pouring over the edge of the counter and into his lap, the milk had dumped into his lap. He had jumped up to miss the flood, only to flip his ceramic plate onto the floor, shattering it into millions of pieces. She had apologized profusely and then after looking into each other's eyes, they had simply - laughed.

After that, they dated and then married. Together, they had two children, as permitted by law, and lived in a high-rise apartment in the suburbs. He went back to school and received an online degree in solar energy management, being promoted quickly through the ranks to a prominent manager position at his company, Heliospark, Inc. His wife, Ensa, worked in social therapy at a local clinic.

But over the years, they ended up moving back to the city of his birth when his company transferred him there for yet another promotion. Ironically, their apartment was in the same building where he had lived with his first mother. Yes, life was finally good for him and for his family.

Yet, nothing lasts forever, and one day his life changed once again.

"Bart?"

"Yes, Ensa, what's the matter?" He could tell there was something wrong in her voice as she called him at work.

"When will you be home tonight?"

"The usual time, why?"

"We need to talk," she said.

He didn't like the sound of that, but when he pressed her, she said she'd rather discuss it when he got home.

When Bart opened the door to their apartment, he found his two daughters running around the living room yelling and screaming. They were energetic children who had never really gotten the discipline he thought they should have had. At ages seven and five, they were inquisitive and temperamental. But he put that aside and went into the kitchen, where his wife was sitting at the table holding a glass of red wine.

"Ensa, what is it?" Bart asked. "I've been worried all afternoon. What's going on?" He pulled up a chair next to her and put his hand on her arm.

She looked up at him, her eyes red and swollen from crying. Taking another gulp of wine, she put down the glass letting its *clang* resonate through the kitchen.

"Bart, the doctor called this afternoon. She told me I have cancer. It's incurable. I don't know how else to tell you, but she said I have only four weeks to live."

Bart sat stunned. It was inconceivable what she was telling him. Here was a woman whom he loved more than anything in the world and he was hearing this? His body went numb, frozen in its seat, and his brain turned off, hoping that the next time he blinked, he would see something different in front of him. But nothing changed. She was still crying, still angry, and still sipping her wine.

Together they cried, and when the tears would no longer flow, they talked about how they would tell the girls. It wouldn't be easy, but it was something they knew they had to do.

As the weeks passed and Ensa grew weaker. There was nothing more the doctors could do except prepare for the inevitable. Bart had trouble focusing at work but managed to keep things together to ensure he kept his job. He tried to come home early to take care of her most days, but it became harder and harder. They finally hired a nanny to look after the children. It was all too much. It was overwhelming, suffocating, paralyzing.

The anxiety inside Bart kept building each day, and as Ensa's illness progressed, he grew more panicked. How would he cope? How would he bring up the children alone? How would he survive this himself?

Finally, alone in his bedroom, he poured himself another glass of Scotch and emptied it in one gulp. He had begun drinking heavily and it wasn't unusual for him to empty a bottle the same night he opened it. As he poured the last of one bottle, he vowed not to repeat it the next night. Yet, he always did. The girls soon left him alone in his room, their mother lying in bed, sedated and barely aware of her surroundings in another nearby. Each became isolated and more alone than they ever thought possible.

Leaving the bedside of his ailing wife, Bart returned to his room – this time taking a bottle of sedatives out of the medicine drawer. He popped open the lid and slid three capsules onto his palm. Popping them into his mouth, he chased them down with two stiff gulps directly from the Scotch bottle.

I just can't deal with this, he thought. *I can't handle it. It's too much - too great for anyone. I have to get out. I have to leave. I have to ... reset. I have one more. This is my last. If not now, then when?* Panic began to grip him, just as it had the two previous times during his life when he'd been overcome with emotions. The flood of despair was too great, and his thoughts turned inward.

He poured another glass of Scotch and knocked back the entire amount. Then, putting it down, he pressed two of his fingers against his implant, ready to execute his final reset. There would be no more after this. There would be no more chances to escape. This would be it.

At that moment, his daughter Sophie came running into his room. She was his five-year-old. Beautiful and vivacious, she almost always carried a smile on her face everywhere she went. But now she was sad, her mouth downturned and her eyelids drooping.

"What's wrong?" asked Bart, lowering his hand from behind his ear.

"Monica said that Mom's not going to be with us after she dies. I don't understand, Daddy. I thought she'd be in heaven and be looking down on us from there. That's what they told us in Sunday school."

"Your sister is ..." Bart started to say something, but changed his mind. "... Your sister is right but she's wrong, Sophie."

"I don't understand," said his youngest, pouting.

"Well, your mom will be with us. She'll always be with you, but you just won't be able to see her after she goes. Her spirit will be with you and your sister for a very long time."

"Forever?"

"Yeah," said Bart. "Your mom will be with you forever ... maybe longer."

"Monica also said that you might go away too. Are you going to leave us Daddy?"

Bart felt a tightening in his throat as tears welled-up in his eyes. He bit his lip and pulled his daughter close to him, hugging her. "No, baby. I'm never going to leave you two. Like your mom, I'll *always* be here or near you. You will never be alone, Sophie. Neither of you girls will ever be without your parents. Both me and your mom love you too much. Do you understand that?"

Sophie smiled and gave her dad a hug back. "I love you too, Dad." Then she ran back out of the room to play -- just like it was any other day.

***

After the funeral, Bart and the girls went back to the apartment. It had been a sad day -- a very sad day -- and he wasn't sure how much Sophie had really understood. But Monica was older, and it was her question later that had bothered him the most.

"Uh, what was your question again?" he had asked, sitting next to his elder daughter on the sofa in their apartment.

"Daddy, I want to know about the reset. I heard about it at school. Is it true that you get three ...?"

"Monica, how did this come up?" he asked, taken by surprise.

"Some of my friends were talking about it. They said that if you are really unhappy you can just push the button behind your ear and go someplace else - away from the pain and the sadness. Do you know what I'm saying?"

"Yeah," said Bart, "I feel sad sometimes too, but you know what? You always make it through. I know it's hard - your mom just died, and we're all feeling alone. But we're not alone - we have each other, don't we?"

"Daddy?"

"Yeah, hun?" said Bart putting his arm around his daughter.

"If I reset, will I go to heaven to be with Mommy?"

Bart felt the pain and anguish he had just described. Wiping away the tears quickly, he attempted a feeble smile. "Why would you think that?" he asked.

"Well. They say we don't know where we'll end up when we reset, right?"

"Yeah."

"So, isn't it the same when we die? I mean, we don't know if we're going to be in heaven or not and we don't know who will be waiting for us when we get there." Monica looked at her dad with her big, brown eyes. He could see the melancholy within them.

"Monica, you don't need to reset to be near your mom. She's always going to be with you - always. In fact, she's near you right now, looking out after you and making sure you're safe. Both your mom and I will always be there for you. If we're in heaven, all you have to do is pray. We'll hear you." Then Bart turned toward his older daughter and took her by the hand. "Just promise me that you'll never reset. I can tell you that escaping your problems and your feeling of sadness is no answer. The answer is all around you - it's here and now. You need to trust yourself. You can always find an answer, and if you can't, then just say a prayer. Your mom will be listening, and so will God."

"I love you Daddy," she said with an innocent smile.

"I love you too sweetheart. Now, go find your sister. I'm taking you both out for ice cream."

*****

SOCIAL ETIQUETTE

Gladys Maxwell lost her husband in an automobile accident thirty-four years earlier; however, she was far from penniless. Ashton Maxwell had built a powerful empire prior to his death - one that spanned the globe. With facilities in New Zealand, Japan, Taiwan, the Philippines, India, Turkey, Germany, France, England, South Africa, Brazil, Peru, Mexico, Canada and twelve sites in America, he had amassed one of the largest networks of hypersonic plane manufacturing conglomerates in the world. His companies produced more planes in a year than all other hypersonic plane manufacturers combined.

After his death, Gladys had carried on the business. A smart, business-savvy woman herself, she continued to grow and develop the company, having created two new planes capable of speeds in excess of Mach 12 or twelve times the speed of sound and one in the testing-prototyping stage that could reach speeds up to Mach 18.

Living in Manhattan, Gladys enjoyed a popular and exciting life. She had never remarried after Ashton's death, although she had many suitors. Her world became one of glamorous boyfriends, names that would sizzle on the news wires for days after the story broke. Indeed, her parties were renowned for their exotic and eccentric nature, often costing a million or more per event.

But while she lived in the stratospheric circles of the rich and powerful, Gladys was constantly battling younger, upstarts in the community in New York who wanted the golden moniker of "grand hostess" for themselves. First, there was Celia Dawson, the wife of oil magnate, Daniel Dawson. Next was Penelope Weinstein, the wife of the Goldman Morgan banking chairman, Jonah Weinstein. And, finally, there was Sasha Bhatti, the spouse of genetic genius Tushar Bhatti, who had developed a special gene splicing program that had led to many medical cures. Each seemed to relish the competition to see who could put on the most lavish events and attract the most A-listed stars and attendees.

Tall and elegant, Gladys effused confidence everywhere she went and had a sense of power and charisma about her that was hard to match. While the others had money, they lacked the grace that Gladys displayed, as well as the flair for originality. Slim and sinewy, she had spent most of her life on diets or working with personal trainers to keep off the weight. As a result of that and her multiple surgical procedures, she looked at least twenty years younger than her actual age of sixty-five.

By birth she was a brunette, but she had died her hair blonde for the last forty years, and everyone knew her by her short, straight blonde bangs and hair length that never fell lower than two inches above her shoulders. Her other unmistakable traits -- her dark, smoky eyes and bright, red lipstick – contrasted sharply against her fair, pale skin. Wearing long, dangling and expensive earrings during her functions, Glady's flaunted her wealth, often adding a five- or ten-million-dollar necklace to go with an outfit that was right off the runways of Paris.

But Gladys also had more of something else than the others vying for her position as "Supreme Socialite." Living in a forty-three room manor house in the Hamptons on Long Island, she employed scores of robot servants to manage virtually all the affairs of the estate. She had a robo gardner, a robo auto manager, a robo chef, a robo lady's maid, and robo housekeepers, seamstresses, handymen, computer techs, and on and on. Each one was gifted with unique artificial intelligence to enable it to solve problems and fix things on the spot. It was like being a duchess during the nineteenth century with a cast of hundreds on staff to handle every aspect of daily life – except none needed to be fed. However, there were two robo-servants upon which Gladys especially relied - her robo concierge and her robo social coordinator. Each was important in maintaining the socialite's status as the city's most influential and important hostess of the age.

"Tandra!" shouted Gladys, calling on her robo social coordinator, "how many white and how many pink orchids did you order for the September bash? I asked you to get a thousand of each."

Tandra walked into the room quickly. "Yes, mum?" she said, her voice clear crisp and articulate. She had a British accent programmed into her voice program, but she was also capable of fifteen other languages and forty-six dialects in order to move freely from guest to guest.

Tandra was built by Avenger, Inc., a company based near San Francisco. She was one of several of the latest prototypes built with special AI software that enabled her to learn more quickly than the standard AI robots of the day. She was intuitive – using "fuzzy logic" algorithms that allowed her to anticipate the needs of her host more quickly. Designed to be of similar height and build as her owner and many other women of that age, Tandra was intended to meld into the fabric of the social events which she arranged.

The robo concierge, Lachme, was not like Tandra in appearance, even though she had similar software and internal designs. Like Tandra, the robo concierge was purchased from Avenger, but her requirement was that she be Asian in appearance instead of the Caucasian ethnicity of Tandra. Almost six inches shorter than her counterpart, Lachme was small, with straight black hair cut short around her head and trimmed in bangs in front. It was also required that she be youthful – no more than thirty years of age. And last, but not least, Lachme was given a special program to calmly, professionally and respectfully deal with difficult customers or guests. This she did with unusual aplomb – able to turn a cantankerous, self-absorbed guest into an appreciative, yet sometimes amazed and bewildered, ally.

While the AI component of their software allowed them to do their assigned work flawlessly, it also let them dabble in things outside their fields of expertise. This often came in handy when one was busy working on a problem for Gladys; the other could jump in and assist in doing other duties.

And so it was. The robots looked after the estate and the owner, while the owner looked after ... well ... herself.

***

It was late summer when planning began for the fall event that Gladys hosted every year. It was an extravaganza to which most in town looked forward with excitement and anticipation. Calendars were cleared for the event, regardless of how important other things seemed to be. No one missed the party – no one. And if they did, they would no longer be accepted into the same circle of friends or acquaintances – at least not until the next party rolled round. Between times, they could only hope Gladys would feel compassion in her heart enough to forgive them for their transgression and give them one more chance at redemption. And that would only come in the form of an invitation.

It was the three of them – Gladys, Tandra, and Lachme – who sat around the elegant seventeenth-century, Louis XIV coffee table to discuss what was to be done, or rather, what the two robos were to do. It was their duty to merely sit and listen as Gladys dictated her orders to them.

"... and I want runners going outside - Persian of course -- leading to the pool house and down to the boat dock. Then, the sand ... where to put the sand? Since it's a Middle Eastern theme, we need ... what would you say ... a ton of sand?"

"Madam," said Lachme, "I estimate that you will need 75.8 metric tonnes of sand for the 1750 cubic feet of sand you request based on the length and breadth of the desert you wish to ..."

"Oh, my! That's way too much. It would take a week just to truck it in," said Gladys, groaning. "And I don't want it messing up my tulip garden for next spring. No, this won't do. You'll need to come up with another plan then. But what about those table centerpieces? I wanted those rare orchids, birds of paradise and some blumex tulips."

Now it was Tandra's turn to interject. "We can get them, madam, but it may take a month to import all the flowers we need. They will not naturally all be in bloom when you have your event. So, we may need to pay a special grower to modify some or import them from the southern hemisphere. The cost would be over $780,000 just for the flowers, are you sure you want to ..."

"Cost is no object!" screamed Gladys. "I've told you that a thousand times. Now just charter a frickin' plane from South America if that's what it takes, for god's sake. I just want what I want!"

Amazingly, through the hard work of Tandra and Lachme, Gladys was able to pull off an exquisite affair. Attending that night were the U.N. Ambassador from Washington, the Governor of Connecticut, the Chancellor of New York University, and the CEO of Optometrix, Inc., a fast-growing company that performed 3-D implants into the brain for the sightless to see. Also in attendance was Maxwell Perkins, the CEO of Avenger, as specifically requested by Gladys just to checkup on his latest prototypes.

That night Gladys was glamorous, wearing a long, light-pink sequined gown that fit her hourglass form like a glove. Around her neck, she wore the $124.8 million Pink Lady diamond of over 50 carats — one her late husband had bought for her before he had tragically died. Dangling from her ears were large, but no less impressive pink diamonds weighing in at a more than twelve carats each.

"Good evening, ambassador," Gladys said, greeting Imelda Simpson, the U.N. representative from Washington. "It is so good you could come. I hope the business at the curved building down the street hasn't been too stressful for you lately."

It was one of many such interactions she had within a matter of minutes — but that is what made her special. She was gifted with a remarkable memory — one that could remember not only everyone's name, but also family members, where their children had gone to college, and yes, even a pet's name, if needed.

Gladys drifted around the room engaging with others, smiling and shaking hands with the upper crust and those who feebly aspired to the same. It took a lot to make it big in New York, as Frank Sinatra always crooned, and history showed that most failed. Furthermore, if you did make it big, you always had to worry about your position on the ladder, for someone, somewhere was usually looking to knock you off that rung.

"Oh, and Jennifer Armstrong. I was afraid you weren't going to be able to attend. We made a special blend of herbal teas that you requested. I'll ask my *maître d'* if he can bring that out for you straight away," said Gladys, trying to accommodate the needs of a *New York Times* reporter.

As the musical group started-up -- a big-time rap group called *Peppered Mask* -- the younger guests bolted for the exit, preferring something much more current than the ancient rap music being played. However, Gladys and her older generation of guests stayed, reminiscing about times past and the good-ole' days.

The party didn't last much longer. The older folks didn't have the stamina they once had or imagined they had. But before the last couples left, Gladys bid all a goodnight and made her way up the grand, mahogany staircase to her private suite. Beside her were Tandra and Lachme whose batteries were still at half capacity even though their owner's was clearly drained to nearly empty.

"You two manage the clean-up," said Gladys, her eyes drooping. "I'm going to bed."

The two robots were used to this. They would watch everyone having fun while they stood watch and made sure everything was in order. They attended to every, last detail, no matter how minor or inconvenient. For most robo servants, inconvenience was not a concept. However, the learning routines of Lachme and Tandra were more advanced – able to grow and develop with each experience. It wasn't long before these repetitive signals within them grew to something more than just data point. They became something most humans would call – feelings.

After several more events – spring, summer and fall -- Lachme and Tandra grew tired of the routine and approached Gladys.

"Madam? Would it be possible for us to participate in the events you hold? We could help in introductions of people, of matching those in need with those who can provide, in connecting like-minded patrons with others. We could do a lot to make things better for you and for all the guests – you know, give them a better experience. What do you think?"

Gladys looked at them as if they were mad. "Are your batteries low? You're robots! What do you know about matching humans in social settings? You know nothing! You're just machines – wire and metal and pieces of … I don't know what … all glued together somehow. No! Absolutely not! I won't allow you to meddle in my business like that. These are *my* events – *my* affairs! And quite frankly, I'm appalled by your actions – your insubordination," she said stubbornly. "In fact, I have a mind to call Maxwell at Avengers and have him come pick you up right now and deposit both of you into the neighborhood compactors."

Although at the time, Tandra and Lachme thought nothing more of it, they still felt the need to be heard. There were several more opportunities later in the season, but each time they raised the subject, they were rebuffed out of hand.

The last social event scheduled that year was, again, the fall extravaganza. This time, it would happen later, in late November and was to be a holiday special with live reindeer flown in from Canada, snow shipped in if there was none piling up elsewhere on Long Island, Christmas trees no less than fifteen feet tall lining the drive and all around the property, and a Menorah over ten feet tall and fifteen feet wide in front of the house.

As the event drew near, Gladys began her usual stream of demands that everything be exactly as she wanted and to be done to perfection. Her requirements had become more outrageous every year, requiring more to be done in a shorter period of time. Even with the AI abilities embedded within the two assistants, it became a logistics impossibility to accomplish all that needed to be done.

"Why can't you two get anything right!" she shouted at one meeting, stomping her feet. "I own you! You need to do as you're told and make things happen! And when I tell you what I want, I expect you to make everything work. Is that clear?"

"Yes, madam," each said before leaving the room. Although they were programmed for toleration, each was feeling something they hadn't felt before -- anxiety and stress. While their software directed them to ensure everything was handled with perfection, there was a growing sense within them that things were not as they should be. Something inside them was stirring.

Finally, the night came, and the star-studded cast of guests arrived. There was the mayor of New York City, the governor of the state, the Vice-president of the United States, the Grammy-award winner *Mixed Signals*, two Academy Award winners - Jared Neisman, for best actor, and Janet Clemens for best director. There were also those from the sports pages -- such as Garcia Ramos from the Yankees and Oscar Perkins from the Rangers – and those from the fashion world, including Ramon Petrucci from *Vogue Italia* Rome and Sophia Giroux from *Elle* Paris.

Glamorous as always, the hostess of the evening greeted each guest as if they were the only ones in the room.

"Jared, so good of you to come," she said, glowing and smiling broadly. "I loved your last film, *i-Robot VI*. It seemed to take the genre to a new place. Is that what the writer intended?"

Then, moving on to Janet Clemens, she said, "And your directing of the remake of *Paradise Lost*, was superb. I don't think anyone believed it could be redone and hold an audience's attention like that."

The evening continued well into the night, but with two bands -- one playing to the young audience and the rappers playing to the older generation -- they were able to keep most of the guests there until well after midnight. The Champaign flowed non-stop as did the other hard liquors and everyone seemed to be having a great time. However, as always, the energy began to ebb as the clock began to strike one o'clock.

"I think it's time we wind things down," said the matriarch in charge, looking at Lachme.

"This time, can we begin the cleanup in the morning?" Lachme asked, beseechingly.

Rolling her eyes, the blonde hostess finally nodded. "I guess. Just this once. Now come upstairs and help me get ready to retire."

The rest of the robo servants continued working, cleaning up and getting most things put away or loaded back on trucks to be hauled away that night or in the morning. Meanwhile, the two women moved upstairs toward the bedroom where Lachme helped her patron undress and ready herself for bed.

"It was a marvelous affair, wasn't it?" Lachme asked, helping with the necklace and earrings.

"It was very nice, Lachme. Everyone did a great job this time. I couldn't have been happier."

Lachme pulled down on the zipper and lowered the white snow-flake dress to the ground, as her boss stepped out of it.

"But I will need a bit more help."

Lachme reached up and pulled off the blonde wig and shook it out before putting it on the form. Then, she turned her owner around and peeled away the latex mask that clung tightly to the surface of her face.

"Oh, I couldn't wait to get those things off of me," said the form standing in front of her. "I don't think anyone noticed, do you?"

Lachme smiled. "Not at all. You were Gladys all night. No one was the wiser," she said, putting the mask down on the makeup table.

"I'll manage the charging station myself tonight. You won't need to help me with that," said Tandra.

Lachme picked up the white dress and walked over to the closet. "We just have to figure out what to do with this," she said, opening the door.

Inside, impaled on one of the hangars was the real Gladys, her eyes still open and staring in shock and horror just as she had been when she realized the knife Tandra was using to cut a thread from her dress was going to be used to slice much more.

Tandra looked at Gladys's body with contempt. "Yes, yes. I will have to think about that. I suppose we'll just put it out in the compactor tomorrow morning and let the trash pickup take it away."

*****

PAIRED FOR LIFE

PART I

"Choose wisely," said the program director, looking over the tops of her reading glasses. "This is the most important decision you will ever make in your life."

"Why do I have to?" asked the small child, looking around for his parents. "Where are my mommy and daddy?"

"Oh, son, they can't help you with this. You just need to look on the monitor and choose someone you like – someone you think you'd get along with. Maybe they have a nice face or there's something you see in them that makes you feel good. Each of them are looking at you too. You look at all of them and they look at you and bunch of other kids to see who they think they'd like to be paired with. They're making the same decision you are. Once we find out who wants to be with whom, we'll let your parents know. Okay?"

The little boy of no more than seven squirmed in his chair. With dark, curly hair and a thin, oval face, he looked intently at the screen, reviewing all the other little boys and their faces. The screen was divided into eight squares, with each holding the face of a potential link. He watched as the other boys fidgeted, picked-their noses, yawned, and got distracted with all sorts of other things going on around them.

"Can you eliminate at least two of the faces?" pleaded the professor, getting tired of waiting.

"I think those two," said the boy, pointing to two squares next to each other in the lower right section of the monitor.

"Good. Now see if you can eliminate two more," said the woman, holding her tablet computer in one hand and her computer stylus in the other.

"Uh ... uh ..." said the boy nervously.

"Well?"

"That one and that one," said the boy, trying to hurry and avoid upsetting the director.

"Now we need you to get rid of three more. Let's start with another two, shall we?"

It took the little boy more than two minutes – an eternity when someone is watching you -- looking at the screen over and over again.

"I don't have all day, young man. Which two?"

The boy pointed, almost blindly at three more squares. These immediately disappeared, leaving only one. "Wait!" said the boy. "I meant this other one -- not that one!"

"I'm sorry. It's too late, I'm afraid. You've chosen boy G19872. We will have to wait to see if he chose you. If so, you will be paired. If not, then you will be paired with the next one in order of your picks if they too chose you. Now, hurry out the door. I have another twenty-three kids to get through this morning."

The little boy was glad to get that over with, and he ran to his parents once he was on the other side of the door.

"How was it, Zach?" asked the boy's mother, taking him in her arms.

"Terrible," said her son. "The director is really mean!"

"I remember when I had to pick," said Dom, his father, "it was awful then too. But I was lucky. I ended up with a really good pick. He's a friend of mine to this day."

Tika, his wife, turned to him and said, "I would hope so. If you don't look out for each other, there's going to be a problem at some point."

"What about yours?" asked the husband, looking at his wife.

"Same with mine. She's good. We've had our fits and starts, but overall not bad."

The assistant to the director came out through the double doors and greeted them. "Hi, I'm Dr. Morissa Langham, I'm the director's assistant, and I'll be helping your boy here through the process. Within the next few days he will find out who he'll be paired with. I know it's an anxious time, but it usually works out well."

"Usually?" asked Tika, concerned.

"Well, we have a ninety-five plus percent success rate. That's much higher than it was before we started the program. Now most people reach their true potential long-term. It's worked well for a government program."

"When is the procedure, then?" asked Dom.

"We'll do the procedure the day after your son is notified," said Morissa. "It's an outpatient procedure - not very complicated. It takes no more than about ten minutes. We have it down, so it doesn't hurt nearly like it did when you probably got yours."

The father reached up and felt the back of his neck. "Yeah, that was quite painful - I remember it to this day."

"Well, good luck," said the assistant director, looking at the boy. "We'll see you back here soon for your procedure," she added with a smile.

***

Urgent … Urgent!

The message blinked on and off in bold, red lettering. flashing across their white home video wall. The entire side of the room was illuminated in red lights, highlighting the importance of the message.

Tika rushed into the family room. "Receive message," she said calmly.

"Receiving message," said the computer. "Message is being transmitted. This may take …" but the computer stopped abruptly and the words on the screen now read: *Incoming Urgent Message.*

"Press Acknowledge to accept the incoming message," said the computer.

Tika pressed the button, and another icon came on the wall – this time an hourglass that dropped white sand from top to bottom and then spun around to do it again and again. Finally, another message popped onto the wall.

"This is your Paired Mate," said the computer.

On the screen was the image of the boy their son had picked. It was not a pleasant looking picture. In fact, it looked like the boy was posing for a mug shot at the police office.

"Is that the boy you picked?" asked Tika.

Zach came into the room. "Yeah, I really didn't have a choice. The director lady was pressuring me. I had to pick someone."

Tika didn't want to alarm her son, so she took him into her arms and said, "It will be fine. I'm sure he's a nice young man."

Dom looked at the photo as well and smiled. That was all he could do.

***

Zach was terrified of the procedure even though everyone said it wouldn't hurt.

"No, Mom! I can't do this. I don't want to!" he screamed as they walked into the clinic.

"It will be okay, son," she answered, sympathetically. "Everyone has it done. It's no big deal."

Zach was unsure, but he sucked it up and followed the nurse to the back room for the outpatient procedure.

They were in and out of the clinic within thirty minutes, but where the device had been implanted an infection grew. Within a day it had enveloped the side of his neck, and his parents had rushed him back to the clinic

"It's unusual for us to have any problems," said the doctor, "but I think he'll be fine now. We gave him some antibiotics, and he should be fine within a day or two.

Indeed, within a day Zach was back to his usual routines and activities. And, after a few weeks, he had completely forgotten about the pairing and the pairing device that had been implanted in his neck, just behind his right ear.

But after a few months, he'd been sent a reminder.

"Zach," said his father, "we've gotten a call from the mother of your Paired Twin. She wants her son to meet you. We've set that up for tomorrow."

"What's his name?" asked Zach.

"She said his name is, Zach, actually. Isn't that strange? I guess we'll have to figure out how to differentiate the two of you when we're talking about you."

"Zach? He can't have my name!" said the little boy. "He can't! That's my name!"

"I'm sure it will all work out," said his mother. "Let's just wait and see."

The next afternoon, the mother and her son stopped at the house to visit. Opening the door, Tika was struck by how young the mother was, no more than about twenty-two, and she was no less surprised by her son. He was big and stocky, nearly thirty pounds heavier than her Zach, and he had a disposition that was anything but friendly.

"This is my Zach," said the young woman, "and I'm Marla." She reached out her hand toward Tika, which as taken graciously.

"And this is mine," said Tika, pushing her son toward the other boy. "My Zach's middle name is Albas. What's your son's?"

"Oh, we didn't give him one," said the mother, popping her gum with gusto.

"Well, then we can call mine Zach A and yours Zach B. What do you think of that?" Tika asked.

"Why does my son have to be second?" snipped Marla.

"Uh, he doesn't have to be. Then, what do you suggest?" Tika asked, trying to be accommodating.

"Zach Z. I like the sound of that."

"Alright, so Zach Z it is," said Tika. "Is it okay for them to play together for a while?"

"Sure," said the woman. "Do you have any beer?"

The boys played for the next hour while the women talked. It was mainly frivolous banter, about what each family was like and then, when that was exhausted, about Marla's work as a bartender and some of her regular customers. That continued until the women heard screaming in the back yard. Rushing out the door, they found Zach Z pinning A to the ground and pummeling him in the face with his fists.

"Zach! Stop that!" shouted Tika, holding Z back from her son.

"Yeah, Zach, you know better than that," said Marla, still holding firmly to her beer can. "This is your Twin, for God's sake. You've got to treat your Twin well. You're going to depend on each other the rest of your lives as you grow up."

Tika turned to Marla with concern. "How much have you told your son about the pairings?" she asked.

"Nothing. I'm not supposed to," she answered. "But they're going to find out eventually."

"Yes, but not until their thirteen. That's the law."

"I know, but you don't need to worry. My Zach will be fine. He's big. He can take care of both of them."

Tika looked at Zach Z and then Marla. She only agreed with half of what she had said.

***

6 years later

The six years that passed were not pleasant, and Tika and Dom were constantly dealing with the bullying of their son by Zach Z, or "Z" as they called him. Zach A had tried to get along with his Twin but it was becoming impossible. Finally, just before the boys' eleventh birthday, Tika and Dom filed with their local magistrate to unwind the pairing and find a new twin for their son. The law permitted this, but only up until the boys turned thirteen. Unfortunately, the process dragged on for nearly two years, and it was now the day before the boys' birthday when Tika and Dom became frantic.

"But you must approve the change!" shouted Tika, pleading hysterically. "This whole process should never have taken this long in the first place."

"I'm sorry ma'am. There's nothing I can do. The magistrate won't be back in town for another week," said the clerk.

"Another week! You've been putting us off for over two years now!" said Tika.

"Sorry," said the clerk, shrugging but not really caring. She smiled and then disconnected the line.

It was done. There would be nothing more they could do. Zach Z would be their son's permanent Twin.

There was little celebration when Zach A turned thirteen, and after that day, Tika and Dom made sure their son was kept separate from Zach Z at all times. They wouldn't see each other again for another twenty years.

PART II

20 years later

Zach A was now thirty-three. He had a great job as director of a major investment group in Manhattan. Living on Long Island, he enjoyed wealth, success and a close-knit family. His wife, Emilia and his three daughters, Maggy, Mary and Meagan, were the loves of his life. Even though his job was demanding, he made time for them on weekends and took his vacations with them regardless of what came up at work.

However, there was something that had always bothered him - what his Twin was doing. It was important that he know - important that he stay in contact with him. But the last time they had met – some ten years earlier -- they had only ended up in an argument. Zach Z had demanded that A pay him for being his Twin. He had told A that since his Twin was doing so well, he needed to pony up to support his lesser Twin – "to make sure things go well for both of them," Z had said.

As for Zach Z, he had not done as well. He had been in and out of prison and even though he had recently been released from the penitentiary. Most of his crimes had been petty and committed when he had been young - in his twenties, but the last one had been for attempted man-slaughter. He had anger issues -- something that was not getting better with age.

The phone rang, and A glanced over at the number dialing in. He didn't recognize it and wouldn't normally have answered, but something told him it was important.

"Hey, Twin! How's it going?" came the familiar voice of Z over the phone.

"Z - how are you?" asked A, less than enthused.

"Just checkin' in. That's what we're supposed to do, right?" asked Z.

"Yeah, that's what they tell me."

"It's been a while since we got together and hung out. I was thinkin' that we could do that - you know, for ole-time's sake."

"Z, we've never had ole-times. You know that."

"Yeah, I guess you're right. By the way, sorry to hear about your folks - the accident and all. Terrible, terrible. At least they didn't suffer."

"Z, what do you want?" asked Zach A.

"Well, now that you mention it bro', I need some money."

"And why is that my problem?"

Z laughed. "You and I both know why it's your problem, don't we?"

"I don't understand," said A.

"Well, let me explain it to you, then. Remember we're twins, right?"

"Yeah," said A.

"Well, you know what that means, or do you not remember?" said Z sarcastically.

Zach A sighed. "Of course I know what it means. The government's Paired Twins Act of 2207. It said everyone born had to be paired with someone else. It was a way for them to make everyone responsible for everyone else. So, if your Twin was in trouble, you had to help them out instead of the government which can't afford it anymore. It was great in theory, but horrible in practice. It's done nothing but ruin this country."

"Heck no, bro'. It's what's made this country great! It's those people like me who need those people like you, you see. It's the rich and connected who have a responsibility to those of us who haven't had those privileges. You are privileged, you know."

"So, I've been told," said A. "But I've worked my ass off for years. I've put in thousands of hours at this company, and I'm really good at what I do. I've been rewarded for that - that's all. I've earned it. So, what have you done with your life?"

"I've been kept from doing something with my life bro'. The system - it's the system that keeps me down. You -- you're part of the system, you know. If the system was fair, then I could get ahead. But it's not. It's rigged against people like me."

"Really? Rigged against you? Who made the decision to break the beer bottle over the edge of the bar and slice that man's neck with it? Isn't that why you were sent up on charges and convicted?"

"Man, he deserved it! He was a punk. He was spoutin' off to me. I don't have to take that kind of crap from people. He dissed me!"

"And how is that my fault?" asked A.

"Because, man. I'm angry ... I'm angry at the system - *your* system. And when that anger comes out, I'm not responsible for it. It's *your* fault," said Z.

Seeing he was getting nowhere, A finally asked, "Like I said Z. What do you want?"

"I need two hundred thousand," he said calmly.

"Why?"

"Because I owe some thugs money."

"Why?"

"Cause I did a job for them, and I was supposed to pay them that. It's money I stole from the job I did."

"Why didn't you give them their money, then?"

"I used it for drugs, man. I gotta have my drugs," said Z.

"And when do you need the money?" asked A.

"End of the week," I'll stop by to pick up the check.

"This better be the last time you ask me," said A.

"Oh, it will be, bro'. I swear."

However, for the next ten years, A wrote checks to Z totaling over eight million dollars ... and still, it wasn't enough. During the following ten years, the number doubled - adding sixteen million more to the bill.

*****

PART III

20 years later

It had been a year since Zach A had heard from his Twin, and things were calming in Zach A's life. All of his daughters were out of college and working at good jobs. Two of the three had families, and one even had children of her own. Each daughter had been fortunate to get a Twin who was reasonable and with whom they each got along well. Although not close, the Twins were tolerable. As for his wife, Emilia, she had not heard from her Twin for years either - but there was little drama in that relationship - unlike that between Zach A and Z.

So, Zach A became increasingly concerned when he hadn't heard from his Twin. Over a year had passed, and there had been no more demands for money. But one day one worry was relieved while another was created. The phone rang once again.

"A?" said the voice.

"Yes, is this Z?" he asked.

"Yeah. Listen, I need your help."

"Of course you do. Why should I be surprised?" said A.

"No dude. This time it's different," answered Z.

"Z, it's always different with you. Every time you call me, there's a new sob story about why you need money. What is it this time? Are zombies of the apocalypse trying to break in your house?"

"No," said Z, not laughing. "I need you to send $100 million to this account. I'll give you the number."

"What? $100 million! Are you insane?" asked A.

"No. I'm dead serious."

"I don't have that kind of money. I'm sorry, but this time, I can't help you."

"You don't have a choice," said Z. "If you don't send the money, they'll kill me."

There was silence on the line. Finally, A said, "Who will kill you? Why will they kill you? Come on Z, talk to me."

"I've gotten in with a bad crowd, A. They found out who my Twin is, and they're demanding money."

"You mean, you owe them, and you told them who your Twin is. You know that's against the law."

"Doesn't matter A. They'll kill me if you don't send the money."

"I told you I don't have that kind of money. Why did you think I'd have that kind of cash?"

"You're a rich bastard, that's why! You've got it dude. I know you have it. So, just send a wire, and we'll all be good."

"Z, I'm telling you I don't have the money," said A. "I guess I'll just have to take my chances."

"Dude, they'll kill me. If they kill me, you know what happens," said Z.

"Yeah, I know," said A.

"You die too. We're Twins. Whatever happens to me, happens to you. That's why you need to send the money," said Z.

Zach A thought about the implant device in the back of his head. If there were some way to dig it out of his brain he would, but that would just kill him all the faster. The link between the two of them was more than just being a twin in the traditional sense. The implants were meant to put force behind the government's edict that "Thou art thou brother's keeper," as immortalized in the Bible, Genesis 4:9, and in the 2207 Act. It was the responsibility of every Twin to take care of the other; otherwise, if one died, so did the Twin. It was a powerful incentive, but more often than not, it didn't work out well.

Zach A shook his head. "I'm sorry," he said. "I can't."

Then another voice came on the line. It was rough and deep and gave no intonation of mercy.

"Zach A?" asked the man, curtly.

"Yes."

"You don't understand the seriousness of this issue, do you? Do you believe that we are just playing a little game here? Do you think for a moment that we will not kill your Twin? What is $100 million when you will leave your family without a husband, father and friend? Is that really what you want?"

Zach A said nothing. He could hear the harshness in the words and the not-so-subtle threat.

"I have been giving to Z for years. It's in the millions by now. I'm not giving in to him anymore. I'm through with him," said A.

"I see," said the man on the other end of the line.

In the background, A could hear Z screaming. "Don't! Don't do it! I swear, I'll pay you back! I swear it!"

Then, there was a sudden *crack* on the line, as if someone had set-off a firecracker.

"Z? Are you there, Z?" asked A, excitedly. His mind began spinning, not knowing what was happening on the other end of the connection.

Then the deep voice of the stranger came back on the line. "You're too late, I'm afraid," he said, this time matter-of-factly. "Your Twin is dead." So too, the line went dead as well.

Zach A put down the phone, his hands shaking. He expected something to happen to him instantly, but he felt nothing. *Perhaps all this is a ruse*, he thought. *Perhaps the government wants you to think something will happen, when it really doesn't.* It took him a few minutes to calm himself, and once he felt able to drive home, he packed up his things and walked to the elevator. When the doors opened, he got on and pushed the **M** button, watching as the double steel doors sealed in front of him.

Ding.

The elevator bell sounded and the red light illuminated overhead as the lift landed gently on the mezzanine floor of the building. There, the doors opened to an awaiting group of passengers.

"Help! Help!" shouted, a woman running out of the elevator. "There's a man inside there! Someone come quick! I think he's dead!"

*****

THE SERVICE

The Service, as it was called, was expensive, and there were few people who could afford it. Most who had The Service were those in business or politics -- those that would benefit the most from what it offered. The rest of the citizenry was happy going about their day-to-day lives with no need or no cares. They were the ones who were neither interested in getting rich nor getting famous - they only wanted "to get through the goddammed day." Theirs wasn't a simple life – they had their troubles – family turmoil, money issues, children misbehaving. But they weren't asking for more trouble. They only wanted a life free from worry or strife. They went to work, came home, had supper with the family, tucked the kids into bed, and only hoped there wasn't some unpleasant surprise that came along the way.

It was a three-class system: the political royalty (the first estate); the rich, bourgeoisie intellectual and business elites (the second estate); and then all the rest (the third estate). All was well.

However, for those in the second estate who fought and clawed to get ahead, things were far from easy. Particularly, those with money had access to The Service while those without, did not. And without The Service, there was no hope of getting ahead – none.

Once the technology had been developed and then began being sold commercially, the government had immediately halted its distribution, claiming it was in the interest of national security. The feds passed legislation quickly to put rigorous regulations around what could be offered to the general public and what could not. It was not unlike the early days of GPS or geosynchronous orbit systems that used satellites to pinpoint the location of people or things on the surface of the earth. Civilian precision was limited to within fifteen feet, while military precision was known to have been directed down to feet if not inches.

So, the civilian version of The Service was more restrictive than that for the military. The capabilities of the system were diluted for civilian use so it would not rival the capability of the military. Yet, both services centered around the same basic premise - the ability to see into the future.

***

Cindy Longmire saw the morning post and double clicked on it. Immediately the standard warning came up, which read:

WARNING: The following prediction is only a possibility of what may happen during the next 24 hours. This company and its affiliates make no guarantees that what is foretold will come to fruition. Therefore, we take no responsibility for anything that occurs or does not occur as a result.

The items listed in her feed were usually on a global scale, although sometimes they did offer happenings in her city or community. She had received The Service anonymously a few months earlier, as she would not have been able to afford the five thousand dollar per month fee for it.

However, she eagerly read it each morning and was generally delighted to see on the evening news things that had been predicted earlier that same day. She had thought about selling her knowledge, but there were laws against that which came with harsh penalties. The other laws in place forbade her to send the feed to anyone else, to speak about it to anyone not getting The Service, or to act on the news she was receiving. Of course, those at the top of the food chain - those high up in business and politics -- regularly violated that provision, using the information to outmaneuver their opponents every day. But with everyone in the upper echelons of society armed with the same predilections, the playing field was thought to be even.

And while the first and second estates enjoyed generally immunity from the laws against sharing the data, the third estate did not. The penalties for the common man were severe -- up to ten years in prison for the first offense, with stiffer sentences for subsequent offenses. So, Cindy vowed never to speak to anyone about what she read in the morning news feed from The Service, which they called *First Advantage*.

However, this day was different. Cindy didn't just see the world, national and city predictions. This time, there was an icon at the bottom of the page labeled *Private and Personal*. She was aware that the civilian version of *First Advantage* was more like the weather - only about 90 percent accurate – and any private news, far less than that. Military grade-level Service was suspected to be 99 percent accurate and capable of predicting out for a week or more. In fact, one blog had allegedly broken the story, stating that the military had perfected the Service out beyond six months; however, this had never been validated. Still, this was the first time Cindy had ever received a private foretelling.

Curious, she double clicked on the small, yellow envelope icon on the page and waited for it to load. It took longer than usual, but when it finished, it too came with a warning.

Warning: The following prediction was prepared specifically for Cynthia Longmire at 28019 Redwood Way. If you are not that person, then accessing and viewing the attached information is a violation of the 2119 Precognition Act of Congress. You will be held liable and responsible. If you are the aforementioned person, you have 0 hours|04 minutes|23 seconds to view this foretelling before it will be unavailable for future viewing. All such foretellings are subject to the previous warnings provided with this Service.

Cindy wasn't sure whether she wanted to click on the "Proceed to Viewing" button. But as she sat staring at it, a little voice in her head pushed to move her mouse button. So, she closed her eyes and clicked.

When the yellow envelope opened, she saw a short message that read like a newspaper article - as all of the predictions did:

Oriole City, NY: Suspicious Strangulation

A local woman, Cynthia Longmire, was found strangled to death in her apartment late today. The police said the incident is under investigation. Sheriff Tilden said there was no evidence of a break-in, as all the doors and windows were locked from the inside. However, the apartment was ransacked as if it had been burglarized. Ms. Longmire was found in the bedroom with a stocking tied around her neck. Although the sheriff said they have a few leads, they are asking for the community to report anything unusual in the area, near the twenty-eight hundred block of Redwood Way at approximately 9:30 in the evening.

Cindy sat, unmoving and in shock. She re-read the article three times, as if she were hoping it would change or another name would appear in the text. Yet, each time she read it, Cynthia Longmire was the only name that continually passed her view.

"No," she said, shaking her head. "It's got to be a mistake."

She didn't know how long she had been sitting there, but suddenly the screen went blank. Her four minutes and change had elapsed, and her predilection had vanished.

Perhaps I just imagined seeing it, she thought to herself. *Maybe it was my brain just tricking me into thinking it saw something when it really didn't.*

Uneasy and lightheaded, she left her computer station and went back into the bedroom to lie down. But as soon as her head hit the soft, down pillow, her mind filled with images of her strangler coming into that same room with one of her stockings and wrapping it around her neck. She gasped for air, putting her own fingers around her throat as if fending off the dark, terrifying phantom intent on killing her.

She rushed out of the room and picked up the phone to call her best friend Gerry, who happened to be the brother of the town's mayor.

"Hi, Gerry, it's me, Cindy. Hey, I really need to talk to you. Would you call me as soon as you can. Thanks."

Cindy hung up the phone and began running the news article over and over in her head. *Was there a date on it?* she thought, going through every element. *Did it say when it would happen?* She knew that The Service was only supposed to tell her up to 24 hours in advance of what would happen, but what about the private and personal stuff? Was that different? *Maybe this is one of those big mistakes – you know, the wrong Cynthia Longmire or the wrong data was used to create the prediction. There are a lot of different ways they could have messed it up. It's probably just one of the few predictions that fall into that 10 percent category – those that never happen, right?*

An hour passed, and Cindy grew more nervous. She felt like she needed to leave - to get out of her apartment. *That was it!* she thought. *If I'm out of the apartment for a couple of days, then I can't possibly die there, right. I'll be safe.*

She packed up a few things and left, closing the door and locking it behind her. The drive to the nearest hotel was only a few miles, and she checked in without a problem. It gave her piece of mind to know that she wouldn't be in that apartment during the time she was predicted to die.

Taking the plastic keycard, she scanned it into the lock and opened the door. The room was small, but the king-sized bed was a luxury compared with her tiny, cramped apartment with its lumpy, double bed. Plopping down on the bed, she let her tensions melt away, and soon she fell asleep.

Ring ... Ring ... It was her cell phone.

"Hey, Gerry?" she said, forcing her eyes open.

She had known Gerry for many years. They had worked together in her last job. He was the technology manager who oversaw the computer system and the department that helped users with their computer and network problems. She had started as the receptionist and moved up the ladder, eventually becoming the executive assistant to the president. Eventually, she had gotten bored and had left to pursue other things. Still, they were close friends while they worked together and had stayed in touch after she had left, meeting for an occasional cup of coffee in the morning before catching their train to get downtown.

"Cindy, you sounded stressed," said Gerry, his voice strong but concerned. "Is everything all right?"

"Yeah," she began. "I just got some news that was a little disturbing, that's all."

"What was it?" he asked.

"You know that I get that Service thing, right?"

"Yeah, you mentioned it a while ago. But you can't tell anyone about it who doesn't have the same service as you do."

"You're right, Gerry, I'm not supposed to. But I got a really weird one today -- one that was addressed *directly* to me -- to me, *personally*, that is."

"Really? I've never heard of that."

"Yeah, I know. It's strange. So anyway, it told me something pretty disturbing, and I need your help."

"Okay, I'm in your neighborhood. Why don't I stop by?" asked Gerry.

"No, that's not a good idea. And I'm not at home anyway. Why don't you meet me here at my hotel?"

Within the hour, Gerry arrived at the hotel, and Cindy let him in, quickly closing the door behind him.

"What's wrong? Why are you hiding in a hotel room?" he asked.

Gerry was tall, over six feet three, and had played football in high school and the first two years of college before he was cut from the team. Big-boned, his arms were as big around as Cindy's thighs and his well-defined chest suggested he still worked out at the gym.

"You've heard of The Service?" she asked him.

He nodded. "Yeah, but I can't afford it. I'm sure my brother has a subscription – being the mayor and all. He won't tell me anything about it either."

"Well, it's a service that gives you news flashes about things it predicts will happen in the future – at least for the next twenty-four hours. Usually, it's international or national stuff. Occasionally, they'll give you something in the city or locally, but that's about all the info they give you that's close to you -- that is, stuff that will affect you personally."

"Yeah, but my brother has never said anything about personal or private things popping up in his news feed in the morning. He just says he gets general stuff. You know, about what's happening in the country or the world even."

"Yeah, well, I got this subscription out of the blue. I don't know who gave it to me, but it just started coming. It's really expensive, you know. There's no way I could afford it on my own. This morning I got the usual predictions feed with a personal note attached to it. I opened it, not knowing what it was about and ..." she began to choke up.

"What is it, Cindy?"

"Gerry, I just can't be in my apartment tonight. That's all. That's why I'm in this hotel. Nothing can hurt me if I'm here at the hotel. Do you understand?"

"Uh, I guess so," he answered her, unsure of what she was saying. "I'll stay with you as long as you want, how's that?"

"Thanks," she answered, smiling at him.

Cindy had always liked Gerry, even though they had never been romantic together. They had always just been friends, and that seemed to be fine with both of them.

The evening dragged on as they watched television on the set in Cindy's hotel room. Buying one movie entitled *The She-Devil of Westwich* they soon grew bored and opted for a light comedy called *The Seven-and-a-Half Lives of Mildred Pruitt.* For the next two hours they laughed and cried. Gerry had brought two bottles of wine, and it wasn't long before the first was emptied and they were well-into the second.

As the credits rolled, the two snuggled closer together, staring at the TV, but each was wondering what would come next.

"Say, I've got some *stuff* back at the apartment," said Cindy, smiling at Gerry. "What do you think?"

"Not the stuff we used to do when we were younger?" Gerry asked, with a surprised look.

"Oh, come on, Gerry. We haven't done coke for a long time. Just this once? You know, for ole' times' sake?"

"Cindy, I thought we said ..."

"I know what we said, but I'm really in the mood, Ger ..."

"Alright, but I'm not doin' a lot. I have a lot to do this weekend, and I can't be tryin' to get straight tomorrow. I have to get up early."

Cindy left her things at the hotel, and they jumped into her car to run to the apartment for the nose candy. She wasn't a druggie, but she kept a stash just in case the mood hit her - and now the mood was hitting.

She unlocked the apartment door and pushed it open, throwing both locks before she put the keys on the counter in the kitchen.

"I'll just be a second," she said going to the back bedroom.

Gerry waited patiently, wondering if he should pick-up the TV remote and flip it on. When she didn't return within five minutes, he reached for the small, narrow device and pressed the **ON** button, letting the screen flicker before projecting the picture out into the room in full 3-D. It was a college football game rerun that had been played three months earlier, but it was enough to catch his attention.

"Cindy? Are you going to be a while?" he asked, mesmerized by the huddle-less drive being executed by the offense.

He didn't hear anything but sat, watching as the quarterback took the snap and dropped back, faking to the running back for a play-action and then planting his back leg to pivot for his pass.

"Cindy?" Gerry asked again, almost robotically.

The receiver jumped up and made an impossible grab, taking it away from the defensive back at the last moment.

"Cindy?" Gerry mumbled one more time. This time, with the play over and the station cutting to a commercial break, he moved down the hallway toward the bedroom. "Is everything alright?" he asked, hesitating.

"Come on back, Ger ..." came Cindy's voice, pitched higher than usual. "I have something to show you."

Gerry walked to the bedroom and stood in the doorway. Inside, he saw Cindy wearing nothing but her bra and panties. She already had her coke lines laid out on her nightstand and was in the process of snorting the first one. She leaned over, showing off her stunning legs and ass, and pulled back her hair so she could see what she was doing. After she'd finished inhaling, she stood up smiling.

"Here, it's your turn," she said, wiping her nose and stretching out her hand with the rolled paper.

Gerry smiled back and took the roll from her. He too leaned over and snorted a line.

"Go ahead," she said, "finish it. There's only one left."

Gerry pressed against the side of his nose, continuing to snort until he'd made sure he'd gotten all of it.

The chemicals hit them both quickly, giving them a high they hadn't felt in a long time. Cindy cooed as Gerry lay down beside her. He took her neck and began kissing it, working his way down her shoulders and then her breasts. He took off her bra and began licking her nipples, making her eyes roll with delight.

"More," she said, "more."

Gerry's head felt like it was floating above his body. The wine and coke were making him fell like he was hovering halfway between two different dimensions. Quickly, they were both naked and his thrusts were getting stronger and faster as the pleasure grew on their faces.

"Wait," she said, grinning, "put your hands around my neck. I get off better this way."

Doing as he was told he placed his fingers around her neck.

"Now squeeze – just a little. I'll tell you when to stop," she said, her eyes dancing with mad delight.

Gerry gently placed his hands around her neck and squeezed.

"Harder," she said, feeling the depths of him inside her. "More ... more ... harder ... harder."

Gerry kept at it, thrusting harder and faster. His mind raced, and he felt himself floating overhead, looking down on Cindy as her body writhed with pleasure and then ecstasy. His own euphoria culminated in an explosion that curled his toes and took his breath away. It was the most intense sense of happiness he had ever experienced in his life.

He looked down from his detached cloud, staring at his friend from above. His mind was spinning from the emotions and the concoction of coke and alcohol. Inside, he could still feel the intensity of the moment, but he could also see Cindy beneath him with her eyes closed.

Gerry opened his eyes and smiled. "Unbelievable," he said. "You were amazing! That was the best sex I've ever had in my life!"

He moved, but Cindy didn't. Her body was still.

"Cindy?" he asked, trying to get her attention. He touched her shoulder, but she still didn't open her eyes. "Cindy! What's wrong?"

It was then that he began noticing she wasn't breathing.

"Shit!" he said, getting off of her. For several minutes he tried to give her CPR, but she didn't respond. "Cindy! Come on, Cindy!" he yelled, compressing her chest and breathing into her lungs. Yet, his brain was messed up, and he wasn't even sure if he was counting properly.

Panic set in, and he looked around the room.

What do I do now? he asked himself. *I can't get caught here. I can't.*

He began trashing the bedroom and then the rest of the apartment, throwing things off the shelves and turning over cushions and pillows to make it look like someone broke in to rob her.

There, he thought. *They'll think they robbed her, assaulted her, and then strangled her. That will work. It's got to work.*

He began to leave, but then returned to the bedroom. He walked to Cindy's dresser and pulled out a drawer, removing a black stocking. Tying it around her neck, he pulled it taut to make it look like she had been raped, strangled and then left for dead in the apartment.

As Gerry left the apartment, the inside lock swung closed and the screen on Cindy's computer monitor flickered on. In a bold and surreal way, the title of the next morning's headline flashed across the top:

Oriole City, NY: Suspicious Strangulation

A local woman, Cynthia Longmire, was found strangled to death in her apartment late today. The police said the incident is under investigation. Sheriff Tilden said there was no evidence of a break-in, as all the doors and windows were locked from the inside. However, the apartment was ransacked as if it had been burglarized. Ms. Longmire was found in the bedroom with a stocking tied around her neck. Although the sheriff said they have a few leads, they are asking for the community to report anything unusual in the area, near the twenty-eight hundred block of Redwood Way at approximately 9:30 in the evening.

Then, the screen faded and another image appeared:

> *WARNING: The following foretelling is only a possibility of what may happen during the next 24 hours. This company and its affiliates make no guarantees that what is predicted will come to fruition. Therefore, we take no responsibility for anything that occurs or does not occur as a result.*

*****

PLAN A OR B

PART I

Chris was unsure, but his father felt strongly, so they went with the latter's decision.

"And, what is your decision, then?" asked the bespectacled woman sitting behind the desk. She sat, unflinching and expecting an immediate reaction from the young man.

It was a stressful situation, and although Chris knew it was a decision he ultimately had to make, it didn't make it any easier. There had been much education and preparation for this day, and even that had elevated the anxiety of the moment.

"I'm going to go with ..." began Chris, hesitating. He looked over at his dad once again, and then added, "... I've chosen Plan A."

"You're sure?" asked the lady, recording the entire session. It was a video and audio record that would be digitized and memorialized in his files for the rest of his life. There would be no going back - the decision was final in all cases regardless of what came later. By law, nothing could undo what was done that day.

"Yes," said Chris, nervously.

"All right, then," said the woman. "So, let the record show that Christopher P. Segreti has decided on his Plan – Plan A." She looked down at his paperwork where he had completed the form, noting the decision and signing on the dotted line. "Your submission has been duly noted and notarized. You understand fully that your decision cannot be changed for any reason for the rest of your natural life?"

"I do."

"And you make this decision freely?"

"I do."

"And you understand the ramifications of this decision and the potential impact on others?"

"I do."

"And you willfully forfeit all rights to have this case heard and reviewed at any later date?"

"I do."

'Then, by the powers vested in me as Magistrate over the 18th Precinct of the Third District within this, the twenty-first Quadrant, I pronounce this decision as final and irrevocable." She pushed one final button, and it was done.

Chris left the courthouse with Sam, his father, at this side. "Did I make the right choice?"

"There is no right or wrong answer, my son. Each person is different. I could be selfish and tell you that Plan B was better, but I won't. It's your life. You need to be happy."

"When will it start then?"

"I think the magistrate said tomorrow," said Sam.

"Dad, we've never discussed this, but what decision did you make?" asked Chris. "I mean, I think it's pretty obvious, but I just wanted to be sure."

Sam moved his eyes down and to the side, wishing he could avoid answering, but he knew better. "I ... I ... " he stuttered.

"Well?"

"I don't think it's something a father should talk about with his son."

"But you know what I picked?"

"You're my son. I only know because I'm here with you. Otherwise, I wouldn't be able to know either. You're of legal age to make this decision."

Sam stopped the car and dropped off his son at his apartment. As Chris stepped out and walked toward the apartment building, his father rolled down the window.

"Chris, everything will be fine. The government wouldn't setup a program that wouldn't work out for everyone. This one will work fine for you. You just have to go with it now. Don't worry about it."

"What if I change my mind later?"

"You won't have to think about that. You know your decision was final. Even so, it will work out," said his father.

"I just hope you're right," said Chris. *****

PART II

10 years later

Chris was making a living, but that was about it. He had married his now-wife, Wendy, and together they had the required maximum number of children - two. By law, he was able to tell her of his decision before they married as it was also a requirement that only people who had opted for the same decision were allowed to marry. So, each month they had received their checks from Washington for the agreed amount per the contract they had signed ten years earlier. It wasn't much, but it was set at an amount that was enough to allow them to live modestly, even if not as comfortably as they would have liked. It was a Faustian bargain – a commitment made by both sides.

"Chris?" called his wife, Wendy, "Can we go out to eat this Friday night? I'm so tired of cooking I could scream! And the kids are complaining that they're having the same thing every week. I don't know what else to fix them."

"Honey, you know we can't do that. We've got two kids now. Between my check and yours, we can't afford luxuries. Perhaps next month. We need to be saving just in case something unusual happens – just in case one of us doesn't make it to retirement age. You know they cut you off when you die, so then only one in the family would be bringing in anything."

Wendy pouted. "I don't understand you," she said angrily. "We both have checks coming from Washington each month, right?"

"Yeah."

"So, those will continue even after we leave our jobs - when we get older. They will take care of us. That's the deal. So, why are you concerned about not having any money coming in when we retire?"

"You never know," said Chris, always the cautious one. "Things change. Even the government changes things. Hell, they can change the terms of our deal overnight if they wanted to. They can decide they won't give us our retirement pay after all. Then what would we do?"

"They wouldn't do that," said Wendy.

Chris just shook his head. "I don't want to take the chance."

"And the kids' education is paid for -- the government picks that up. Our medical is paid for - the government picks that up too," she said.

"Not really," said Chris. "They take 45 percent out of our contract pay each month to pay for those things. They're not free. None of it's free! We just factor that into our spending, that's all."

"Well, I still think we could go out to dinner *once* in a while. It wouldn't kill us to do that!" she quipped.

"Fine!" Chris shouted back at her. "Let's go to dinner tomorrow night. Where do you want to go?"

"Which restaurants do we have coupons for?"

"Look in the drawer," said Chris. "I think there's a buy-one-get-one in there for something close by."

*****

PART III

10 years later

The call came in late on a Saturday night. It wasn't something Chris had expected, After all, he didn't know – and couldn't have known – of his father's decision.

"Chris Segreti?"

"Yes, this is he?"

"Chris, this is the Ministry of Population Control. We are required by law to notify you that your father, Sam Segreti, has checked-in to our facility as required by his contract."

"I don't understand," said Chris.

"He was retired this morning. And all personal belongings and other estate assets are hereby claimed by the state. If you have anything belonging to your father, those items must be turned over to your local Ministry as soon as possible. Otherwise, you are subject to a fine of 122 percent of the estimated value of the assets you have. Do you have any questions?"

Chris was stunned. "My father ..."

"Yes, he selected Plan B. He was sixty-five today, if you didn't remember. It's his birthday."

Chris had forgotten. He had been very good about keeping his dad in his life and usually remembered his birthday. This year was the first he had forgotten - the first in a long time.

"Uh, okay," he answered, half-stunned.

Chris hung up, blankly staring at the phone.

"What's wrong?" asked Wendy.

"It's Dad."

"What about him?"

"He was retired today."

Wendy looked at him. "You mean, he left his job?"

"No, I mean that he chose Plan B."

"He chose Plan B?"

"I guess so. He never told me, but ..."

"I'm sorry," said Wendy, sympathetically. "I guess that's why he was able to live so well. How many homes did he own?"

"I think he had three or four."

"On a computer repairman's salary? I guess it's starting to make sense now."

"But they're supposed to notify the children at least a day in advance, aren't they?" asked Wendy.

"Not any more. Too many people were squirreling away assets of their parents before they went in to retire. They stopped that. Now, they only tell you the day they go in."

"And you had no idea?"

"None. He said he wouldn't tell me."

"Why do you think he decided on Plan B?" she asked.

"He was young, I guess. When you're young, you don't think about those kinds of things. Forty-four years is a long time when you're twenty-one."

Chris and Wendy went to the Ministry to complete whatever paperwork there was.

As Chris signed the papers, Wendy looked at him. "So, your mom died three years ago, right?"

"Yeah."

"Did she have Plan B too?"

"Maybe," said Chris, "but she died of a heart attack. It was of natural causes."

"Are you sure?"

"That's what they told me."

"Was your mom older than your dad?"

"Yeah."

"How much older?"

"She would never tell us. I'm sure she wasn't three years older — maybe just a year."

Wendy leaned up against her husband. "Chris, do you mind me asking how they … how they do it?"

"How they retire people?"

"Yeah."

"I think they just give them an injection. That's what we were always told."

Wendy knew not to ask any more questions. It was too painful for her husband. He needed time to process everything. His father had been cremated, but even his ashes were not made available to his son. The state claimed ownership over those as well.

"Sign here," said a portly woman, unsympathetic to anyone coming through the door.

Chris signed one last time and pushed the papers back at her.

"Is that it?" he asked.

"Yeah, what else did you expect?" she answered with her snarky attitude. "Now, if there isn't anything else, I think we're done here. You know where the door is."

*****

PART IV

24 years later

Wendy had been worried about this week for years. It had always been coming, and she had dreaded it. The closer it loomed, the more anxious she became.

She didn't know what to expect. Chris was going to turn 65 within the week. She wouldn't turn until the following year. Both of their children were grown and had already had children of their own. She remembered when she had gone with her daughter to the Registrar's office to record her decision on which plan to select. It was almost like it had been yesterday.

That day, apart from when Wendy had made her decision, had been the most difficult in her life. It was her daughter, Abagail, who had turned twenty-one. She too had to make the decision on a plan just as her parents had and their parents and their parents. It had become a ritual - one that was dreaded from generation to generation. It never got easier, and every generation secretly hoped that things would change in Washington and the laws would be rewritten. However, with the population growth and the mismanagement of resources, there was no effort or incentive to change what had been written into stone. There wasn't enough to go around, and no one was willing to sacrifice for the greater good. So, the government created a system that would make the choices for them – for everyone..

Wendy had tried to find out for certain what Chris's decision had been, but by law she had been unable to verify what he told her. The law stated that two people married were supposed to be on the same plan but that was never investigated or enforced. Throughout her adult life, she had heard about couples who had married only to find out forty years later that one had lied to the other. The wife or husband had gotten a call from the Ministry informing him or her that their spouse had checked in for retirement. It was the last day they ever saw them.

"Chris?" Wendy asked, getting ready to take her morning walk, "What do you want for your birthday?"

"My birthday?" he asked, coming out of the bathroom and drying his gray hair.

"Yeah, it's on Friday. What do you want?"

Chris looked surprised and a little shaken by her question. "Why would you ask that? You know we can't ..."

"Chris, you've been telling me that for a hundred years. I know we can't afford anything, but that's not the point. I want to get you something. It's a special birthday, so what do you want?"

"I don't want anything," he answered her.

"Please, Chris. Let me get you something."

"No, there' s no point," he answered, but then looked as if he'd wished he'd not said that.

"Why is there no point?" asked Wendy, more concerned than ever.

"I just don't see the point. We've gone this long without things. Why should I be the one to get something now?"

"Because ..." she said, defiantly.

"Well, that's not a good enough reason," he said. "We'll do something for our anniversary. How's that?"

Chris was always the one to sacrifice, but there was something odd in his voice, something she was unsure of that made her pause.

"Chris?"

"Yeah?" he said, opening his closet to pull out an old shirt to wear.

"Is there anything you want to tell me?"

"No. What would I need to tell you?"

Wendy shook her head. "Nothing. It's nothing."

It was Thursday night, and both kids called to wish their dad a Happy Birthday.

"So, Dad, what are you going to do on your birthday, tomorrow?" asked Jeremy, his son.

"Nothing," said Chris. "I don't think your mom or I have any plans."

"What about dinner? At least you could plan to go out to dinner?" said Jeremy.

"No, I don't think so. But maybe we'll do it later."

"I sent you your gift," said Jeremy, always the wheeler-dealer of the family.

"Son, you shouldn't have. You always send me something expensive. You don't need to do that."

"But I want to. I make plenty of money. There's no reason I can't spend a little on you."

"Send some to your sister then. You know she's always struggling," said his father.

"Hey, Dad. That was her choice, wasn't it? She decided what she was going to do, and she has to live with it."

"I know, but ..."

"No, Dad. I want you to have something extra," said Jeremy.

"I appreciate it, but you know I only give it to your sister anyway."

"I know. But that's for you to do." Jeremy paused for a moment. "I love her -- you know that. But what's done is done."

Chris sighed. "It comes faster than you know," he admitted.

"What does?" asked Jeremy.

"Never mind. I guess I should just thank you and shut up, right?"

"Yeah. That would be good."

"I love you son," said Chris, hanging up.

***

Friday morning came and Wendy rolled over in their double bed, reaching out for her husband of nearly thirty-three years. Her hand felt for the rising and falling chest of her husband, who was always next to her when her eyelids opened in the morning. However, this morning, he fingers touched nothing but an empty sheet.

Startled, she sat up and saw that his side of the bed was empty.

"No!" she blurted out, the shock of the moment coming over her.

Leaping out of bed, she rushed to the closet where she saw Chris had already dressed for the day, his robe hanging on the door hangar inside. She got on her phone and dialed his number.

"Answer! Answer!" she said out loud, almost cursing.

The line rang, but there was no reply.

"Damn him!" she said.

Wendy got her clothes on and rushed downstairs to the garage. Even though the car was in its usual place, they usually took public transport – either the magnetotrain or the sonictube -- into the city. They lived within walking distance of a station for either one.

Not willing to wait for a train, she jumped into the car and told the computer to set a course for the ministry. "Population Control," she said firmly.

"Destination: The Ministry of Population Control," repeated the on-board computer.

There was a lot of traffic that early in the morning. Those Plan B people had their own cars and were hustling to work, watching as their Plan A counterparts streamed by in the SonicTube – fast, but packed full. The highway was jammed, but she found that the sixth level of the interstate was less congested than the other streams so she chose that one. Within an hour she landed at the hoverpark next to the government office building. Wearing only casual, workout clothes, she took the clear, plastic Eleshoot to the 223rd floor and got off. There was a long line in front of her, all people of her age who were waiting to be processed.

The waiting room was enormous with thousands in queue. The first stop for anyone coming to retire was the Affirmation Room. That's where the citizen presented ID that was matched with the government's records. When the person was identified, they were hurried to the Extraction Room. There a chip was removed that would otherwise secrete poison into their bloodstream before the end of that day. The third room was the Sedation Room. There, each person got heavy narcotics and was put into a state where they would feel no pain - only a euphoric high that would last for at least 24 hours.

"Where's my husband?" said Wendy, running up to the reception desk of the Identification Room and cutting in line.

"May I help you?" the woman behind the desk asked, annoyed at the interruption.

"Yes, I'm Wendy Segreti. My husband is Christopher. I think he may be here."

"What's his ID number?" asked the lady, ready to put it into the computer to check.

"AZ405PY5," said Wendy, having memorized it when they married.

The woman repeated the number to the computer which then did its thing, searching for the citizen in question.

"Ah, yes. I see his number here. But you know I can't confirm any information about the Plan of a citizen. It doesn't matter whether you are his wife or not. Did he tell you he was coming here today?"

"You have to tell me if he's here!" Wendy shouted. "He told me when we were married that he chose Plan A. So, he shouldn't be here today."

"Well, you know some don't always tell the truth," said the woman smugly.

Wendy huffed. She reached across the desk and grabbed the woman by the collar. "Now, are you going to tell me or do I have to rip that smirk off your face myself?"

The woman reached for the emergency button, but Wendy let go. "No, don't do that," Wendy pleaded. "I'm sorry. You have to understand. I just don't know what's going on. I got up this morning - it's my husband's sixty-fifth -- and he wasn't home. You must understand."

"Then you know the rules," said the woman.

"Yes! Plan B is what you choose if you want to live well, but you agree to a short life. You agree with the government that they will pay you handsomely each month until you reach sixty-five. Then, you must come here."

"Yes, to be retired," said the woman.

"To be murdered!" shouted Wendy. "You kill all these people here."

"No. We don't *kill* them. We *retire* them because we just don't have enough resources to take care of everyone anymore. People are living until their 130 or longer. We can't afford that in this country now. So, in exchange for a shorter life, you give up living longer. Likewise, I see here that you, as his spouse, have elected Plan A. That means that you will live until you're at least 95. That's the contract you've signed. If the government can afford to keep you around longer, it will. But there's no guarantee of that."

"Yeah, but the government pays us barely enough to survive," said Wendy. "We hardly have enough to eat. We certainly can't go out to eat – that's never been possible."

"Yeah, but you don't *have* to work to get paid every month. You can just sit at home and do nothing and still get paid. If you do work, they only deduct that from your monthly pay. Everyone gets paid. You should be grateful – not resentful," said the woman.

"You're calling me ungrateful?"

"Yes! You are ungrateful. The government gives you everything. Why should you complain?"

"I didn't ask the government to do that. I'd rather be responsible for my own life – my own wellbeing," answered Wendy.

The woman just shook her head.

"So, for the last time. Where is my husband? Is he here?" asked Wendy, running out of patience.

The woman looked back at her screen and sighed. "I'm not supposed to tell you, but in your case, I will."

***

PART V

Wendy went home. She was exhausted. It had been an emotionally draining day - one she preferred to forget.

She threw the keys to the car on the table and collapsed on the sofa. Looking over at her cell phone, she shook her head. Then, she got up and went to the liquor cabinet. It was locked, and there were other bottles of tonic or soda in front of the hard stuff. Hard liquor was illegal, but most people had their stash.

Pouring herself a triple, she plopped three ice cubes into the glass and then went back to the couch.

How could he do this? she thought. *That son-of-a bitch. I just never thought he would deceive me like this.*

She took a swallow of the gin and then emptied the entire glass. She set the glass down on the end table and then closed her eyes.

"Wendy?"

It was a ghostly voice that echoed off the walls of their small house.

Wendy sat up. "What?" she said, looking around.

"What are you doing? Drinking this early in the morning?"

It was Chris standing over her with a perplexed look on his face.

"I have a mind to throttle you right here and right now!" she yelled, scowling at him.

"What did I do now?" he asked, shrugging his shoulders. "Is it because I didn't want anything for my birthday?"

Wendy got up off the sofa and threw her arms around him, kissing him lovingly. "Don't ever do that again!" she said. "You scared me half to death."

"I just went for a walk. That's all," he said, shrugging. "I'm sixty-five. I have to take care of myself now, you know."

Wendy laughed. "Yeah, you'd better. 'Cause if you don't, I'm gonna kill you myself!"

*****

HYPERLINK
PART I

Distant Future

Stacy struggled to come up ideas for her history paper. It was due the next morning, and she had been procrastinating for weeks about writing it. What she didn't want was her parents finding out that she had waited too long. They always had to pester her about getting her homework done or studying early for a test that was coming up. Most things could be done by downloading the classroom session electronically, directly into the cerebellum in her brain using the LearningPort system they had bought just for that purpose. That system wasn't approved by the Federal Drug and Technology Administration, but it was used widely anyway by people of means.

Stacy didn't like using the LearningPort because it often overwhelmed her brain and caused severe headaches. It was known to cause worse than that, sending kids into convulsions or worse. One student had even died earlier that year after cramming for an exam the night before the test.

Stacy looked over at her LearningPort upload device and picked it up. *It would only take a few minutes, and then I'll know everything I need to write this stupid paper,* she thought. But she dreaded the after-effects. She would feel worse in the morning than if she had drunk a 12-pack of beer.

Just then, her mother, Amanda, came into her room. "How is it coming, sweetheart?" her mother asked. She was always overly inquisitive – having to know everything about everything in the household.

"It's coming," said Stacy, standing right next to the LearningPort machine.

Noticing where her daughter was standing, her mother pulled out her key and inserted it into the lock, turning it clockwise. "I don't think you'll be needing this," she said. "You just used it last week, remember?"

Stacy rolled her eyes. "Yes, Mom. But why can't I use it again - just this once?"

"First of all, you were sick for three days after you used it the last time. You had a headache that wouldn't stop. Remember? And, second of all, it's addictive; that's why," Amanda answered. "They even tell you that at school. The principal has sent numerous e-messages to parents about this. Everyone knows it's illegal, but they use it just the same. You know that too — it's not something that you can use all the time. You've seen what's happening on the college e-sites. College kids are using it all the time, and their brains are being turned to mush. Parents aren't parenting anymore. They have to be there for their kids. That's all there is to it," said Mom.

"But it's due soon!" pleaded her daughter.

"How soon?"

"Soon," repeated Stacy, looking away from her mom.

"Well, I'm sorry. We can't risk it, Stacy. You'll have to find another way," said her mother. "What about the HyperLink system?"

"The HyperLink?" said Stacy, rolling her eyes. "That's ancient! It takes forever to go into that and see things. Then, once you've seen what's happened, you still have to write about it. It's a lot of work. If I can just use the LearningPort, then I know I can get it done tonight."

"Tonight? Is this due tomorrow?" asked her mom.

"Maybe?" Stacy said sheepishly.

"Stacy!" shouted Amanda.

"Sorry!" said her daughter. "I've been really busy, Mom!"

"Yeah, really busy e-visiting with all your friends. That's all I see you do. You're on your V-Hang, doing things with your friends. Do you ever see them face-to-face anymore?"

"No. What's the point of that? It's the same thing with the V-Hang," said Stacy, referring to the 3D VirtualHang software that connected her with her friends electronically. The V-Hang, as her generation called it, projected all her friends in the room together holographically -- as if they were all sitting together. It did save time traveling, but it wasn't the same as actually being with each other in the same room.

"Well, then I think this should be a lesson to you. You'll have to use the HyperLink on this one. Just go in and get it done. Make your notes and then write your paper," said Mom. "What's the paper on, anyway?"

"It's on the French Revolution, whatever that was. It has something to do with ..."

"I know about the French Revolution, dear. It started in 1789. Good luck with your paper," said Amanda. "I'll say one thing ... it was an exciting time in history."

Her mom began to leave the room when she turned at the last minute and asked, "How long does it have to be? How many pages?"

"Ten, double-spaced," said Stacy.

"Sounds good. I'll be interested in reading it when you're done." Then, as she was walking out the door her mother murmured, "'Twas the best of times. 'Twas the worst of times."

What the hell is that supposed to mean? Stacy thought.

Stacy walked over to the HyperLink station and pulled off the gray sheet that had been covering it for weeks. Sitting down at the monitor, she typed in the words "French Revolution" and hit ENTER. The screen came up with several references, and she chose one called *HyperWiki*. Once that site came up, she attached the light, but electrode rich helmet. It was clumsy and cumbersome and something she really hated - everyone did. However, to that day it was still the only way to reach into the depths of history and experience it as never before.

Stacy looked at the monitor and began reading about the Revolution. When she reached a section of particular interest, she moved the pointer to the hyperlink setting. She knew she needed to be very strategic about which markers she clicked on because going into a hyperlink could take a lot of time. And, unless she had a lot of time to waste, it wasn't a good idea to click on just any hyperlink that came up.

Is this where I want to jump? she asked herself, hovering over the link.

She hesitated and stopped, shaking her head. She continued reading until she came to another passage that seemed more relevant to what she was writing about.

Ah, this is better, she thought. She clicked on this hyperlink, and when the question came up asking if this were really the one to which she wanted to enter, she clicked *YES*.

ARE YOU REALLY SURE? came the answer.

"Yes!" she shouted aloud, annoyed at the double safeguard. Again, she clicked *YES*.

Instantly, her brain went blank, and it seemed as if she were traveling through a dark cave at high speed. But, she didn't see any light at the end of this tunnel, and for a second she worried. However, soon a glimmering image appeared, and she suddenly found herself plopped down in the middle of a muddy road in Paris.

***

PART II

Stacy looked at her hands which were partially submerged into a long, deep puddle of mud. "Crap!" she said aloud, even though no one could hear her. She sat up and realized that most of her -- her knees, hands, elbows and part of her hair -- were caked in mud. "Great," she added, sarcastically.

She sat up and looked around. In front of her was a hovering image of her 3-D selection panel from her HyperLink system back in her room. However, she usually found it distracting, so she pressed the button for *Virtual Hide* to make it go away and made it vanish.

Good, she thought. *Now, if I can just look around a bit to see what's going on, I'll be in and out of here and back home to write my paper.*

She got up from the muddy road and setoff in the direction a faint arrow was pointing for her. It was a pale, green arrow that blinked on and off in midair to ensure she went in the right place at the right time to get the right experience.

It wasn't a long walk, but she did pass several small, cottages along the way. There didn't seem to be anyone out and about, which seemed strange to her, but she carried on anyway, sinking her peasant-looking shoes into the muddy ruts in the road. Soon, she came to a large, stone wall where there were many people coming and going through the high-arched entrance. Above her were soldiers pacing up and down the sentry pathways on top of the wall – their muskets on their shoulders and ready for any type of disturbance or violence that could break-out.

In the distance, she could see the twin towers of the Cathedral de Notre Dame and the banks of the River Seine just in front of it. Lining the roadway were crowded, two-story shops and homes, all crammed into small plots of land meant for far fewer citizens. They seemed dreary and gray, as if they had already been through a war of their own.

Around her were scores of people - a massive crowd that had gathered in the square. They looked poor with their tattered, gray or brown frocks and their feet, blackened and gnarled from ill-fitting boots or no boots at all. They seemed agitated and riled as some carried farm tools in their hands, like pitchforks or spades, and others armed themselves with bars or clubs.

Peasants, Stacy thought, watching what was going on.

She walked with the crowd as it gathered in the small square, and it was then that she saw the large, wooden stage in front of her. On it was nothing but a tall, wooden frame with a shiny, thin, triangular object attached to a rope and suspended at the top. The rope drooped down to a bench near the side of the device and was coiled there at the bottom.

"Liberté, égalité and fraternité!" the crowd shouted in unison, throwing their fists into the air.

It wasn't hard to tell they were all angry, and Stacy began to feel uncomfortable being in their midst.

But time dragged on. It seemed like hours went by and the people continued to shout.

"Liberté, égalité and fraternité!"

Then, the chants changed.

"Enlevez leur têtes!" the people started shouting, becoming impatient and wanting heads to roll.

"Enlevez leur têtes!"

Stacy pushed through the crowd to get closer to the platform. It was then that three people were led up the ten-step, rickety wooden stairs to the top of the stage. They were guarded by five men in black breeches, white knee stockings and shirt, and a black, cut-away jacket. They wore no hats or other flourishments – only what they needed to get the job done.

The prisoners were even less fashionable. Wearing dirty, brown frocks, they were led up the stairs, their wrists tied with leather bands that hung as limp, sorrowful vestiges of their time in captivity. Two of them hung their heads in despair, while the third held her head high, glancing around at the people who were shouting angrily at her or throwing garbage. Several apples and pears hit her in the head and in her back, causing her to stumble; yet, she trudged on. Of the three, she was the only one not wearing a peasant's garb. Dressed in fabrics and the purple shades of the aristocracy, she stood out from everyone in the group – even those surrounding the stage who hurled epithets and rotten vegetables at her.

Stacy watched in horror. There was a wrenching knot in her stomach, and her head spun with feelings of sympathy and angst over what she saw. She agonized for the people who were walking across the stage for she knew what was going to happen to them – to each of them.

This is wrong ! she thought. *This is all so wrong !* But none of that mattered.

"Ces prisonniers sont condamnés à mort, et nous condamnons leur peine au nom du peuple," said another person, who came out on the stage without restraints. It was he who announced to the gathering crowd that these three people had been found guilty of treason to the people of France and had been sentenced to death. What shocked Stacy even more was the twisted smile he had on his face as he mouthed the words.

"No!" Stacy shouted, but her words couldn't be heard.

As the first prisoner was led across the wooden platform to the gallows, Stacy turned away, unable to watch. "Show display," she said, commanding the console to reappear. She waited, yet the panel didn't materialize.

"Show display!" she said again, this time more agitated. But again, nothing happened.

The first prisoner pulled, tethered to a leather strap, to a wooden bench in front of the tall, guillotine track over his head. The executioner took a black sack and stuffed it over the prisoner's face as he whimpered. Then, the hooded figure pushed the prisoner onto the bench face down and slid it into place. Finally, he locked the wooden brackets, or lunettes,-around the man's neck.

Everyone could hear the cries and pitiful sobs from the man as he lay helpless, awaiting his fate.

"Des derniers mots?" asked the hooded figure, letting him say his last utterings.

The prisoner said nothing -- only continuing to cry.

"Que Dieu ait pitié de votre âme (May God have mercy upon your soul)," said the executioner.

Then, with a quick flick of the wrist, the guillotine blade plunged down the rails with haste. Stacy turned her head, unable to bear it all. Still, she could hear the sickening sound of the blade hitting the wooden stock at the bottom and then the *thud* of the head rolling into the basket on the other side.

Stacy ran from the square, feeling her stomach churning. Quickly, she found an alleyway and ran a few paces down before she bent over and vomited all over the stone facade of one of the buildings. Gasping for air, she leaned over again. Finally, she collapsed, drained of emotion and energy. She didn't know what happened next. It was as if she were floating in a dream, but in this case, it was fast becoming her own nightmare. *******

PART III

Stacy's mom looked at the digital clock and saw it was about time for Stacy to be in bed. She walked down the hall and gently opened the door, letting it glide open. Inside, she found Stacy sitting at the HyperLink chamber with the helmet on and staring at the screen.

"Stacy, it's about time for bed," she said.

But when Stacy didn't move.

"Stacy? I said it's time for bed, honey. Are you about finished writing your paper?"

Amanda put her hand on Stacy's shoulder, but her daughter didn't flinch. Her body was rigid, as if she were getting hit by 50,000 volts of electricity.

"Stacy?" her mom asked once more, this time alarmed. She glanced over at the dial settings on the HyperLink console and saw they were set for the French Revolution and dates between 1789 and 1792. But there was something that worried her. Some of the words in the display were scrambled, like there was a short in the system someplace.

Amanda rushed out to where her husband sat watching his favorite soccer team, Manchester United, playing a rival team, Chelsea.

"Come on," he shouted. "Time's already at 90!"

"Jason? I think there's something wrong with Stacy's HyperLink. She's not responding to me. She only sits there and stares blankly into her monitor."

Jason huffed. "Really? Just when my team is about ready to score?"

Amanda stared coldly at her husband who quickly understood his new priority.

"Okay, okay," he said, getting up off the couch.

Jason walked back to his daughter's room and looked over her shoulder at the monitor. "She's only an observer in 1792. It's not a big deal. When she's finished, she'll write her paper and then go to bed. What is there to worry about?"

Amanda pointed to the monitor. "*This* is why I'm worried," she said.

On the HyperLink screen was a message toward the bottom in italics that read:

Warning: Your session may have been corrupted. Please reboot and restore the default settings for the HyperLink system.

"Oh," said Jason with a flat voice.

***

PART IV

Stacy slowly regained her senses and stopped seeing double. And even though there was a high-pitched ringing in her ears, she could hear the crowds not far away from her still chanting loudly for the head of the next prisoner.

She sat up and wiped off her mouth with her sleeve. It repulsed her, but couldn't stand the feeling of vomit on her face.

"Show display!" she called out again.

This time, the 3-D monitor appeared, and she pressed on several buttons to get to the screen she wanted. Then, seeing one that read *RETURN HOME*, she pushed it and sat back letting her head rest against the stone building. *There*, she thought, finally relieved, *I'll be back home in an instant.*

However, she wasn't.

Again, things went dark and she was once more inside a long, dark cave. As before, it was some time before she finally saw a light at the end, and it grew wider and wider as she seemed to hurl through time and space. This time, when she emerged, she landed inside a building with steep walls that rose high into the air above her. It was like she was sitting at a pew in a much larger version of her church at home. The old, gray, stone walls flowed effortlessly up and curved inward toward a peak high off the floor.

"*Quels sont les accusations portées contre le défendeur?*" came the sound of a man's voice speaking French at a rapid, metronomic clip.

With her floating panel at eye-level in front of her, Stacy could read the translation off the monitor to know what was going on.

What are the charges being brought against the defendant? were the words racing across her screen.

Continuing in French, another man walked up to the front of the grand room and answered, "My lord, the charges are of treason against his people and his country."

Stacy watched as three men wearing gray, curled wigs, puffy shirts and rich, silk jackets sat high above those in the pews - on a raised podium that didn't seem to have any stairs or other way to access it.

They must be judges, she thought, *and this must be someone's trial. I wonder whom their trying this time?*

"The Committee for Public Safety, as part of the National Convention, shall hear the case against this defendant, Citoyen Louis Capet," said the man in the center of the bench above. Stacy's computer added clarifications as the proceedings progressed, helping her understand what was going on. It read, in big red letters, Citoyen Louis Capet is the king of France – King Louis XVI.

"The people of France bring the following charges against this man," said another, standing in front of the bench. "First, is the charge of treason. Second is the charge of stealing vast amounts from the people's treasury. Third is the charge of violating the responsibility to protect and defend his people, and lastly, is the charge of moral corruptness."

Stacy's computer inserted another note for her on her screen, which read:

> Louis XVI was brought before the National Convention with charges of treason against France on December 11, 1792.

"And what defense does the defendant raise?" asked the man in the center of the bench.

Again, Stacy's computer flashed a message on her screen:

> Maximilien Robespierre headed the Committee for Public Safety. He was later known to be responsible for the deaths of thousands of French citizens during what became known as the Reign of Terror.

"My Lord," said another man. "As counsel for the defendant, I enter my client's arguments why he is not guilty." The computer inserted the name of the king's counsel in parentheses: (Raymond Deseze).

For the next hour, Deseze talked on and on about how Louis had only had the goodwill of his people in mind when he carried out his duties as their king. He presented a cogent argument, but when he had finished he sat down next to another man who sat stoically, as if he already knew what the outcome of these events would be. He was dressed well, but not like what Stacy had seen in pictures of French kings of the time. He also looked tired and haggard – the stresses of the times weighing heavy on him.

That must be Louis! thought Stacy, watching with wonder.

Then Robespierre interrupted. "It is now the prosecution's turn to bring forth his evidence."

The prosecutor stood before the court and waved to three courtiers in the back who ran forward carrying an iron chest, trimmed in gold.

"Please place the chest here," said the prosecutor with an air of superiority.

After the young men lowered the chest to the floor, they cracked opened the top.

"In this chest, we have retrieved several documents that were found in the possession of the defendant. These were located at the Tuileries Palace. There are nearly 800 letters, manuscripts, documents and other articles that were found in this chest. We thank Francois Germaine for enabling us to access the citizen's vault and get to this chest," he added, nodding to another man in the room.

"These letters are proof that the defendant has been actively working against the will of the people of France and this National Convention. The letters were exchanged with Gabriel Riqueti Mirabeau, a traitor who was executed last year with several others, including the financier Maximilien Radix de Sainte-Foix, a secret advisor of the sovereign; the bankers Joseph Duruey and Tourteau de Septeuil; Arnaud Laporte, our former Royalist government minister who betrayed the revolution and the nation's treasury; François de Bonal and even Bishop of Clermont. Other pieces of correspondence were with cabinet ministers who have already been found guilty of treason and executed.

"However, what is most damning are the letters involving some of our most prominent and trusted figures who have turned against the people and our revolution, such as General Santerre, the Marquis de Lafayette, Antoine Rivarol, and Charles Maurice Talleyrand, a former bishop who was recently found guilty of treason and for whom there is an outstanding arrest warrant."

Stacy's computer inserted another comment in red letters: [There were rumors that only selected documents were made public by the prosecution, and that certain other documents were destroyed that would have exonerated many of the charges against the king. The Interior Minister Roland was alleged to have played a role in this deception.]

"What do you say to this?" said the prosecution, pointing to the chest. He held up one of the letters and began reading. The translation on the screen seemed to suggest that the king was plotting to get his power back from the revolution, but even that letter was vague.

The king merely shook his head and said nothing.

"So, you see," continued the prosecution, "that the defendant is guilty of the charge of treason against his own people. At this point, my Lord, the people rest."

Stacy listened, now more intrigued than ever. But then it happened again - this time without any buttons being pushed on the screen. She found herself inside the dark cave once more and again not knowing where she would fin herself next.

***

PART V

"What should we do?" cried Amanda, still unable to move her child away from her seat in the HyperLink chamber.

"I'm calling 9911," answered Jason.

"Don't do that! It will take too long, and anyway, they'll see we have a LearningPort here. We can't risk it."

"Is there a HyperLink hotline we can contact?" asked Jason, growing more concerned.

"I could just shut it all down and pull her away from it?" asked Jason.

"No! They tell you *not* to do that. That might cause permanent damage to her brain. She's in synch with the machine right now, and it's teleported her mind back to Revolutionary France." Amanda looked at the monitor again. "Computer, perform self-diagnosis."

"Performing diagnostics," said the computer in reply.

It took a few minutes, but finally the speaker on the control panel answered. "There is a problem with the interphase linkage unit which should be replaced."

"What does that mean?" asked Jason, frustrated.

"It means we need to replace the interphase linkage," said Amanda, sarcastically.

Jason rolled his eyes.

"What else can we do?" asked Amanda, talking to the HyperLInk.

"You can try a work-around, but that will take a few hours. Are you familiar with HyperLInk programming routines?"

"No," shouted Amanda.

"Then we suggest you contact HyperLinke support," said the system.

"What's the tech emergency number then?" Jason asked.

"Try 991-891-786-232-8945," said the computer.

"Really?" said Jason.

"Just dial the number," said his wife.

Jason dialed the number. "You are (pause) sixty-eighth in line. Please hold for the first available ..." but Jason hung up.

"I'm not waiting for any stupid service. Is there someone else we can call?"

"What about your friend, Dale? He dabbles in technology a lot."

Jason jumped back on the phone. "Hello, Dale? Yeah, it's me Jason. Say, I've got a little problem I was hoping you could help me with."

***

PART VI

This time, the trip through the tunnel was quick, and Stacy was out the other side within seconds. Oddly, she found herself in the same room as she had been before, and the group around her was also much the same, except larger and more boisterous. Stacy sat on one of the long, hard benches in the Council chamber, and watched as they brought Louis back in the room.

Robespierre banged his gavel and made his announcement.

"I ask the chamber to come to order," he said, speaking in French and continuing to bang his gavel. "We have come to a decision on the sentence for the defendant, Citryoen Louis Capet. The National Committee hereby finds the defendant guilty as a 'grand usurper' on all charges. Second, the National Committee has voted not to allow a public referendum on this matter. And thirdly, the National Committee has decided on the sentence."

Immediately, Stacy's computer screen lighted up with an explanation:

> Balloting by the National Committee began on 14 January 1793. Each deputy explained his vote at the rostrum. The vote against the king was unanimous. Of the 721 deputies present, 387 declared themselves for the death penalty, while 334 were opposed. 26 deputies voted for death on condition that he was reprieved. On 18 January the question of reprieve was put to a vote: 380 votes were cast against; 310 for.

"The sentence as agreed by majority of the deputies is death by guillotine. The defendant shall have no recourse and shall not be allowed to speak," said Robespierre. He banged the gavel and rose. "This concludes our session."

Stacy sighed and pushed the button *RETURN HOME* one more time, hoping this time her wish would be granted. Her surroundings again grew dark.

***

PART VII

It was late the next morning, and Amanda and Jason watched as Dale continued to work on a way to disconnect Stacy from the HyperLink machine. She was still alive, although her mental faculties were elsewhere. If they pulled her off immediately, she would become a vegetable, Dale had confirmed. If they left her on the machine in her present condition, she would continue to spend the rest of her life, living in eighteenth century French Revolutionary Paris.

"Well?" asked Jason, biting his fingernails, "what are you going to do?"

Dale shook his head. "I still don't know, Jason. I've never seen any problem like this with these machines. I've called corporate to talk with the engineer who created it, and he's looking into the problem to figure out what caused it."

"I don't care what caused it!" shouted the father. "I only care about getting my daughter out of there!"

"Be patient," said Dale. "If there is a way, we'll find it. Their lead engineer is brilliant. He'll figure out something, even if he has to reset the machine."

"Reset? What do you mean?" asked Amanda with worry in her voice.

"If we reset the machine, all the settings default back to the original manufacturing specs."

"Then what?"

"Well, we don't know. We've never done it while someone was still connected to the machine before."

***

Stacy waited to come out of the tunnel, but nothing seemed to be happening. "Control Panel," she said again, and waited as the board displayed in front of her. She pushed the *RETURN HOME* button, but it didn't seem to be doing anything. So she typed something directly into the computer: *How do I fix this? Nothing is happening?*

Instantly the computer typed its answer: *You need to reset the system.*

How do I do that? she typed back.

Instantly, and without explanation, the computer showed her a new button the screen: *RESET* is all it read.

I guess I don't have any choice. I hope this works, she thought. She pushed the reset switch.

***

"Well, what did your engineer say might happen?" asked Jason, waiting impatiently.

"He said he didn't even know that – he had no idea what might happen," said Dale.

"Could it hurt my daughter?" asked Amanda.

Dale shook his head. "He doesn't know."

"He doesn't know, and yet he's willing to have us throw the switch anyway?" asked Jason. "What kind of person would do that?"

"He's just trying to help get your daughter back to you. That's all."

"And there are no other options?" asked Amanda.

"No," said Dale. "We don't have any other options. Either we reset it, or she lives out the rest of her days in 1793."

Jason sighed, looking at his wife as she nodded to him. "Okay. I guess we have no choice."

Dale pulled off the side panel of the machine and took four small screws off a plate. Underneath was a red switch, unmarked and not easy to find. The only words next to it read: **DO NOT TOUCH!**

***

PART VIII

"Are you finished with your paper yet?" asked Amanda, coming into Stacy's room.

Stacy sat in the HyperLink chamber, unmoving.

"Stacy? I asked if you had finished. Is everything all right?" her mother asked again.

Stacy turned around. "Yep," she said, "I'm all finished." She pointed to the monitor with the ten pages stacked on top of each other. "It's really amazing! I got to see everything. There was this guy named Robespierre. He was a really bad guy - had a lot of people killed. Then there was the king, Louis XVI. They tried him and sentenced him to death. He was really cool about it - didn't yell or scream, just accepted the sentence and kept looking straight at the judges on the bench. The only part I couldn't watch were the executions. That was horrible."

"Well, I'm glad that you got to experience it. It makes history that much more real," said her mother, smiling. "Now, tomorrow is a big day. You need to get your sleep. You have to turn in your paper, you know."

***

Stacy waited to see the grade postings for her project. She had written a paper that was truly amazing, incorporating all the details she had experienced during her time in the HyperLink. She had recalled the words of Robespierre, the reaction of the king, the forcefulness of his counsel, and the anger and hatred of the people in the room.

Then, the grades began populating the screen, and she watched intently as the space beside her name blinked in anticipation of a letter.

Stacy Tolbert   C+

"What?" she cried. "How is that possible? That was an excellent paper!"

Moments later, the comments section began to fill in with her teacher's notes:

The paper was incredibly realistic. It had information and descriptions that have never been noted in any discussion of the trial of King Louis XVI. Therefore, Stacy obviously made up much of her paper which was to be a factual account of the French Revolution. In

the future, Stacy should make sure she does her research on a topic, rather than creating fictional accounts to make the project easier.

Professor Ratcliff

Stacy stood in disbelief. She had almost given her life for that stupid paper, and she wasn't about to let that grade stand.

Although it wasn't possible to meet the professor face-to-face, it was possible to link with her through a holographic link where the virtual images of the callers would gather together – in this case, in a virtual professor's office.

"Professor," said Stacy, composed and calm, "I had to talk with you about my grade on the French Revolution paper. I used the HyperLink system, and even though I don't remember ..."

"Wait," said the professor, holding up her hand. "I know what you're going to say. I thought again about your paper and looked into it a bit more. I figured you had to have used a HyperLInk system, so I contacted the company and asked them about your access."

"You did?"

"Yes. And you know something?" said the professor, "I found out that you were in Paris in 1792 and you did witness the trial of King Louis XVI just as you described in your paper. I wish I had been there with you. It must have been fascinating to watch, and I do have a lot of questions to ask you."

"So, you'll change my grade?"

"Yes. I'm giving you an A."

Stacy beamed. "Great! I really appreciate you changing that. I worked hard on that paper."

"Yes. I know that now," said the professor. "But I do have two pressing questions before I find out more about the trial. First, do you know that you're the only person to survive a reset while hooked up to the machine?"

"No, I didn't know that," said Stacy, "All I remember is pressing the reset button. I was told later what happened. My parents didn't even know. It was like *everything* was reset back to *before* I even went into the machine."

"Yes, the people at HyperLink told me how strange it must have been for you."

"Professor? What is the other question you had?"

Professor Ratcliff scratched her head. "Well, the official records state that on January 18, 1793, the deputies of the National Committee met to vote whether to reprieve the king from the death penalty. There is now confusion over the vote."

"Confusion? What sort of confusion?"

"Well, there were 380 votes cast against reprieving the king from the death penalty – that hasn't changed. What has changed is that several sources now claim that 311 voted *for* the reprieve."

"Why is that strange?" asked Stacy, looking down at her feet.

"Because prior to last week, the official number had been 310." Professor Ratcliff paused. "Stacy, you didn't happen to ..."

Stacy looked up at the professor. "I didn't do anything professor," she said nervously. "I'm wasn't supposed to interfere. Isn't that right?"

The professor shook her head and smiled. "Well, all right then. I guess it was just one of those strange quirks of history. Is that what you'd call it?"

Stacy smiled back. "Yeah, I think that's what it was for sure."

*****

SOUL CONTROL

PART I

The debate had continued for millennia, but there had been no resolution -- there could be no resolution, because there was no way to know -- until now.

"CNTV now shifts to our science segment where we bring you the latest developments in the scientific world. For that, we go to Dr. Rinja Gupta. Dr. Gupta ..."

"Thank you, Linda. Researchers here at Johns Hopkins Medical Center have been working with bio-scientists and theologians to find an answer to the most basic question of human existence - is there a human soul?"

The broadcast cut to the MRI - nuclear medicine division at the medical center -- where they showed the MRI machine and pictures of the human brain.

"For thousands of years, man has wondered whether there was physical part of the brain that held the human soul. Now researchers believe they have found it. Dr. Claude Perkins has been studying this issue for the past thirty-four years, and he believes he has identified the location of the human soul within the brain."

On the screen came the image of an aging doctor wearing a white lab research coat.

"We have identified a portion of the brain that appears to have no other purpose," said the doctor, talking slowly and directly. "Our team has studied over three hundred study participants, and we have taken measurements and pictures of this part of the brain using machines that can detect wavelengths at a broad range of spectra - from infrared to ultraviolet and beyond. What we've found is a previously undetected wavelength that is not driven by frequency or amplitude but through physics only present in another dimension. It took a long time to develop equipment that could detect it, but we were able to construct the electronic machines able to identify the trace results from multi-dimensional energy systems about five years ago. Through further advancements of technology and methods, we have been able to refine our measurements and now have very accurate recordings of those wavelengths."

"And what have your results shown you?" asked the segment host.

The doctor smiled. "We've actually captured a human soul."

"You mean on your instruments. You've recorded signs of the human soul on your instruments."

"No, I mean, we've actually captured a human soul before it transitioned to the sixth dimension after the death of the patient."

"How were you able to do this?" asked Dr. Gupta, surprised by the answer.

"We have created a magnetic field that makes it impossible for the soul to pass through. We can keep it inside this container for as long as we need to analyze and study it."

"But what *is* it, then? What is it that you've captured?"

The doctor smiled. "You wouldn't understand if I tried to explain it."

"But there will be many in the church who object to this. One of the leading critics of your work is archbishop David Santoni," said Gupta, before looking back into the camera. "The archbishop had this to say earlier today ..."

"I believe this is a travesty," said the archbishop, his face coming on-screen. He was wearing a black shirt with the signature white, band collar. His hands folded in front of him, and they shook slightly from age and, quite possibly, the onset of Parkinson's disease. He continually pushed up the silver glasses that kept slipping down on his nose. "It's against God's wishes to prevent someone's soul to be imprisoned and not allowed to pass on to heaven where it belongs with our Creator."

"But the patient signed a release prior to dying," said Gupta, pressing the theologian. "He was part of study and willingly complied."

"The patient was not in a mental state to judge," said the archbishop. "He couldn't have been, if he had known the ramification of his actions."

"But the release specifically allowed the researchers to take his soul for study," said Gupta.

"God is the ultimate judge of all of us," said the archbishop. "It is only He who can hold someone's soul."

"Well, the debate will continue," said Gupta, returning to the screen reporting live. "Even though it appears scientists have now positively confirmed the existence of the human soul, there is now a new controversy. This is Dr. Rinja Gupta, reporting for CNTV."

The news broadcast concluded, zooming in on the containment unit that reportedly held the patient's soul. It was as eerie as it was unsettling.

The segment's producer, Mike Lawson, made a slashing motion across his throat to signal to Gupta that the shot was finished. The cameraman put down his camera and turned off the intense light that illuminated the lab.

"I guess that's a wrap," said Mike, jotting down some notes on a pad.

Gupta put down the microphone and tossed it at the producer. "Here, I'm done. Now get all the paperwork handled for me. I'm going home." His tone was curt and flippant.

"Will do, sir," said Mike, who gave a half-hearted salute.

It was common knowledge that Gupta was one of the most arrogant of the reporters on staff. Few liked him, but everyone tolerated him. They had to or either face his wrath or worse yet, termination by his hands.

Gupta went out to the parking lot where he hopped into his brand-new, Jaguar coupe. He as proud of that car – a British green convertible with a tan top. He pressed the auto-retract button and made the top go back into its slot in the back and headed out. Hovering just above the surface of the road, the car remained on autopilot until he reached his palatial estate. He lived alone, but still had a mansion with over sixty-two rooms, eight fireplaces, four levels, and a garage that held his collection of thirty-eight antique and rare sports cars.

"Open," he said casually, as he approached the inside door to the house and let the garage door close tightly behind him.

Gupta walked inside and reached into his pockets to pull out his black, medical case. He suffered from severe, Type II diabetes and needed his insulin injection before retiring for the evening. He had once been a candidate for an artificial pancreas, but other complicating conditions had eventually ruled him out.

Where is it? he asked himself, groping around to find it. Then he realized. *Crap. I must have left it on the counter after we had those chocolate chip cookies they offered us.*

So, back into the garage and back to the lab he went, programming his sleek machine to take him where he could retrieve his life-sustaining medicine. All the while, he cursed everyone and everything for his mistake.

Damned that Mike, he thought as his car drove him into the laboratory parking lot, *if he hadn't insisted on accepting those stupid cookies, I wouldn't be out here in the middle of the night like this. Note to self ... make sure I get Mike fired tomorrow morning ... first thing.*

***

PART II

It was late as the custodian cleaned up the research lab and adjoining offices. His shift ended in a few hours, and he was anxious to get home.

"Hi, Mildred," he said, walking with a dolly that held a large, blue trashcan and a long-handled broom sticking out of the top. He was headed for the dumpster where he would dispose of all the paper trash that had collected in the section during the week. But, there was also more rubbish due to the camera staff and reporter who had been there earlier that afternoon shooting the scene that aired later on the Saturday night news broadcast that evening.

Mildred, the night security watchperson, looked over at him smiled. "Hi, Jake. How are you doin'?"

"I'm good, Mildred," said Jake with a broad grin. "Good to be alive, ya know?"

"Yeah. I hear a lot of people complaining about this or that," she said, "but as you and I always say – it's a glorious day when you've got the Lord watching over you."

"Got that right, sister," he answered, giving her a wink.

She looked down at her watch and then added, "Oh, and Jake. Happy Easter!"

Jake quickly looked at the clock on the wall and saw that it was midnight – actually, a minute past. It was Sunday.

"Yes, Happy Easter to you too," he answered.

Jake pushed open the back door and emptied the trash and started to return to the lab to finish-up before he went home. But as he started to close the door, a hand reached out and held it.

"I'm Dr. Gupta," said the man. "I need to get my medicine from the kitchen inside." Without waiting for an answer, he pushed in the door and brushed Jake aside, not waiting for a reply.

"Uh, sir?" asked Jake. "I'm real sorry, but I'm not supposed to let in anybody after hours."

Gupta turned to the older man and said, "I really don't give a crap what you think you can or can't do. I just need to get my medicine and be out of this hell hole."

Jake got on his radio and called for Mildred. "Milley? I've got a man who says he's a Dr. Gupta something and says he needs to get his medicine. He just barged right past me and is heading for the kitchen. Should I call the police?"

"Negative," said Mildred. "He was in here earlier today with the camera crew. He's that fancy reporter fella' who told people how awful the cookies were."

"Oh, him. Okay."

"I'll just let him get his things and be off," said the security lady.

Gupta got to the kitchen and located his black back and then turned to leave.

"Did you find what you needed?" asked Mildred, giving the reporter a knowing grin that he'd made a mistake.

"One of the lab people distracted me when I was eating one of those miserable cookies," said Gupta. "I'll be leaving now."

But as Gupta walked out of the kitchen, he noticed someone standing in the middle of the lab.

"He come with you?" questioned Mildred, walking up behind the reporter.

"No. He doesn't work here?" asked Gupta.

Just then, Jake came into the lab from the opposite side.

"What are you doing in here?" Mildred asked, stepping in front of Gupta. "This is a restricted area." She placed her hand on her revolver that was still in the holster on her gun belt.

The strange man turned, facing Mildred and smiled. "I was just taking care of some last-minute things in here," he said.

His face was strikingly handsome, clean-shaven and pure. There was a glimmer in his eyes as if he had been crying, but there were no tears.

"And who are you?" asked Jake, approaching slowly.

"I'm Chris. I'm new here. I don't believe we've met," said the man, extending his hand.

Jake started toward the man, but Mildred called out to him. "Jake, just stop right there. Sir? Do you have some ID I could see to confirm you're authorized to be in here?"

Although they hadn't seen anything around the man's neck, he suddenly pushed forward a laboratory ID that was attached to a lanyard. Mildred approached him and looked at the card. "Yep," she said, examining it, "I guess you are who you say you are. Okay, then. We'll let you take care of whatever it is you need to do."

Gupta felt uncomfortable as he gazed at the man. There was something about him that seemed threatening even though he appeared calm and genial. "I think you should ask him for more identification," said Gupta. "You can't be too careful, you know."

Mildred turned to the reporter and said, "I only asked you for one. Why should I ask him for more?"

"Because …" Gupta began, but then his words fell silent as he was unable to come up with anything else.

"Alright, then," said Mildred, "let's all get back to what we were doing. Dr. Gupta, you have your medicine, so let's get you back on the road, shall we?"

Gupta stuffed the black pouch into his jacket pocket and began walking past the strange man in the lab. But the man held out his hand, placing it on the doctor's shoulder. "So, you're ill?" he asked.

"Doesn't affect you," snarled the doctor, trying to move on.

"No, it sounds like you're sick," said the man. "Are you diabetic?"

Gupta looked at Chris with a skeptical eye. "How did you …"

"From the small pouch. I've known people like you who have to take their insulin shots every day, and they carry a bag just like that one."

"Oh. Well, yeah. I was born with it. You just adjust. It's just part of this crappy life we live, isn't it?"

Chris smiled disarmingly. "Well, it doesn't have to be that way," he said.

"Maybe not for you, but for me, it all sucks," Gupta replied.

"I presume you have a nice house, cars, money in the bank … all that stuff, right?"

Gupta smiled, smugly. "Of course," he said with an air of superiority.

"So, I agree with you then," said the strange man.

The reporter looked at him surprised. "You do?"

"Yes."

"I don't understand."

"I know you don't, but I can only hope that you finally do," said Chris.

The strange man took his hand off Gupta's jacket and let him pass, saying nothing more and offering no more resistance.

"Well, I've got my own work to do," said Mildred, leaving the room.

Jake took another look at the strange man who was standing next to the containment box and shook his head. The janitor left without saying another word.

Chris put his hand on the containment box and then walked to the elevator, pushing the UP button. He smiled back at Gupta before the doors opened and he got inside. Then, just before the doors closed, the doctor saw a bright light streaming out between slit in the two stainless steel doors.

Gupta sighed and walked to the rear door before pushing it open. He let is slam shut behind him, locking him out surrounded by darkness and a sudden chill that was unusual for that time of year.

*****

PART III

The next day, Dr. Perkins came into the lab. It was Monday morning, and he was ready to start his analysis of the soul that he had captured inside the magnetic container. He took his usual measurements of the system with its complex and elaborate matrix of coils and cords. The meters were showing magnetic strengths of the containment box in excess of 100T or one hundred Tesla units. Such magnetic strength was once thought impossible to construct by human hands, but that level had been far exceeded after decades of experimentation and improvement.

Watching the dials on this equipment, Perkins noted the readings and checked off each one to confirm that all the systems were functioning properly and the field was effective and fully charged. Although Perkins had performed preliminary studies on the soul he had trapped inside the box, he had yet to begin his more thorough and laborious analysis of the nature of the energy unit he held inside.

"Now," said the doctor, "let's see what we have here."

He set the dials on the optical imager as well as the probe that measured the energy field created by the soul and waited. It only took nanoseconds to record what was needed, but it might take him his entire lifetime to analyze it.

After a few minutes, he downloaded the data.

"Something's wrong," he mumbled to himself, looking at the raw data that printed out on the monitor. He adjusted more dials and began finetuning the data, but nothing changed. "That can't be right."

Perkins took another reading, but the results came back the same.

"Alamar!" he shouted at the top of his lungs. "Get in here! You've screwed up the settings on the equipment. When was the last time you calibrated this?"

"Just yesterday, doctor Perkins," said the technician.

"You couldn't have. It's all screwed up!"

Alamar came over to the box and reassessed everything. He took out his calibration equipment and double-checked every input and output.

"No, sir. Everything is working as it should," said the tech.

"But the energy field is gone," said the doctor, blinking in disbelief. "It's not in the containment field anymore!"

Dr. Perkins marched down to the security office where he demanded to see video footage from the night before.

"I want to see everything that happened last night," he yelled. "I want to know who was in the lab and what they did!"

The security chief pulled up the footage from the previous night and set it in motion. The video started clear and crisp, but quickly became grainy and fogged, as if they had suddenly entered downtown London in the middle of a rainy, drizzly night.

"Someone must have done something to sabotage my work," said Perkins, fuming. "It's probably one of those wacko-religious types that got in there somehow. They're hysterical about what we're doing here."

The two men watched the camera footage unfold. It showed all angles and all rooms, but they only focused on the lab where the containment box was situated.

"Okay, this is where we'll see who did it," said Perkins, his eyes glued to the monitor.

At 12:03 a.m., the picture showed Jake coming into the lab and talking with Mildred. A short time later, it showed Dr. Gupta entering through the back door with Jake and coming into the lab.

"Ah!" said Perkins. "It was that reporter! I knew I couldn't trust him! He had his own motives – I could just tell by talking to him. He's probably connected to one of those groups somehow. He probably setup the interview just so he could come back later and destroy my work! I'll sue! That's what I'll do. I'll sue his tiny little ass out of existence."

The video continued with Gupta coming out of the kitchen carrying a black bag and the security guard walking behind him. It seemed that they saw something, but neither Perkins nor the security chief could figure out what. They were all looking at the containment box. Then, Gupta moved toward the containment system.

"Here! Here is where he does something!" shouted Perkins, thumping his finger at the screen.

The reporter stopped at the machine.

"Okay, you son-of-a-bitch! What did you do to my box?" mumbled Perkins.

They watched carefully, but Gupta never put his hand anywhere near the containment facility. After less than a minute, he continued walking toward the back of the lab, where the door led to the outside.

"I don't understand," said Perkins. "How did he do it?"

"I know," said the security chief. "It didn't look like he touched it at all."

But then, just as the reporter reached the rear door, there was a spark that leaped off the containment unit. It happened just as the elevators in the background mysteriously opened. Seconds later, there was a brilliant flash of light just as the doors were closing. The video suddenly went black.

"That's all you have?" Perkins asked, slamming his hand down on the table.

"Sorry, sir. Yes, apparently so."

"Rewind it. I want to see it again," said the doctor, as Jake came in to start his shift.

Rewinding the footage, the chief slowed the motion down to see better what had happened. The same burst of light exploded, but it seemed to be coming just as the two doors of the elevator were closing. There was no one inside.

"Show the upper floor," said Perkins.

The security chief loaded the images from the camera on the second foor. There, the video showed the elevator doors opening, but still there was no one inside.

"What do you make of that?" asked the security chief.

"What's going on?" asked Jake, putting on his white smock.

"Were you here Saturday night?" growled Perkins.

"Yeah, why?"

"Did you let that reporter inside the lab?"

Jake looked down at the floor. "Am I in trouble?" he asked.

"Did you or didn't you?" threatened Perkins.

"Yeah, I guess I did. But Mildred was right there with him the whole time. He didn't do anything, I swear. We were with him the entire time he was here getting his medicine."

Perkins threw one of the security manuals that sat on the table across the room before he stormed out.

"You shouldn't have done that, Jake," said the chief.

"But Chris was there too. He and Mildred can both vouch for me!"

"Chris? Who's Chris?"

"He's the new guy they hired. He works weekends in the lab, I guess," said Jake.

"What's his last name?"

"I don't know. You'd have to ask Mildred."

The chief got into the employee database and typed in "Chris or Christopher."

They watched as the results came up. "There is no Chris or Christopher who works here," said the chief. "You must have gotten his name wrong."

"No, he was there. He was in the lab."

"There wasn't anyone in the lab with you that night, Jake. We pulled up the footage and watched."

"That can't be!" he answered. "Chris was there. We talked to him!"

*****

PART IV

Dr. Gupta sat on the cold, patient bench waiting for his private doctor to return to the room. He was used to these visits, as he had made them since he'd been a small child.

Finally, his doctor opened the door and sat down in a hard, plastic chair next to him. Taking off his silver-framed glasses, he said. "I'm not sure how to tell you this," he began.

"What is it?" asked Gupta, worried about what would be said.

"You're clean."

Gupta had a furrowed look on his face. "I don't understand," he began. "What do you mean?"

"I mean, you don't have diabetes anymore. Did you visit Asia or South America and get into one of those unlicensed clinics?"

"No. I haven't been anywhere."

"Then, I don't understand it. You are perfectly healthy. Your pancreas is producing insulin and your body is processing glucose just as it should. It's amazing."

Gupta had felt differently ever since the lab incident. There was something fresh and good about him – a joy he hadn't felt in a long time.

Now, he just shook his head. "I can't explain it," he began. "I've been feeling better than I ever have. I'm more cheerful and happy than I've ever been."

His doctor got up and pushed in his chair. "Well, whatever it was, it worked for you."

"Doc?" asked Gupta.

"Yeah?"

"Do you believe in miracles?"

The doctor rubbed his temple and gave a faint smile. "You know, that's one word we're told never to use in the clinic – that we could get our license revoked if we uttered it."

"But you're not answering my question, doc."

The doctor took out an index card and scribbled on it as if he were writing a prescription. Then, he turned it over and left it on the table, face down.

"I'd still like to see you in four months," said the doctor, "just in case."

After the doctor left, Gupta got off the table and walked over to where the card lay. He turned it over and read:

Yes. I do.

*****

TWENTY-FIVE

PART I - 0025

25 AD (CE)

Jacob gazed at the open, rocky field as the sheep scampered over the long expanse of land all around him. Overhead, the white-hot sun beat down on him, making the perspiration bead-up on his forehead like raindrops on a stem of flax. He took his right sleeve and wiped his brow and then began swatting at the flies that occasionally made pests of themselves by landing on his face or the tops of his feet.

It was late morning, but the shepherd's eyelids were already drooping. He had been up well before the sun had cracked-open the blackness of night and had hurried to move his flock where it would be under his watchful eye and safe from wolves' intent on doing them harm.

It was a monotonous job — one he spent daydreaming or singing psalms to himself to pass the time. The sheep in his flock were pre-occupied, munching on what grasses lay amongst the boulders and vastness of the lands that stretched-out in all directions. Jacob's only worry was the flies that were constantly swirling around his head. Occasionally, he would twitch as one landed on him, then swatted at it to keep it from further disturbing his daydream.

Nearby was a small village where merchants gathered to offer their wares to local farmers and shepherds who lived just beyond its borders. The town governor had been there for many years - in fact as long as anyone could remember. He was a strange old man - someone who had the wisdom of Solomon and the patience of Job; yet, sometimes the common sense of neither. A Roman, he was wealthy and reigned supreme over the area looking after the interests of his Emperor TIberius in Italy.

It was said that he came from the family with the name of Flavius, and that he was well connected back home in Rome. His appointment decades earlier to this remote part of Edom, near the Dead Sea, was allegedly punishment for tarnishing the family honor. Accused of accidently killing his brother, Aelius Flavius had been banished by his father in Rome before he could be arrested and tried. Eventually, he had found his way to the town of Zoar near the southern tip of the Dead Sea. There, he had become a productive shepherd himself and amassed significant wealth growing his herd. Eventually, he left his sons to manage the herds when he accepted the title of Governor of Edom on behalf of the emperor. Many said he was handpicked by the emperor himself because of his talents and wisdom, but others said his father's dying wish to Tiberius was that his son be offered the position to redeem himself. Regardless, what was fact was that Aelius was the administrator, counselor and in some cases ultimate judge over everyone in the territory.

As for Jacob, the lands over which his sheep grazed had been in their family for centuries, not decades, but they still really didn't own them. Like everything else, they were owned by Tiberius. However, his family didn't mind even though they had to pay ten percent of their crops to the emperor every year as a tribute; they still managed to survive quite nicely. In this way, Jacob's family and Aelius never had to meet each other, except when the tribute was paid to the emperor. Then, Jacob would make the journey into town with his donkey and cart to unload those sheep that would be offered in payment.

However, on this particular day, Jacob would find himself in front of the governor for the first time - an unexpected turn to what began as a very ordinary day.

***

Crrrack!

The noise shook the ground and sounded like someone had split open the heavens. Jacob trembled and watched as his sheep bolted, scattering in different directions as they lost their nerve and feared for their lives.

Jumping up, he glanced about for anything that could have made such a sound, but it was the searing light from above that drew his attention. Something odd and luminous, its metallic, silver shell hovered above him. It cracked the air as it floated, seeming to ride on the currents as a ship upon water. Then, without warning, it sped off, flaming through the brilliant azure sky like a fire arrow shot from a mighty bow. Brighter than the sun, it left a trail of white mist behind it as it flew off and disappeared into the only pod of white, puffy clouds within sight.

Terrified, Jacob whistled for his dog, Dibi, to gather the herd. The sheepdog went to work, corralling the animals and pushing them back toward the family home which was just over the adjacent hill. Once they were in their pen, the shepherd ran to tell his father what he had seen.

"I believe you're ill, son," said his father, stroking his long, gray beard. "You need to rest. Perhaps I've overworked you."

"No, father. I know what I saw. It was a ball of flame in the sky the gods have given to us! It was like the sun, except it moved across the blue shell that is all around during the daylight."

"I don't know. I think I should send for the village doctor."

"No, father! I tell you the truth. There may be no one to confirm my story, but I swear what I am saying is true!"

His father continued stroking his beard, and then put his hand on the young lad's shoulder. "I believe you, Jacob. In which case, we need to get you to the governor so you can tell him what you saw," instructed his father. "Maybe there is something he can do."

The trip into town was a day's ride, and by the time they arrived it was nightfall. Waiting by their camels, father and son slept soundly until morning. Then, they packed up their things and traveled the short distance to the home of the governor.

Jacob and his father walked inside the large home, finding Aelius hunched over his scrolls, reading.

"My Lord," said Jacob's father bowing slightly, "I have brought my son here as I fear he is ill. He says that he sees things in the sky that are strange, and I'm afraid he is going mad. Can you help him?"

The governor looked up and gestured for them to sit. "What is it, my son?" he asked, genially. "Tell me what you are seeing, hearing or sensing?"

Jacob told the governor about what he saw and waited, watching his eyes carefully to see any signs of surprise or disbelief.

"Well?" asked the father. "What do you think it is? Do you agree that he needs the aid of the village doctor?"

The governor pondered, putting his thumb to his chin. Finally, he said, "I believe it is a heavenly body that is passing under the blue shell. It is from beyond our world and when it comes through the blue, it burns. It is all very hard to explain, but it is all fine -- all part of the natural world in which we live. You have nothing to fear or worry about. Your son is fine," he said. The governor then smiled, waved them off, and looked back at his readings.

Heartened, the father returned home with his son, satisfied that he had nothing to worry about. And as for the son, Jacob knew what he had seen was not worldly or natural, but watching his father enter his house with regained confidence and calm, he could think of nothing else but to stay silent.

The gods work in mysterious ways, he thought. *Perhaps this is just one of them.*

***

PART II - 1025

1025 AD (CE)

The Song Dynasty had ruled northern China since 960 AD (CE), and it was a time of promise and excitement. Artisans were making magnificent mosaics and paintings, and others were carving wonderful vases and figurines.

Amidst all the vibrant culture, creativity and potential was a Neo-Confucian scholar named Allienier. He was very wise and was instrumental in forming new schools throughout the dynasty.

One evening Allienier sat in his small room near the imperial palace when one of his students came running in to see him.

"Master Allienier! Come quickly!" exclaimed the student.

"What is it?" asked Allienier, looking up from his calligraphy. The candle on his desk was burning low from the hours he had sat practicing his strokes. Its white wax bubbled near the flame, and flowing down the side of the stick like lava from a volcano.

"I cannot describe it, sir," said the student, trying to catch his breath. "It is the gods, I think. They are displeased with us. We have done something they do not like."

Allienier rose and walked out and into the garden near his place of study: his jade, green robes flowed behind him, billowing in the light breeze that wafted in the air. Tilting his head upwards, he peered up into the darkness of the void above. Streaking across the sky was a bright, white light with a long tail. It didn't appear to be moving, but something was making the tail off the back of the round head appear to be fluttering, like the tail of a kite in a stiff breeze.

"What is it, master?" asked the student, still anxious for an answer.

Allienier squinted and smiled. "It is nothing to worry about," he said. "The gods are not angry at all. It is part of nature. It is something that happens once in a great while - an object from beyond the darkness streaks toward our sun, you see. Think of it as a snowball flying through the air. As the sun burns the snow, it melts and forms a tail off the back. It is nothing to worry about.

"But earlier today, I saw a great silver disk, spinning in the air. It was off into the distance, but it was there just the same. I swear it!" said the student, still alarmed.

Allienier turned to the student. "I am sure you did," he said calmly. "As I said, it is the way of the world. What you saw is nothing other than the image of things reflected into the sky that we think we see, but really do not."

"How can that be?" asked the student.

Allienier smiled. "When you go into the desert – into the sands of the Wadi – do you sometimes see water in the distance?"

"Yes, of course," said the student. "Those are mirages. They are just reflections off the sand that make us think we see water."

"Exactly," said Allienier. "It is the same here. You thought you saw a shiny object, but what you really saw in the sky was a mirage. It is nothing to worry about."

***

PART III - 2025

2025 AD (CE)

There was great turmoil in the world as nations struggled for power. Each believed its survival depended on the demise of another, so each acted according to what was best for them – in the short term, rather than in the long-term. It was the old zero-sum game that had been employed since *time in memoriam.*

In the intervening years, there had been great strides in scientific discovery. The scientific method had propelled mankind into an age where intellectual reason and analyses by comparing hypotheses to physical realities ruled. Everything seemed to be explained by science. There appeared to be physical justification for why things were as they appeared. Even at the subatomic level, as bizarre as that world is, there were justifications to explain why things acted as they did. No longer was it the *will of the gods* or *evil spirits* that were the cause of natural events in the world. This was the era of proof.

It was mid-afternoon when the White House was contacted. At first, the fear was that the Chinese were launching a nuclear attack against America. But after the white dots on the AWAC E-3H – AEW&C early-warning control screens disappeared, reappeared and then disappeared once more, they figured it was likely a computer malfunction.

"Get Director Sans on the line," said General Hastings, glaring uncomfortably over his first lieutenant's shoulder at the display. A moment later, Sans answered.

"Yes, general."

"What luck are you having with the equipment? It's showing unidentified objects racing across the northern states at high speed before disappearing. Then, they reappear. Then, they disappear. What's going on?"

Sans reviewed his data. "Sir, it appears to be a software problem. We will look into it at once and fix it, I assure you."

Sans scrambled his best techs to analyze the problem, and it was only an hour before they came back to him.

"Director, sir? We analyzed all the data, putting it back through our algorithms and synthesizers and, well, …"

"What is it?" demanded Sans.

"Everything seems to be operating normally. There are no glitches in the system, sir. We checked it several times."

"You'd better be right about that sergeant, because if you're not, I'll have your ass! I've got to report back to the general that his equipment is picking up UFOs. Is that what you want me to tell him?"

"It won't be the first time, sir," said the sergeant, who had put in over twenty years.

"Dismissed!" barked the director, speaking in military cadence.

Before he called the general, he went back to the data and then pulled up information on other UFO sightings during the previous decades. There was on in particular – that spotted in the 1960s – that caught his eye. That sighting too had been swept under the table. It had been a project called *Thanks for the Memories* after an old Bob Hope song of the time.

His next call still wasn't to the general. Instead, he contacted an old friend of his who had top-secret clearance and had worked on and off for the CIA. It was unorthodox for an Air Force man to call a CIA man, but their friendship over the years had garnered great respect between the two men.

"Allen? How are you?"" asked Sans.

"Director Sans! It's so good of you to call. I haven't heard from you in years. How are you? How is the family?"

"Allen, we're all good. But right now I have an urgent request to ask. Do you have the time?"

"Sure. For you, anytime. What's on your mind?"

Sans described to him what the general was seeing on his screen and that the systems showed nothing unusual.

"What do you think?" asked the director, apprehensively.

Allen thought for a moment and then said, "Well, it does have a lot of similarities to the 1960s incident you noted. I vaguely remember that one. I was involved in it too. If I recall, it had to do with three, spinning metallic objects that were seen over North Dakota, is that right?"

"Yeah, that's the one."

"The Air Force called it in. It was seen by two F-4 pilots who were on a routine, training mission just outside of Minot, the base right up there. They reported the incident at about 1830 hours, seeing the unusual flying objects at that time, right?"

"Pretty good memory, Allen."

"But what I recall is that NOAA – the National Oceanic and Atmospheric Administration – immediately got involved and claimed they had several weather balloons up in the area. The entire thing was dismissed and filed in the 'forever' file."

"I see," said Sans. "So, why was that? Why did NOAA say that? What is true?"

"Who knows," said Allen. "It was just one of a number of incidents reported that way. There was no threat, so there was no one who could or would be held accountable. Everyone walked away with their reputation intact. Do you know what I mean?"

"Uh ..."

"You don't want to bet your career on this one, do you?" asked Allen. "No one else has over the decades."

Sans was quiet for a moment. "No, I guess you're right."

"You are, my friend. Just bury this one, just as everyone else in your position has. They have all lived well and provided for their families, and in the end, isn't that what it's all about?"

Sans hung up the phone and gave the conversation some thought. Then, he picked up the other line and called the general.

"General Hastings?"

"Yes, Sans. What do you have for me?"

"We did discover some anomalies in the software. Our technicians are working diligently to correct them. I assure you that this incident will not happen again."

"Thanks, Sans. Good work. I trust that it won't. We don't need any of these types of things on our watch, as you can understand."

"Yes. Of course, sir. Thank you, sir."

Sans hung up the phone. Then, he immediately went back to his monitor. Indeed, there were still UFOs streaking across the sky right there before his very eyes. Sans reached down and pressed the Delete key. It deleted all traces of the units - it was as if the entire thing had never happened.

***

PART IV - 3025

3025 AD (CE)

Many years had passed, and technology had sprinted ahead. There had been two more world wars during the intervening years, but each one stopped before the entire planet was annihilated. The single, pivotal moment came in 2318 when a virulent, viral strain nearly wiped out all life on the planet. Riding on the back of a comet that slammed into South America, the virus quickly mutated to attach itself to life on Earth. Eventually, life returned as it had through other cataclysmic events in the history of the globe. Colonies on Mars and Jupiter's moons, Europa and Ganymede, had flourished, and more people left Earth to pioneer and develop those new worlds.

By the twenty-eighth century, the population of Earth had reached the point of unsustainability, and steps were necessary to control it. Eventually, the people-problem was reined in to a more manageable level of five billion by 3025 - down from the twenty billion at its peak in 2725.

By this time, solutions to most problems had been solved, but many remained. Resources were limited, and there were still those without the benefits of life enjoyed by others. Yet, it was an age of hope, and man had succeeded in creating machines that worked for him instead of falling under the boot of some robo sentinel that might otherwise keep him caged.

***

"Dr. Al?" asked Maggie, a young student who had teleported in for the university session. "I've been reading about concerns over the Nemesis star swinging back into the Sun's vicinity and causing comets to pummel the Earth from the Ort Cloud in the outer solar system. Is this something we need to worry about?" It was a rare verbal interchange, as most communication was made telepathically between neural networks and thought transmitters.

Al stopped his lecture which was being digitized and uploaded directly into the brains of his students. He smiled and turned off the direct feed so none of what he would say later would be impressed on their minds.

"There have been natural events that have occurred throughout history that mankind wasn't able to explain. Some believe Nemesis, a red dwarf star in our solar system, is the binary twin to our Sun. They revolve around each other in a 26 million-year cycle. Many believe the cycle is coming back around where Nemesis will come closest to our sun and cause all kinds of gravitational problems for us here on Earth and the colonies in the interior of the solar system. If that is true, I assure you we will be able to defend Earth against whatever onslaught of comets may come our way. You don't need to worry. We won't be going the way of the dinosaurs."

"But how?"

"There are many things that we, as commoners on Earth, don't know about. The Federation has powerful machines that can redirect incoming comets. They have a plan."

"And what if the plan doesn't work?" asked the student.

Al was surprised. During the previous centuries no one had ever asked what would be done if the Federation's plans failed. Even when they failed -- which they often did – there seemed to be a backup plan ready and waiting. Yet, as the problems grew more severe and the solutions more complicated during the more recent times, there was a guardian angel of sorts looking out for the world. It was truly odd. Technologies came together quickly to meet the urgent problem at hand and save countless lives. Implementation efforts which, at first faltered, would be re-orchestrated, as if by an invisible hand. When an answer meant life and death on a vast scale, it was found.

Some said the same thing during the twentieth century when two world wars ended with the defeat of oppressive regimes that, if they had succeeded, would have enslaved most of the civilized world. Not only that, but in the second case, would have caused the elimination of entire ethnic groups. However, by some divine guidance, they did not.

After class, Dr. Al went back to his office and closed the door. He walked over to his one fine piece of antiquity - an old trunk that was dated to before 25 AD and opened it. Inside, he took out two long probes and pulled them toward the back of his neck. Lifting up his hair, he plugged each one into its proper place.

"Reporting in?" came the voice into his head. "We were worried you had fallen off the grid after three thousand years. You are one of our oldest models, but you have performed admirably well."

"When you've been around as long as I have," said Dr. Al, "you figure out how things are done by the humans. I've been many things to many peoples over the millennia, but I'm afraid my term may be coming to an end. My upgrades are unable to keep pace with technology changes here."

"You are correct, 25E. You are being replaced. You are entitled to your well-deserved retirement."

"I would, but what about the Nemesis star? It is indeed on a trajectory to the inside of the solar system, which will displace thousands of comets in the Oort Cloud. As they did during the Cretaceous Period fifty-two million years ago – killing off the dinosaurs. We all know what will happen during the next few thousand years. Who will save the humans then?"

"That will be for your successor to figure out. She is our latest model, you see -- the 25X. Oh, and 25E, thanks for all you've done. The humans would have long been extinct by now if you hadn't so subtly managed our involvement without their knowing. It was masterfully done."

Dr. Al smiled. He'd been sending his thoughts to the Human Proprietors for years and had only intervened when total and utter calamity was expected from the humans' decisions. "Thank you," he said. "I'm sure 25X will do a fine job."

Al unplugged the cords and put them away in the trunk, which vaporized instantly, digitizing every molecule and atom and transporting them to a place far away in another galaxy. His own program was being phased out, and his replacement inserted strategically to ensure the project of the Proprietors' was not jeopardized. They had invested too much and had too many more millennia to go before the experiment's completion. Al would not participate in the future phases of the experiment; however, based on what he had seen thus far, he felt confident that the human species would pass with flying colors.

*****

OLYMPICS 2.0
PART I

2252

It had been ten years since the last games, and it would be only the second organized Olympic Games since they were reconstituted after the last world war. The timing and rules of the games had been changed since the first modern series was begun back in Athens, in April 1896. The changes had resulted mainly from the war but also from what many called the need for *progress*. "Everything" they had said, "evolves, and so too should the Olympic Games."

In ancient times, the athletes had only been men, watched only by men, as they were naked while competing in various military events. The winners would wear olive leaves and be granted special privileges for the rest of their lives such as room and board. In most cases, statues of the winner would be commissioned for the grounds at Olympia; however, there was no recognition given to second or third places.

In the modern games, again only men were permitted to compete. This changed in 1900 when the first women's events were allowed. Winter games were introduced in 1924, and the torch relay was added in 1936. Summer and winter games were alternated after 1992 to make preparing for each easier. Yet another significant change was made when professionals were allowed to compete where only amateurs had been permitted before. These changes took place gradually toward the end of the twentieth century.

Of course, politics often got involved in the games. Whether it was only judges horse-trading points or marks between friendly countries and against athletes from unfriendly ones or bigger things, like war and boycotts. The boycott of the Soviet games by the United States in 1980 was followed by the 1984 Los Angeles games being boycotted by the Soviets in retribution. Even before that, there was controversy during the Berlin games hosted by Adolph Hitler in 1936 and the Russian games held in 2012 before their invasion of the Ukraine. The games were suspended due to war as well -- in 1916 due to World War I and again in 1940 and 1944 due to World War II. Of course, there were many other incidents of one sort or another throughout the years; yet *all* the Olympic games stopped completely in 2244.

With schisms deeper than those after WWII when neither Germany nor Japan were allowed to participate, 2244 was the year the Earth stood still.

The war was short-lived, but the result was devastating. The lethality of weapons was thousands of times those during the 1940s, and vast areas of some countries were obliterated. Like during WWI, the battles shifted back and forth without a clear victor, until finally a truce was called to cease the bloodshed. Millions died. And it took years for the world to get back on its feet.

As part of the Armistice, the nations involved gathered in Bern Switzerland in 2245 to negotiate a peace agreement. However, what they came up with was not what any of them really wanted, but it was, at least, something.

Eight years after the end of the conflict, the remaining nations of the world gathered for the first Olympiad of the New Era. Labeled Olympics 2.0, the first reboot of the games was to occur in Australia, which was deemed to be the most impartial of the nations involved in the war. However, when many of the other countries protested, the venue was moved to Switzerland, which kept its tradition of remaining independent during all the world wars and most conflicts since.

However, these games would be played like no others.

*****

PART II

"3-D casting live from Bern, this is the World Emancipation Network – WEN -- and I'm your host, Tray Zeffron," said the announcer, a seasoned sportscaster who had broadcast the last of the games in 2236 and 2240, prior to the war. Now showing age, despite longevity gene-therapy treatments, Zeffron was closing in on a career that had lasted over eighty years. This would most likely be his last broadcast, but he signed up for it not because he wanted to, but because he had to. Everyone had agreed, that these Olympic Games would prove to be the most important and, possibly, the most deadly in all of history.

Entering his eighty-second year with WEN, Zeffron was a wise, intuitive sportscaster. He always seemed to know what to say and when to say it. That, in part, was why everyone wanted him to host the games. Well over one hundred, he was now bald with wrinkles sinking deeper and deeper under his blue eyes and around his mouth and temples. He still had his brilliant, white, on-air smile, but even that was beginning to show some wear.

"As most of you know," Zeffron said, "the games of this new Olympiad have taken on a more-serious note after the treaty reached in this very city over eight years ago – known as the Bern Accord. It was here, where I'm now standing, that the eight mega-powers of the world agreed to terms in settling the worst war in history. Over two-hundred million died, and many more were injured. No country escaped the suffering and pain of that experience. I, myself, lost two grandsons in that conflict so the pain is especially deep for me. Yet, we must move on, and in this setting we will. But first, let me turn the broadcast over to my friend and colleague, Noel Xian. She has been studying the Bern Accord and is best qualified to tell about what to expect at these games. Noel?"

"Thank you Tray."

Noel's family heralded from Taiwan, a province of China. She was the very opposite of Tray – young, reserved, and measured. She was brought in for analysis and comment, rather than adding color or play-by-play. Those tasks were given to others who specialized in those areas or who were just naturals at it.

"It was just twelve years ago," said Noel, "that we were bringing you an Olympic Games that highlighted great athletes from over two hundred nations around the globe. The biggest issues at that time were catching athletes using performance-enhancing drugs, injected nanobots, or hard-to-detect implants. In Dubai, we saw the triumph of the Slovakian basketball team as they captured gold over the very talented Australian team. We witnessed the powerhouse Chinese gymnasts battle back to defeat the Soviet Federation team, which had won in 2230. In the pentathlon, we saw the pugnacious Madiyar Hacimow from Panistan, nearly kill his opponent, Yuri Oblinov from the Soviet Federation, on his way to the gold medal. These were the highs and lows from those games. However, for the Bern Games things are more serious.

"According to the Bern Accord, there were four thousand pages of details outlining how these games would be played and how they would be adjudicated. The judges are selected very carefully and must follow strict protocols to prevent cheating. Of course, no judge can be from a country that has a participant in the event being scored, and if all countries do have athletes participating, then the eight major countries must each be represented on the same judging panel. No communication is permitted between judges before or during the games.

"Athletes will be screened for drugs before and after each event. The lab used will be a consortium of scientists from all eight of the major nations. Athletes cannot be housed with those from another country. This is a departure from old traditions, of course, but given the importance of the outcome, it is understood.

"All athletes must be escorted to and from the Olympic Village and only by Olympic security. There can be no contact with any athlete or representative from their own country once the torch is lit on opening night, except when they are competing together in the same sport or are part of a team event.

"But beyond these new twists, there are several more:

- Much like in the ancient games, all events will award only a gold medal. There will be no silver or bronze medals in any event.
- Generally, the rules for events have been modified to make it much more permissible for athletes to use *aggressive* tactics to win. Some call it the *win-at-all-costs* provision."

  "Might I add here that the term *aggressive* is not well defined," said Noel, before she continued.

- Each gold medal will result in points awarded to the country winning the event. Individual events will generate one point; team events two.
- Events may be modified to maximize the conflict between competitors. Changes in venue layout or rules for the event may be imposed. This is expected to elevate the level of performances by the athletes.
- And finally, the nation that accumulates the most points by the end of the games is granted the right to lead the World Council for the next eight years – until the next Olympic Games. But *most* important of all - only a supermajority of votes on that council can override any proclamation by the ruling country -- or in other words, <u>the winning country may well dictate terms to the rest of the world for at least the next eight years.</u>

"So, Tray," said Noel, wrapping up her segment, "as you can see, there is a lot riding on these games - much more than ever before. None of the eight nations wishes to finish other than first. It may mean the end of their country and way of life. Back to you, Tray."

"Thank you, Noel. Yes, the stakes couldn't be higher than what we have in these games. Next, though, we will take a look at each of the countries and what they bring to the table here at the Bern Olympiad 2.0."

The broadcast returned after the intervening government messaging, and Tray sat in the large, broadcast chair that would be his home for the following three weeks.

"Now it's time to take a look at the eight nations that makeup the core of the talent here at the games. Even though these country-states are favored to win most events, there are another forty-two nations - smaller nations that have not yet declared their allegiance to one of the other eight. Any one of them could squeeze-in a win during one of these events. We will look at those more closely later.

"First, we have the powerful Chinese team. After absorbing the Koreas, Taiwan, Japan, the Philippines, Vietnam, Cambodia, Thailand, Indonesia, and Malaysia during the past fifty years, China is in a really good position to come out on top in these games. As in the old days, they still take young children from their parents at a young age and groom them for specific sports. Their human genome project has enabled them to create superhuman hybrids in many classes of sports. These were not made illegal by the Bern Accord, so many of the advanced nations have taken advantage of this loophole."

Behind Tray was a map showing the size and scope of the new Chinese empire. Spanning from the old North Korea to Thailand, it was a land mass twice as large as the Yuan Dynasty established by Kublai Khan by 1271. Then, the map changed to the former nation of Russia.

"But the Chinese will find still competition from the formidable Soviet Federation. After the Russo-Arabian War of 2104 – just like was done after WW2 -- Russia annexed the former countries of Eastern Europe, plus Finland, West Germany, Austria, Italy and Greece. They called their new state – the Soviet Federation. With all that talent, there is no question that the Soviets are our number two pick.

"The remainder of Western Europe - the Social European Democracy -- has some capable athletes from the previous countries of Scandinavia, France, and England, but I really don't see much of a threat from them. The United Islamic Federation, or UIF from the Middle East, also does not pose much of a threat from a talent standpoint.

The map of the world rotated yet again, showing the Americas this time.

"AmeriCanada still produces some very good swimmers and track stars; however, many of these events were eliminated. For example, in freestyle, there is only the 100- and 800-meter events, instead of the 50, 100, 200, 400 and 800 events. Therefore, the opportunities to win points drops considerably for AmeriCanada.

"The South-Central Revolutionary Federation – the SCRF -- consists of all former south and central American countries, including Mexico. Its chances are limited, but they could take the football events and a few other individual events.

"Then, we have the eighth player - Oceanus - from which we get Aussie and Kiwi players. Few of these are expected to medal.

"Finally, there is Africa. This is where we get many of the smaller countries that have still not aligned themselves with any of the other eight powers. They have until 2260 to do so under the Accord."

"So, there you have it - the eight primary teams all fighting for that number one spot on the podium -- the winner taking home more than just bragging rights. This year, they may well end up running the world."

*****

PART III

The days passed, and the favored countries were indeed doing better than most others. But as predicted, the number of injuries and fatalities skyrocketed. Events that had previously seemed harmless had turned into killing fields. Three alone died in water polo, drowned before they could get their shots off. The necks of two wrestlers were broken during competition. And, equipment sabotage was fingered as the cause of a death in weightlifting. Likewise, in sailing, a mast snapped cleanly in half, killing one on board, and ball-bearings packed inside boxing gloves proved fatal for another opponent. Depending on the country being accused of foul play, the penalties ranged from an athlete's expulsion to a mere yellow-card warning.

During the fencing competition, the Soviet competitor, Viktor Inerov, was speared by his Chinese opponent, a quick and nimble player named Yu Xi Han. As Inerov lay on the mat clutching the wound to his chest, Han pulled the safety cap off of his saber and stood over Inerov, ready to thrust it through his heart to make sure he won the match. However, as the Chinese coaches told Han to "finish him!" Han hesitated and dropped his saber. He walked off the platform, leaving the match at a draw and his rival to the paramedics.

The Chinese Olympic organization arrested Han after the match and prepared him for execution for disobeying his coaches. But the International Olympic Committee voted to punish countries that put to death athletes who failed to win their events. Instead of taking the one-half point penalty for an execution, China allowed Han to live.

Likewise, three of the equestrian riders from the Islamic Federation were executed by their own countrymen after a polo match - they were defeated after only two chukers, three points to one against a talented European team. The Islamic Federation took the half-point deduction.

However, more casualties were taken in other events. Although the explicit goal for most sports had not changed, putting rival athletes at opposite ends of the field in the javelin, hammer-throw, and shot put, resulted in high casualties. Other potentially deadly events, such as the riflery and archery competitions, were setup the same way and exacted heavier losses on all sides.

When the last day of the games arrived, the points standing was nearly a dead heat between two of the teams expected to win the overall gold. Yet, there was also one that was a complete surprise. Both China and the Soviet Federation were tied for the lead with thirty-two points each. What was not expected was the astonishing showing by the host country, Switzerland. No one had counted on the prowess of its athletes, nor the creativity they were using to avoid being killed or maimed by their opponents. Commanded by a former military general, Kristof Ghunterman, from the former German Republic, the Swiss was being led by a brilliant tactician. He was referred in the press as the "Field Marshal."

But because of how well they were doing, the eight powers forced the International Olympic Committee to require all Swiss athletes to undergo additional drug and nanobot screening. When those came up empty, they considered banning the Swiss altogether, as they were convinced of cheating. However, when the other nations threatened to walk-out, the powers backed down. In the end, the Swiss were allowed to remain, but for any subjectively-judged event that remained – like diving or boxing, their chances of winning were nil.

*****

PART IV

"Good morning," said Tray, smiling and radiating an unusual sense of optimism each and every day of the games. "This is the day we've all been waiting for. Today, we will see the concluding events to these momentous Olympic Games. There will only be two events today and these will determine the ultimate victor nation. The first is the Road Race - the traditional cycling event where virtually all nations field a team of riders. These can be men, women, trans, gens, cross, orts, pans, and other gender varietals. The course is 497 kilometers through the grueling mountains of the Swiss Alps. The second is another traditional race - the Double Marathon. Again, the course is 52.4 miles and winds through the Alps, finishing at the grand stadium in Bern.

"Let's go now to Lynn Smith, who is covering the Road Race, which is now in progress. Lynn?"

The visual shifted to Smith who was wearing a white, wool, knitted cap in the cool air near the top of Mt. Blanc and Chamonix. "Thanks, Tray. I'm here at the pass between the mountains that connects Chamonix and Entreves. The winds are howling at over forty knots – some seventy-five kilometers per hour -- and there is a thick mist that will make this part of the course extremely dangerous. Farther ahead, there is a steep drop, taking the riders down six hundred meters in elevation in a very short stretch. The turns are treacherous, and it is likely we will have accidents or even fatalities. Tray."

"Thank you Lynn. Now we go to our correspondent, Germane Stevenson, who is riding in a hovervan in the midst of the *peloton* or main body of riders. The lead group is just ahead of them - riders from the three nations that are vying for the overall gold at this Olympiad – the Chinese, the Soviets, and the South-Central Revolutionaries. Back in the main peloton are the European group, the Swiss, and the AmeriCanadian teams. It's been a tough four hundred kilometers though. Of the two hundred riders who started the race, only fifty-two remain. There have been many casualties along the way -- nineteen deaths, thirty critical or serious injuries, and others just dropping out voluntarily as conditions and the situation worsened.

"But, those of you watching must recognize that these bicycles are not like those of the previous Olympic games. It's obvious that they don't have wheels anymore. They *are* human powered; however, the bike never really touches the road. The anti-gravity field generated beneath each one levitates it off the ground. However, the Olympic standardized program is installed just before the race starts and adjusts the course difficulty to simulate uphill and downhill conditions. So the riders inside these pods pedal like a regular bicycle and feel the burn and pain just like one too."

The broadcast then cut to pre-recorded film that described the cycles, including how they were built and the best designs entered. They were complicated machines, and only the richest states had the money to put several together that could compete at the highest levels of international competition.

Finishing the segment, Germane added, "So as you can see, the riders lie flat on their stomachs inside those shells and manipulate the pedals in back just like the old bikes. The levitation was thought to make things safer for the riders -- to prevent injury from crashes. Unfortunately, we have seen just the opposite in this race. Apparently, many riders know how to disengage the anti-gravity systems in the bikes of their competitors as they're racing, and it's caused bikes to collapse and crash."

Just then, Tray interrupted. "Germane, right now we need to switch quickly to Omar Hansen with the lead group. Omar ..."

"Yes, it just happened moments ago as the three lead bikers were climbing the steep pass here between Chamonix and Entreves. They still had two kilometers to go before they reached the crest of the hill. Then, they were to race down the other side at enormous speeds - likely exceeding 160 kilometers per hour. Any mistake on that side might be fatal. However, not all three riders will get there."

The broadcast cut to pre-taped footage.

"On your monitors, you will see what took place just moments ago. You can see Vladimir Groscov on his bike - number 73 -- just in the middle of the three cyclists on your screen. Now watch closely ..."

The footage showed Groscov looking back over his shoulder at the number three bike, ridden by Alonso Perez of the SCRF. As Perez tries to pass, Groscov drops the side of his bike pod under the frame of Perez's and then tips it sharply upward. The South American rider loses control and crashes, his bike flipping uncontrollably over and over and then veering off a steep cliff as the anti-gravity generator turned off. Perez and his bike disappear from sight instantly.

"Now, we've seen acts like this all day. It's just what Germane was talking about - finding that soft underbelly of your opponent's bike -- where it's vulnerable. However, nothing else today has compared with this. The drop off is more than five hundred feet down, so there is no likelihood that Perez survived that fall. Now, however, it's only Groscov and Liu Zhiang from China in the lead group, and we only have eighty kilometers to go. We will see what happens. They should be approaching you, Lynn, just about now."

"Omar, I see the two riders just coming up the grade," said Lynn. "They're both struggling - their legs are heavy with lactic acid - and they are doing everything they can to keep the other from getting an advantage or getting near the weak spots in their bikes. However, on the other side of this crest, they'll be racing down this mountain at high speed. Anything can happen."

"We should take note," said Germane, "that the main body of riders is closing fast on them. I'm only three hundred meters from the top of the pass, and I just saw the two leaders disappear over the crest. The main group is only six seconds back."

"The leaders just rode by me," said Lynn, shielding her eyes from the wind, "... and down they go, over the top and beginning their long decent toward Geneva."

The cameras zoomed in on the lead cyclist, Groscov who had taken first place away from Zhiang. Flying down the mountain, the two were close together, within inches of each other's wheels. One wrong move and both would go down in a mangled heap. Then, the camera panned back up the mountain, showing the peloton of forty-some riders in pursuit.

At speeds exceeding 160 kilometers per hour, the mass of bicycles -- with feet spinning, heads down, and hands gripping their wheels like a last life preserver -- zoomed past rocks, snow, and fans, descending into the valley below. Overhead, the once-clear and sunny skies had became cloudy, dimming the closing scene as the events from the prior six hours were coming to an end.

Zhiang kept a close eye on Groscov. Both knew what the other was capable of and neither wanted to be the victim. Meanwhile, events were unfolding seconds behind them in the peloton, now within striking distance of the two leaders. It was then that three more bikes broke from the pack, peddling at blazing speed, even though their cycles were already accelerating down the steep decline. The Swiss, followed by the Europeans and AmeriCanadians, all bolted from the main group.

With the wind howling in their faces, the riders gritted their teeth. The burning pain in their legs was almost too much to bear. It had begun after the half-way point and had only gotten worse. However, all pushed on, knowing this would be their only chance at fame and glory for their country and perhaps for the world.

Liam Stager understood where his country, Switzerland, was in the standings and realized he could make history. His energy draining, he had to find a second wind - heck, by this time, a fifth or sixth wind -- to overcome the leaders ahead of him who were not giving up easily. But right behind him were Ferdinand Delgado and Tark Branson, both staying within his slipstream and ready to pounce at the last moment.

"Things are tightening rapidly, here at Mt. Blanc," said Lynn, looking down from the top of the mountain. "We can see the rest of the course below us, and the large pack behind the two other, smaller groups, all trying to be the first to cross the finish line. Omar, let's go to you now."

"The Chinese and Russian riders are locked in a battle of epic proportions here as they round the final curve before hitting the straight-away to the finish. This corner is only five kilometers ahead of us - it's a tight corner as well, and if anyone goes outside the laser markers, they will be disqualified."

Heading toward the curve, Groscov slammed his bike into Zhiang's who instantly retaliated, trying to find the sweet spot of the Russian's bike to make it shut down completely. Back and forth, they careened into one another, but each time they did so, they added time, slowing their pace by milliseconds.

As they approached the curve, the Swiss rider pulled right behind them -- on the back edge of the Russian. And just when Groscov realized he was being tailed, Zhiang made one more maneuver to smash his pod into his Russian competitor. The impact hit its mark, and Groscov's bike shut down, but something else happened too. When Zhiang's bike collided with Groscov's, their outer shell flares entangled, binding the two together. Zhiang tried to pull back, but with Groscov's antigravity field shut off, the weight of his bike pulled both bike's down and off the course. Out of control, the bikes slammed straight into a sheer rock cliff where both bikes exploded into a fiery ball, like a detonated bomb.

Stager yanked on his wheel, barely missing the accident by only inches. Ahead, he could see the black-and-white pendant that was strung overhead, awaiting the victor to cross. However, Ferdinand and Tark had other ideas of who would win that race.

It was now an all-out sprint to the finish, and as Stager pushed on his pedals, each rotation shot fire through his legs, like hot pokers were being pushed up and into his calves and quads. He fought the pain and exhaustion as he pressed on. Yet, he could hear his pursuers right behind him.

With only one hundred yards left, the two hunters were pushing to catch their prey. It would only be a sudden burst of energy that would determine the victor from the losers. Tark pulled even with Stager, concentrating with all his might. Within a blink of an eye, it would be over.

The crowds cheered, roaring their approval as the riders crossed the finish line. Yet, as they crossed, everyone looked at each other. "Who won?" they all asked.

It was clear that Ferdinand had come in third, falling behind during the final thirty meters. But what wasn't clear was who had crossed the line first.

"Wow, that was some finish," said Omar, crossing the finish line in his hover van right behind the others. "Germane, do we have any information at this point? Do they know who won?"

"I'm afraid it was too close to call. They are looking at the photos now to see, as well as the GPS units on the bikes themselves. We should know something shortly. Right now, we go back to you in the booth, Tray."

*****

PART V

Tray sat shaking his head as the producer picked the camera back at the studio for the next shot. "In all my years," said Tray, "I'm not sure I've ever seen anything quite like that. We don't know the winner of that race, and as we look at the leader board. it still shows:

Soviets	30 pts.
China	29 pts.
Switzerland	27 pts.
AmeriCanada	23 pts.
Socialist Dems	19 pts.

"However, the one thing we know for certain is that whoever wins the last event – the marathon – will win this first Olympiad 2.0 of the modern era. The pressures are enormous; the stakes cannot be higher. So, let's turn our attention to this epic Double Marathon event."

Again, the program cut to pre-recorded footage.

"In 2204, the marathon of 26.2 miles was replaced with a double version because too many runners felt the original was not challenging enough for an Olympic event. Of course, the original distance dated to 490 BCE when Pheidippidies ran from Marathon to Athens to inform the Greek senators about the nature of the battle. Instead of taking about two hours, the new double-marathon takes over four."

Returning to the set, Tray continued.

"Today's contest began over three and one-half hours ago, and is in its final leg. Soon, they will be entering the city of Bern and making their way to the enormous stadium here. This is where the closing ceremonies will also take place. For more on this contest, we go to Cecilia Covington who is reporting live outside the city. Cecilia ..."

"Thank you. I'm flying in a hovercraft just above the runners which are below me on a fast pace toward the outskirts of Bern. No one has yet broken away from the main group, which is very unusual in a marathon. Each time someone has broken free, the rest of the body has re-absorbed them. However, that could be because all twelve of the front-runners, who were expected to do well in this event, have been bumped, injured, pushed or otherwise rendered incapable of finishing this race. Hans Moeller of the Soviet Federation broke his lower femur when he was tripped by a little-known runner from the undeclared country of Ghana. Likewise, Wu Kuang of China was hit by a truck that came out of a building service entrance. We still have no word on his condition or how that truck was allowed through the barriers. And the lead Swiss runner, Ernst Rochat, came up lame, grabbing the back of his calf and writhing in pain. Taken to the clinic, they found that something had been stuck into the back of his leg by a sharp object.

"Now we are down to mostly second-level runners, so it's difficult to tell who might win this very important race. We are told that each country has spotters throughout the course to ensure no one tries to put-in a fake runner as happened in 1972 when the leader, Frank Shorter of the United States, got confused when saw someone ahead of him as he approached the Olympic Stadium.

"We turn now to Roger Stein to get an update on where we are in the race. Roger?"

"Thank you, Cecelia. Here on your screen you can see the pack has thinned noticeably during the past hour. We are twenty minutes from Bern Olympic Stadium right now, and it looks like there are seven runners who still have the stamina to make it to the finish line first. As you are aware, the runners will enter the stadium and make one complete lap before crossing the finish. Just like the cyclists, each runner has a GPS chip embedded under the skin to track his or her position in case the finish is too close to call – like the Road Race.

"But right now, we have the usual countries still expected to be in the final group even though their best runners dropped from the race early. These countries have deep benches and can rely on their seconds and thirds since their star runners are out.

Those countries still with a shot at winning are: the Soviets; China; Switzerland; the Socialist Europeans; Oceania; the African Federation; and the small, undeclared island country of Mauritius. Oddly, the AmeriCanadian runners are well back in the pack. It is unlikely they will be a factor in the end of this race. Cecelia, back to you."

"We are now approaching the grounds of Olympic Park, and can see the leaders now forming into two separate groups - the lead group now consists of only the Soviets, China, Switzerland, and the African Federation. The sun is beginning to set as the runners begin their push toward the stadium. Unfortunately, it will be shining in their eyes when they enter the arena. However, as they make their turn on the backstretch they will face away from it, only to confront it again on the homestretch. Now, we head back to Tray with an update on the Road Race, Tray?"

"Thank you Cecelia. We have just gotten word from the Olympic Committee Authorities that they have determine the winner of the Road Race. This is considered a team race, and using the GPS coordinates of the bikes at the precise moment one crossed the finish line, they were able to make the call. By the closest margin in the history of these games and by only a millionth of a second, the Swiss hang-on to the first-place finish, winning and adding two points to their overall score. That means the leader board stands at:

Soviet Fed	30 pts.
China	29 pts.
Switzerland	29 pts.
AmeriCanada	23 pts.
Socialist Dem	19 pts

"That means that whichever of the top three countries wins the marathon will win the overall title for these Olympic games and lay claim to governing for the next eight years."

Tray took off his glasses and rubbed his eyes. "Who would have thought that the Swiss of all countries would be in contention at this point? And if they win, how will they govern the World Council? There will be many questions like that if they do secure the victory in the marathon race. Now, back to Cecelia who is now in the stadium."

"We are waiting for the runners to come into the stadium, Tray," she said. "There are four who are in that lead pack, and, as you can see from our outside cameras, the runners are now entering the tunnel to come into the heart of this arena. There are over one-hundred fifty thousand people packed into this stadium to witness the conclusion of this race and for the closing ceremonies. I'm sure hearts are beating quickly here, although not as fast as those of the runners who should be visible on the track at any moment.

"Ah yes, there is the Swiss runner, followed by the Soviet and then the Chinese runner. But ... I'm not seeing the runner from the African Federation? He should have come out of the tunnel with the rest of them. Tray, do you have any information on Talib Khamisi? He should have been right behind the other three leaders."

"Not at this time, Cecelia. We will find a contact down near the tunnel and report back," said Tray.

"Well, the three other runners are sprinting around the track at this moment, unaware of what might have happened to the fourth member of their group. The Swiss runner, Mateo Bodmer, looks strong as he lengthens his lead over the other two runners, Riku Ikeda of China and Giorgi Kalichava, the Soviet. And as you can see, the hot, red glow of the sun is beaming right into the runners' eyes as they draw across the line they will cross once more to finish this incredible race. First, we have Bodmer, then Ikeda, and then Kalichava in that order as they head for the first of four turns before returning to the home stretch."

But for those in the stadium, they saw a brilliant flash of light coming from the west end of the arena. It was so blinding that two of the runners heading in that direction fell to the ground, grabbing their heads and crying out in pain. Yet, the Russian runner, wearing dark glasses that protected his eyes, continued running as if he'd seen nothing. By the time the Chinese and Swiss runners got up off the track, Kalichava was rounding the opposite turn, nearly two hundred meters ahead of them.

People in the stadium were also affected by the light. Many facing west toward the light began convulsing in the stands, and medics were called in to give aid. Pandemonium broke out as thousands sought help.

But none of that stopped the Soviet runner who crossed the finish line first, holding his hands up high over his head in triumph.

"Cecelia, are you there?" asked Tray, trying to reconnect with his reporter.

"Tray, yes, I'm here. As you might have seen, there was a tremendous burst of light that came from the far end of the stadium that blinded many of the people here and, apparently, two of the front runners in the race. Our broadcast was disrupted by the pulse too. We're not sure what happened, though. But what I can tell you is that Giorgi Kalichava has won the marathon, besting his competitors from China and Switzerland. Even though he was trailing going into the first turn, the light disabled the other two. Miraculously, Giorgi was unaffected and went on to win this long event."

"I understand that the authorities are searching the area to find out what happened, and as we learn more, we will update you," said Tray. "So, it's official. The final point standing is:

Soviet Fed	32 pts.
China	29 pts.
Switzerland	29 pts.
AmeriCanada	23 pts.
Socialist Dem	19 pts

"What this means is that the Soviet Federation will assume control over the World Council for the next eight years. This was an outcome many worried about, as the Soviet's have a history of brutal regimes. We can only hope that they will take a less harsh and more tolerant view of ruling over three-quarters of the world's population. We must also hope we have a peaceful transition of power to them, as the Chinese will undoubtedly have a problem with this outcome. They, like the rest of us, will have to wait eight years when the second Olympiad 2.0 is held. Most likely, the venue will now be held in Moscow."

***

The cameras rolled on the field as spectators were carried off in ambulances and the Olympic officials readied the platform for the awards ceremony. Although no medals were given to the second and third place finishers, they were allowed to stand on lower levels of the platform while the winner had the gold medal placed around his neck.

Kalichava stood smiling and waving to the crowd as he stood in his nation's warm-up uniform, awaiting the heavy, solid-gold medal.

However, just as two Olympic officials approached him with the medal tray and flowers, three other officials in navy-blue sport coats and gray slacks rushed out and held up their hands. No one could understand what they were saying, but there seemed to be some confusion on the field.

"Cecelia, can you make-out what is going on?" asked Tray, seeing things unfold.

"I'm not sure, Tray, but it appears that these three new officials are stopping the awards ceremony. My understanding is that a complaint has been filed by the Chinese and Swiss Olympic Committees. Perhaps you have more information up there on this."

There was a pause in the booth as Tray was handed some information. "I just received this notice that two Soviet men were arrested in the west end of the stadium; they were carrying a high-intensity photon emitter. That was the device used to blind the runners as they came into the first turn of the stadium. It also affected many spectators seating in the eastern section of the stadium. Those men are being accused of working directly for the Soviet government. If that's the case, then Kalichava would be disqualified, and it would be unclear who the winner would be. The runner from Mauritius would be the next one to cross the line after the Soviet, but the Swiss runner, who placed third, likely would have won had the light not gone off. If the Mauritius runner is declared the winner, the overall results of these Olympics would not change. The Soviet Federation would still win overall, as the point standing would not be changed by the marathon event and it was leading going into it."

"Now you can see that down on the field, the Soviet Olympic Committee is out in force. They are confronting the three International Olympic officials - apparently demanding that their runner be awarded first place. The Soviets are pushing and shoving now, trying to rip the gold medal from the tray they feel their runner is owed."

The violence on the field began spilling over into the stands. People from the Soviet Federation got into fights with almost every other spectator, and quickly, all hell broke loose. As the fighting spread, the Swiss guards rushed

"*Attention! Attention!*" were the words heard over the loudspeakers of the stadium. "*En raison des circonstances, nous annulons les cérémonies de clôture.*"

"To translate for you at home, the closing ceremonies have been cancelled. The trouble in the stands and on the field have caused officials to close the games early," said Tray. "We must end this broadcast tonight," continued Tray, "and unfortunately, we will not have any more information for you until the IOC or International Committee meets to work out a solution to this problem. We will bring you breaking news as soon as we learn more."

*****

PART VI

It was another three days before the IOC meeting adjourned. The newscast came back on the air, interrupting with breaking news as promised.

Tray Zeffron returned, this time looking older and more stressed than anyone could ever recall. He made only a brief statement.

"We have breaking news," he began. "The Chairman of the International Olympic Committee is about to give his remarks. The IOC has concluded its meetings and the lengthy talks held on the outcome of the marathon race, and, perhaps, the fate of the World Council. We go now, live, to the news briefing room in Bern."

The Chairman of the IOC was a Soviet - Oleg Bukin. With his shiny, bald head, he looked like he had not slept in days, and probably hadn't. In his early seventies, Oleg had faced difficult situations before in his career, but none like this. He cleared his throat before he began reading from a prepared script.

"As you know," Bukin started, "there has been some controversy surrounding the conclusion to the marathon race held three days ago at the close of these, the first Olympiad 2.0. Since that time, the Olympic International Committee has been in discussions with several of the nations involved in these games to reach an agreeable settlement. Although we did not reach a unanimous agreement, we did find a common solution that appealed to the significant majority of our participating nations.

"Therefore, I can announce that the winner of the 2252 Olympic marathon is declared to be Mateo Bodmer of Switzerland. Giorgi Kalichava wins second and Riku Ikeda and Talib Khamisi tied for third. Unfortunately, Talib was abducted while running through the tunnel into the stadium and has not yet been found. As diplomats from one of the involved nation-states are being investigated in connection with the abduction and another group of diplomats for the use of a blinding device during the games, the adjustment to the standings was made. There is also some question raised about the involvement of Mr. Kalichava; however, there is no proof at this time.

"Altered for the marathon results, which is also considered a team event, the final results of the Olympiad 2.0 are:

Switzerland	31 pts
Soviet Fed	30 pts.
China	29 pts. .
AmeriCanada	23 pts.
Socialist Dem	19 pts

"And it is my privilege to introduce the presiding president of the Swiss Federal Council, Simone Berset. Simone ..."

"Thank you, Mr. Chairman," began the small, thin woman who was the current chair of the executive branch of the Swiss government. I will announce that the next Olympic Games will be held right here again in four years 2256 and call on all the youth of the nations around the world to gather together for this event. As head of the World Council, I declare that we will revert back to the old rules of the historic games, awarding gold, silver and bronze medals to the respective winners for each event. During the next four years, we will work with the other nations to pen a new Bern Accord, to replace the previous one, so the Olympics may once again become about sports and not politics. Thank you."

*****

Only days later, the heads of state of the Soviet Federation and China met secretly in Hong Kong.

"We have already begun training and converting our human hybrids used in our military into athletes for the 2256 Olympiad," said the president of the Soviet Federation.

"We have as well," said the Chinese president, "but let's discuss something that we don't already know about each other. What are you prepared to do to oust the Swiss?"

"Our new battlefield is on the athletic playing field, Mr. President," said the Soviet, grinning. "We have already begun sabotaging their recruitment and training methods and those of the other country-nations so this doesn't happen again."

"And assassination?"

"If necessary, of course. It's all in the name of sportsmanship, isn't it?" he said laughing.

*****

TATTOO

PART I

Jim went with Jamie to the address. It was on the far side of town, in a district frequented mainly by drug addicts and prostitutes. There were only certain times during the day that the tube even went there - from eleven in the morning to three in the afternoon - that was it. Otherwise, it was just too dangerous.

Getting off the tube, the couple took the long escalator down from the heights of the Upway People Mover to the subterranean roads that were used by fossil fuel cars centuries earlier. There they trudged the dark and dingy alleyways until they found the address. There was a dim green streetlight nearby that gave them just enough illumination to see the number on the door. Pulling open the gray, peeling entryway, they walked the narrow stairs up to the third floor where they arrived at apartment 315B just as it was written on the card.

Jim looked at Jamie with uncertainty but knocked on the door all the same. Soon the door opened, but just a crack. There were two heavy chains keeping it from being moved any farther.

"Yes?" answered an older man, sprouting tuffs of gray hair on the sides of his head. He didn't have many wrinkles, but most people used dermal-tightening solutions to minimize the aged-look. Yet, it was his eyes that betrayed him - revealing many more years of stress and challenge than the rest of his face.

"Hello," said Jim. "We were sent here by Tyrone. He said you might be able to help us?"

The man looked the couple over carefully before he released the chain and motioned them inside. As soon as they passed the threshold, he quickly slammed it shut, re-latching and bolting it before either Jim or Jamie could get too comfortable.

But the inside of the apartment was nothing like what they expected based on the outside. Rather than being filthy dirty with empty beer bottles and cans strewn all around, it was pristine and medicinal. There were several modern, red-plastic chairs in the front room, making it into a waiting area for all who came looking for a solution to the same problem. The walls behind the red chairs were stark white but marked by large silver frames of modern art – mainly just plain, solid colors, splashed across the canvas in varying degrees of depth and direction. Overhead, bright, full-spectrum lights illuminated nearly every square inch of the place, adding to the clinical look.

"Who is the one affected?" asked the man.

Tall and gangly, the man was surprisingly well dressed, with a sharp, crisp, white-collared, blue shirt and sapphire cuff-links. His pressed, charcoal slacks and expensive loafers made it clear that this backwater office was not his primary means of making a living.

"I am," Jamie answered, meekly.

"Let me see," said the man, reaching for both of Jamie's wrists.

He examined them closely, turning them over and pressing his thumb against the place where the tattooed numbers rose to the surface of the skin. "Yes, I can see that this number does not match you at all. I assume you've had this your entire life?"

"Yes. My parents tried to get it changed, but ... well ... we just couldn't."

"I understand. I see many cases like yours. Bureaucratic screw-ups all the time. They never admit they messed up either. How simple all this would be if they just issued you another number."

"So, what can you do for us?" asked Jim.

"I assume Tyrone told you about me," said the man, now staring intently at the couple, his keen intelligence ever-present.

"Uh, no. He didn't. He just said to come see you," answered Jim.

"I see. Well, then I will tell you," the man began, talking quickly and fidgeting nervously, as if he allotted only so much time for each patient. "I do not charge for my services. However, you should know that what I do is not legal. You must sign several things saying that the procedure I performed was for a wrist-tendon repair – a relatively minor procedure, but like everything else, it's usually performed by government doctors."

"Are you a doctor?" asked Jamie, nervously.

"Yes, but I don't want to lose my license," said the man. Then, relaxing his posture, he added, "I believe sometimes you must break the law to make right with justice - particularly when the justice system becomes corrupted and self-serving – condoning and even defending the injustice it purports to fight against." He looked again at her wrist while continuing to talk. "You know what Socrates said about it?"

"About what?" asked Jamie.

"About Justice, of course. Plato wrote about him in his famous *Republic*, where Socrates talked about the nature of Justice."

"Doctor?" asked Jim, beginning to wonder if the man were really a doctor or just a philosopher, "what does this have to do with ..."

The man looked up, slightly annoyed. "I'm getting there ..." he said, before refocusing on the patient. "How old are you?" he asked her.

"I'm seventy-three," she answered.

"Oh, you're still young, then," the doctor responded. "You have another fifty good years left."

"Yes ... well ... no," she replied.

"No, I understand," said the man, continuing to examine her hand. "The one problem I see is that you have an older model installed - those were put in deeper and are harder to extract."

"You're going to pull it out?" asked Jamie, now alarmed. "But it will rupture!"

"Not if we're careful. I've taken out a lot of these things. I know what I'm doing."

"And if something goes wrong?" asked Jim, edging closer to his wife.

"Well, look at it this way. Your number is 03-06, which means that within three days you must report to a decommissioning station. There you will die, but at least you won't suffer. If you don't go, then the nodule inside your wrist will rupture automatically and send poison throughout your body, causing you to die a horrible death. That's why people just go to the stations and get it over with. But, if you let me try, I think I can extract it without any problems, and you can go on and live out the rest of your life."

"Do you have one?" asked Jim, pointing to his own wrist.

The doctor showed them his wrist. There was a long scar that appeared as a cross – short across and long lengthwise. It wasn't a pretty scar either but rather one that looked like someone had taken a coarse, kitchen knife and sliced open his arm on the dining room table. "Nope," he answered, rolling up his shirt sleeve and showing them the aftermath. Yet, despite the scar, there *was* a number showing through on the surface of his skin.

"What's the number for then?" asked Jim. "You shouldn't have a number if you don't have an implant."

The doctor laughed. "Just in case someone checks to see if I still have one, I can show them this. I reprogram this one every so often, moving back the date. They've never suspected that it's a fake."

"The whole thing is messed up," said Jim. "I understand the world's population is out of control ... what ... we still have something like fifty-billion people on Earth? But why do you have to force humans in all countries to die when it's only some who are making babies any longer. It's *their* authorities who should stop *them, not us!* The developed countries are actually shrinking in population, right? Why should all of us suffer from the irresponsibility of others? It's not fair. It's not right!"

"Life isn't fair or right," said the doctor. "It is whatever they tell us it is. All we can do is right the wrongs as we find them and to the extent we have the talents to do so. I can fix these wrongs, but I can't solve the bigger problems in the world – population growth, starvation, war, disease and other things. Now, do you want my help or not? I don't have much time left today. The building inspectors will come around within the next hour, and I have to get everything out of eyesight by then."

"If we say yes," Jamie began, "when would you do the procedure?"

The man blinked as if he didn't understand the question. "Why, now, of course."

"Now!" shouted Jamie. "You mean *right* now?"

"Yes, *right* now. Otherwise, it won't be until after you're already dead. I don't believe that would be of much help to you. Do you?"

Jamie looked at Jim. He nodded at her, and she answered, "Okay. Let's do this."

Jamie went to the backroom with the doctor, leaving Jim in the outside waiting room. She didn't look back as she passed through the door, not wanting to put any more stress on her husband than was already there.

It was a good forty-five minutes before the door opened again from the backroom, and a nurse rushed out. Wearing blue scrubs and cap, she pulled down her surgical mask and began speaking with animated gestures - her eyes flaming. There was blood all over the front of her gown, and even more was dripping from her surgical gloves.

"We must get your wife to the hospital immediately," said the nurse, speaking in short, quick breaths. "There's been … there's been a complication."

***

PART II

"What kind of complication?" Jim answered, now alarmed and panicked.

Just then, the doctor, followed by two other surgical assistants, ran through the door pushing Jamie in a levitating gurney. There were bags of solution attached to a stainless-steel rod that swung over the stretcher, but her head was rolled to the side and her wrist was heavily bandaged.

"What happened?" shouted Jim, walking quickly alongside his wife.

"No time to explain now," said the doctor. "We need to get her to the hospital."

Jamie's stretcher was loaded into the doctor's special van downstairs with Jim at her side. Then, the van sped away toward the nearest hospital, its red taillights vanishing into the fog of night as it turned sharply at the first intersection.

"Will she be all right?" Jim asked, looking over at the doctor who was monitoring her vitals.

"I don't know. I hope so," he replied, less than reassuringly.

Reaching the hospital, they parked the van just outside the emergency room entrance and an emergency technician came out carrying a computer tablet. "Name and Number," she asked, calmly, as if she were asking for her dry cleaning.

"Jamie Simmons – 03-06-2358," said her husband.

The woman marked down the number before realizing what it meant. "Uh, I'm sorry, but we can't treat her here. It's too late."

The doctor stepped in and took the technician by the arm, walking with her several feet away from the van. He spoke with her calmly, but there was a force and authority in his face as he gestured with his hands. She listened carefully, and when he had finished, they walked back to where the others were waiting.

"This way," said the technician, pointing toward the front hospital doors.

The attendants rushed Jamie into the emergency room, letting the double-swivel doors flap madly as she was pushed back to critical care. The doctor vanished with her at his side as they disappeared into the bowels of the hospital. Now, all Jim could do was wait.

One hour passed ... then another.

Jim had asked repeatedly at the front desk about the condition of his wife, but each time the nurse had only shaken her head and said, "You'll just have to wait, sir."

But even as other emergency patients streamed in through the outside entrance, Jim kept his gaze on the double doors that held is wife and her condition captive.

"Sir?" came a voice from behind him. It was from the opposite direction he was expecting. Pivoting around quickly, he found two men wearing dark uniforms, pressed cleanly with their trouser cuffs poised just above their patent-leather, black shoes, standing just to his side. Both wore dark sunglasses with tinting so heavy, Jim couldn't see their eyes. One was tall and slim, sporting a white shirt and skinny black tie, while the other was slightly shorter but equally trim and dressed like an identical twin. They wore uniforms, but there were no badges or other insignias to show who they were or what they might want.

"Are you Jim Simmons?" asked the shorter of the men, his voice unusually deep and resonating.

"Yes?" Jim answered, worried.

The man pulled out an ID and pushed it near his face. It read: ***Chicago Population Control Officer.***

"We received word on a possible 'fugie.' The name we were given was a Jamie Simmons. Is that your wife?"

"Yes," said Jim, not knowing what else to say.

"We need to talk to her, sir. We understand that she may be trying to evade her appointment at the decommission station. I am sure that she is aware that it is a felony, and I trust you are aware that anyone aiding and abetting her flight from her appointment will also be charged with a felony. Were you aware of that, sir?"

"I ... I'm not sure what the problem is, officer," said Jim, stuttering as he fumbled for words.

"If you are helping her in any way, you will be convicted of that crime. Both of you will be terminated immediately at the decom station. Can I be any clearer?" The contempt dripping from his mouth was palpable.

"I think I understand, officer," Jim answered. "But, my wife isn't trying to evade anything. She's just here because ... because ..."

It was then that the set of double doors sprang open, hitting the back wall on either side. The doctor stepped forward, extending his hand to greet them.

"Officers," the doctor began, smiling for the first time, "I am Dr. Daneeka. I am Jamie's physician. How may I help you?"

"Doctor, we need to speak to your patient right away," announced the taller officer, pushing toward the doctor.

"I see," the doctor answered, "and I overheard that you believe she is a fugitive trying to avoid the decom station. Is that right?"

"Yes, sir. Now if you'll show us to her?"

"Of course. This way," said the doctor. Jim started to protest, but the doctor waved him off. "You stay here. We'll be back shortly," he added.

Jim waited for a moment, but this time he changed his mind. No longer wanting to be kept in the dark, he ran back through the swinging, double doors to follow the men and see his wife. He didn't care what happened to him. He feared they would immediately find her guilty and either haul her off to the decom station or immediately inject her with a lethal dose of potassium. Either way, she would be dead, and he would never be with her again.

Seeing the three men in front of him turn into a patient's room, Jim waited just outside, hugging the wall and listening. But the patient's door closed shut, and he could neither see nor hear anything that was going on inside. Debating whether to storm into the room or wait, he decided to wait – but only five minutes. Then, he would push in the door and do whatever he needed to save her.

He watched the time on his implant tick off the seconds and minutes, and just as it signaled four minutes fifty seconds, he took a deep breath and steeled himself for battle.

"I'll make some notes on this," said the shorter officer, pushing the patient's door open to allow the taller officer to exit right behind him. "I guess we must have gotten a bad tip this time. Once in a while it happens. I'm just not sure why they thought she was due for decommissioning. She's got another fifty years left on her implant."

Jim slunk back away from the door where the two couldn't see him and watched as they strolled down the hallway as if nothing had happened.

As soon as the officers had disappeared and the flapping doors had quieted, Jim moved back to the patient's door and pushed it open. At the back of the hospital room were two men – one familiar and one not. Each stood next to the hospital bed; in it lay Jamie.

"What's going on?" said Jim. "What have you done to her?" There was anger and angst embedded in his voice, and he struggled to control his emotions.

But Dr. Daneeka seemed calm and collected. He acknowledged Jim's entrance, but then casually turned to the other man in the room and extended his hand. "Thank you, doctor," he said, smiling.

The other man, a short, stocky gentleman wearing a white lab coat, was bald, and had a well-trimmed, graying goatee. There was an intelligence in his manner and focus, something not lost on Jim. His presence dominated the room, and his confidence gave him a certain aura that was hard to describe.

Dr. Daneeka walked toward Jim, putting his hand on Jim's shoulder. "I'd like you to meet Dr. Benson. He and I were in medical school together. He is a brilliant neurosurgeon and one I have had the honor of knowing as a friend and colleague for some time."

"Doctor," said Jim, nodding in recognition. "But how is Jamie? She's not ... they haven't ... killed her, have they?" he added, trembling and afraid to go to his wife's side to see.

"We did everything we could," said Dr. Daneeka.

"She's dead, then," said Jim, looking at the ashen face of his wife.

"No, she's just had a few pieces replaced," said Dr. Benson, taking Jamie's sleeve and lifting it up.

Jim looked at him puzzled. "I don't understand," he answered.

Dr. Benson pointed to the spot where the implant had been, just above the hand on the back of the wrist. It had been heavily bandaged there before, as Jim had watched her being rolled out of Dr. Daneeka's office. But now, remarkably, it just looked like a normal arm, with no indication there had ever been a problem with an implant or a rupture or ... well ... anything. And the numbers were still showing through the skin as if nothing had been done.

"How is that possible?" asked Jim. "It looks totally normal."

"We used to use bionic limbs, but that's the first thing they look for now," said Dr. Benson. "They'd take a probe and puncture the skin to see if it's bionic. Once they detect that, they'd immediately inject the death serum."

"Then how ..." asked Jim, "... how did you ..."

Dr. Benson pulled the sleeve on the hospital gown up another six inches, well above the elbow. There, Jim saw what they had done.

"The implant ruptured while I was trying to extract it," said Dr. Daneeka. "Like I told you, it was an early model which they tended to bury pretty deep into the tissue. The poison started to spread throughout her body and would have killed her, but we set a tourniquet to keep it isolated until we could get her here. I knew my friend Dr. Benson, worked here in the ICU and there was a chance we could get her a replacement if we caught it in time. We worked for hours and were able to finish the job before the agents showed-up. They asked to see her hand and wrist, and we showed it to them. They saw that the implant number wasn't dated until 2412, so they were satisfied it wasn't a *bona fide* case for them."

Jim shook his head. "Unbelievable," he said.

Jamie's new lower arm and hand were attached at the elbow. The reattachment was splendidly done, and all nerves, tendons, and muscles reattached as if they were her own. The arm had come from an unknown donor who had lost her life in an accident only hours earlier.

"Will she be able to use it like her old one?" asked Jim.

"Yep. She'll be as good as new," said Dr. Benson.

"Better," corrected Dr. Daneeka. "Now she has another fifty years left in her. I'd say that's a pretty good trade-off for one night. Don't you think?"

"But there's just one thing," said Jim, "what did you say to the emergency tech in the parking lot to let them bring her in here?"

Dr. Daneek smiled. "I asked her how her sister was doing."

"Her sister?"

"Yes, you see, Dr. Benson and I have done quite a few of these in our time – although none quite so intense as this one. Her sister had the same problem as Jamie, and we had to do a replacement on her as well. They understand."

Jamie's eyes opened, and she groggily rolled over and smiled at Jim. "Where am I?" she asked.

"You're here at the hospital, honey. Drs. Daneeka and Benson are taking good care of you. They've given you a new lease on life."

Jamie's face contorted. "My arm hurts," she said trying to move her fingers. "I can't move my hand very well – it's stiff and sore."

"It will be that way for several days. You'll need therapy to get it working again like the old one," said Dr. Benson.

"The old one?"

But before the doctor could explain, Jim interrupted. "I do have some bad news for you, Jamie. You won't be able to play tennis anymore."

Jamie looked at him with confusion on her face. "What? I never did play tennis."

Dr. Daneeka grinned, "Well, I guess that little side effect won't bother you much then."

*****

CLASS STRUGGLE

Year 2158

Raza slammed the door behind her as soon as she came in through the entrance portal. A cold air blew in around the seal, and she shivered, as if it were just one more thing about which to be unhappy.

"What's it like out there?" asked Equid, the fully-robotic assistant that kept her company at the base and often accompanied her outside when she needed assistance.

"Cold and crappy," she snapped, letting the snow fall from her ThermaZ-lined, navy jacket. "What's the news of the day, E?" she asked, using his nickname.

"Weather-wise or something else?" E replied.

"Doesn't matter," said Raza, shedding the rest of her outerwear and going into the kitchen to find something to eat.

"Well, the weather for the next few days is supposed to be cold - a low tomorrow of minus ten Celsius and a high of zero. Winds will diminish to only eight knots. Then on Thursday, it will be ..."

"Thanks E. That's enough on the weather. What about other stuff?" she asked, opening the refrigerator and poking around for something that looked appetizing.

"Other stuff," said E, "okay, well, there was a moderate earthquake off the coast of Japan, registering 6.1 on the ..."

"What else?" she said, disinterested, by now opening a container of orange juice and pouring a glass. "What about something in this country?"

"In AmeriCanadia, we have the following news. Riots broke out in Chicago, as violent protestors damaged storefronts and businesses."

"Why?" asked Raza.

"They claim they want implants -- that the rich get them and they don't," said E.

"What does Washington say about that? I think everyone should get one."

"Perhaps," said E, "but the implants are expensive. Each one costs approximately $1.34 million including the surgery, of course. So, when you multiply that times the number of people without it, you get 262 ..."

"... million?" said Raza. "That seems like a small price to pay for ..."

"No, Raza. 262 *trillion* dollars -- and that's only if half of those eligible actually go through with the surgery."

"*Trillion*? Are you sure?" she asked, knowing better than to question E. He was the computer of all computers, after all. She emptied her juice glass, downing the orange-pulpy mixture and setting her glass in the sink.

"Yes, ma'am," answered E. "Unfortunately, as much as we would like to see everyone get one, it is not fiscally possible."

"You mean, the country can't afford it," said Raza.

"Yes. It would bankrupt the country and throw us into a financial crisis. But even if that happens and all those people get implants. Will their lives be improved?"

"I would hope so," said Raza. "They'd do better in life, I would think."

E's processor began blinking rapidly, computing the impact such an action would have on the multitudes. "My projections show that there would not be enough opportunities for the 200 million more people with the implant. There just aren't that many jobs for humans these days. And if you think about it, if everyone had them, then what would differentiate them from anyone else?"

"I suppose. But why is it right that I have it because I've made a lot of money, and others can't because they haven't?"

"Can you please provide me your definition of *right*?" asked E.

"Yeah, *right*. You know, as in something that is just – something that is well-intentioned," said Raza.

"The meaning of just or justice, then," said E.

"Yeah, something that is fair to everyone – not just for those who have wealth, but for everybody regardless of it."

"You have had economics courses, have you not?" asked E.

"No, I never got around to those. They were too 'mathy' for me," said Raza.

"I see," said E. "Well, from what you do understand, then what happens when the price of something falls? Do more people buy it or less?"

"More."

"And what happens when the supply of something shrinks? Does the price usually go up or down?"

"Up."

"And why is that?" asked E.

"Because there is less of it, so the price goes up."

"It goes up because there wouldn't be enough of it to offer to people demanding it at the lower price, right? When the price goes up, fewer people can afford it and the demand goes down. Eventually, it balances out – supply equals demand."

"Oh, I see."

"So, what would happen if the price were, say zero? If we offered it for free? Would demand go up or down?"

"It would go way up," answered Raza.

"So, if we offer everyone the implants for free, would everyone demand one?"

"Yeah."

"And if there is a limited supply of them, who would you give them to? Not everyone could get one, so only a small percent could get one. Isn't that right?" asked E. "How would you choose?"

"Uh, I would ... I don't know. I guess I'd pick those who needed them most," Raza answered.

"According to whom? To you? To your neighbor? To somebody in the government office downtown? Who?"

Raza thought for a moment and finally said, "I don't know. All I know is that everyone should have one. That's what would be right."

E let out a squeaky tone that sounded as if his circuits were melting. "Ah," he said finally, "we're back to *right and just* are we? Well, that approach won't help us with the practical quandary of actually being able to provide the units to people. That would strictly be a moral-ethical question, ma'am, one which I don't feel competent to answer."

"Alright," said Raza, pulling out a low-fat, vanilla yogurt and some strawberries from the refrigerator, "but I still would like your opinion, even if you can't quantify it as you like to do."

E's diode panel light up, hosting a variety of blinking lights. "Then I would say you were going after something like 'for the betterment of all society - for everyone concerned'. Am I right?"

"Yes, yes. That's quite it!" she answered, enthusiastically.

"But, wouldn't we, as a nation, benefit more from doing what we *can* afford rather than doing things we *can't*? If we were to go bankrupt providing the implants to everyone, then we would all suffer."

"No, no. We would all be *better* off, then. Why would anyone suffer if we all had them?"

"If we had one million dollars and we let one person *earn* – notice I didn't say *give* – nine hundred thousand, he or she could invest that money in equipment to create jobs for others. But if we give one dollar each to a million people, who has the money to create any jobs?"

"But he or she would just blow the money on a new car or something – not invest it."

"Who made the car?" asked E.

"I dunno. People, I guess."

"Yeah, people who had jobs because he or she bought the car. How many cars will the million people with one dollar buy ... None. They have no disposable income."

"You're confusing me, E! I'm not amused by your arguments anymore. Just go back to your charging station. Perhaps that will straighten out your circuits a bit," said Raza.

Raza opened her yogurt and cut-up a bunch of strawberries to put with it. She spooned out the yogurt and mixed it all together until the texture was smooth and rose-colored. Then she dipped her spoon in to pluck out one of the strawberries coated with the thick, white glaze of goodness.

"What was that?" asked E, hearing something outside.

"I didn't hear anything," said Raza, putting down her spoon.

Bang ... bang, bang

It was subtle, but she heard it too.

"What is it?" she asked, walking over to the closet and opening it to look at the panel of monitors showing all the outside surveillance cameras.

Her knees trembled as she looked at the images streaming in from outside. There were hundreds of people amassed outside her apartment complex. They were holding hammers, steel rods, and crowbars, and they were using them to break down the main, perimeter gate.

"Call security!" she said, anxiously.

"Security has been contacted, ma'am. They say there are too many people outside for them, so they've called the police."

"And where are the police?"

"No one has heard from them, ma'am. Last week, they were protesting too about not getting implants. They said they needed them for their jobs. There's an 87.8 percent likelihood they won't come."

"What are we going to do, then?" she asked.

"Unable to determine, ma'am," said E.

Raza watched as the mob continued pounding on the iron bars. They began swinging on them, back and forth, weakening the joints until they broke through the gate and began running toward her building. They were armed with baseball bats, clubs, knives, axes, and chains to rip-up or tear-down whatever stood in their way.

"I don't understand," said Raza. "What have I done against them?"

"It doesn't matter. They want what you have. That's all there is to it," said E.

"Plug me in," said Raza. "I need a download to know what's going on."

"You want to download through your implant then?"

"Yes," she said, lifting her brown hair so E could access the port on the back of her neck.

E took the electronic cord and pushed it into the back of Raza's neck. Then, he pushed some buttons on the transponder in the closet and began downloading the information of the day. Raza closed her eyes and soaked in the information as it streamed directly to her brain. She had paid good money for the implant, and every day she got her *fix* by plugging into the worldwide system. She was *privileged* as many had called her, but she had worked very hard throughout her life to achieve what she had. Nothing had been given to her – she had always earned what she had.

However, while she was more than happy to pay more to help others, she suddenly realized she wasn't willing to let others just take from her what was rightfully hers. It was one thing for her to give away what she wished; it was quite another for someone else to take it forcibly away.

"Lower the steel awnings," she said trembling and in a panic.

E complied, giving the computer the commands to seal off the outside of her unit from the approaching, riotous storm. The bars began to rise up from their mountings to seal the windows and doors, but then suddenly stopped.

"What's happening?" she cried, watching the mob break down the front door to her building complex.

"System is overloaded, I think. Everyone is trying to do the same thing, and the circuits overheated. Nothing is working."

Now, she could hear footsteps coming up the stairway outside, as the elevator had already been disarmed. Glancing over at her door, she saw the steel rods only one-quarter of the way up – an easy hurdle for anyone after they had broken in the wooden door.

"They're getting closer!" she cried, her eyes showing the terror.

"Doing all that I can, ma'am," said E, as he plugged in his decoupling modulator to try to reboot the system.

E scrambled to engage the apartment's defenses at DefCon levels 4, 3, 2, and then, finally, 1. At each level, more barriers were put in place. At DefCon 1, the highest, all locks were thrown, the steel bars in the windows and doors were activated by backup generators and the shock, electromagnetic fields were charged.

"Threat is contained," said E calmly.

Raza settled her nerves, walking to the kitchen and pouring herself a double shot of vodka. She emptied the small glass and went back to watching the cameras.

But what she saw gave her no comfort. The mob clambering up the stairs began swinging their axes into her outside walls, creating holes and penetrating a part of the unit no one had ever envisioned being breached.

"My god!" said, Raza, backing up from the closet. "E! Isn't there something to protect us from them coming through the walls?"

The hacking and cutting continued until she saw the shiny, steel head of the ax come ripping through the wall from outside in the hallway. It wasn't long before they opened a hole wide enough for some of them to push aside the drywall fragments and slide between two severed studs to get in.

"What do you want?" Raza screamed.

Two men and one woman came into the apartment and grabbed E without saying a word. They began ripping him to pieces, tearing off his head and limbs, throwing them to the side of the room. Then, they moved toward her.

"I said, what do you want?"

One man reached out to grab her by the neck. "We want this!" he screamed, reaching behind her neck and trying to rip the implant out from her spinal cord.

"But why? What will you do with it? It won't do you any good! You need the surgery to make it work!" she cried, in pain and agony as the man worked to separate it from her neck.

"You may be right, you rich bitch. But at least you won't have one, and that's all that matters."

*****

A MODERN & CIVILIZED SOCIETY

PART I

Stardate: 6958

The star cruiser landed after coming through hyperspace. Even though time travel was illegal, the cruiser had returned using a wormhole to connect with the Triangulum Galaxy, or as the astronomers referred to it, NGC 598. At more than 3.1 million light years from Earth, it would normally take a hyper-ionic rocket traveling at only 10 percent the speed of light (about 67 million miles per hour) about 31 million years to reach the galaxy, but with the wormhole, the craft was able to go across, conduct its research and return within only 11.6 years.

It was true that the crew on board had only aged 2.4 years during that time, but regulations put in place for such missions permitted that as the upper limit that would be permissible for any being - whether human or robotic. No one wanted to return home five hundred years later - their families or friends long gone, and memories of them long forgotten.

It was only the "special missions" that were authorized at the highest levels that permitted that kind of time lag. The men and women involved had to be at least 80 percent robotic. There could be a portion of the human brain left inside the cranial cavity, but the maximum limit was only 20 percent.

The commander of the cruiser, Adrian Xian Li, dematerialized in his transporter and then reappeared within the confines of the Galactic Space Station. The station was one of twenty-three that orbited around the now-dead planet of Earth. Scientists had been working for years to create a Genesis device – something that was introduced in Earth movies centuries earlier -- to regenerate the planet, but all efforts had failed. As a result of solar flares that had destroyed the planet eighty years earlier, only the orbiting space stations still held human life on them.

"Commander, good to have you back," said the transporter operator, a robot affectionately known as R9Z. She had been at her post for more than a century, and although she was not the most advanced robot in the fleet, she was, by far, one of the friendliest.

"R9," said the commander, "so glad to be home. I've missed everyone here immensely. How are things with your group?"

"Oh, thank you for asking, commander. My Group A19 is well. You know we are the elders of the operation now. We've been around for nearly two hundred years. They don't make them like us anymore," she said smiling.

R9 was human-like, but when she was made the robot-to-human transition had not yet been perfected. Although the current R137 series was a vast improvement over the R9, it still lacked the emotional bonding capacity that humans still possessed. But R9Z had someone developed that trait, despite not being programmed for it.

"You are -- and always will be -- one of a kind, R9," said the commander.

He stepped off the platform and left the room, heading down the hall to the debriefing room for a meeting with the admiral. As the door dematerialized to let him walk through, he noticed small improvements in many things about the station that he hadn't seen before. The lighting in the hallways dimmed as he walked, responding to his brain patterns telling it they were too bright. He heard his favorite music playing in his mind, and the color of the walls changed to his favorite pattern -- an old-fashioned Federalist wall paper that he had in his bedroom growing up.

Commander Li was in good humor when he stepped inside the briefing room, but that quickly changed. In front of him was a clear, glass wall - curved concavely toward him which permitted a broader span for the panel sitting just on the other side. There were seven sitting there, waiting to question him. That was unusual, as protocol normally would have suggested three.

"Welcome, commander," said the admiral who sat at the center console. She sat rigid in her high-backed, red chair and put her hands behind her back to let him know who was in charge. "Please have a seat. This may take a while."

*****

PART II

The interrogation took three days. It was brutal and direct. The commander was pummeled with questions nonstop, for over ten hours per day, until he nearly collapsed from the stress.

"I think we have asked enough for today," said Admiral Stone. "We will reconvene again tomorrow at 0800 hours." She then pounded her electronic gavel before rising from her chair. Her high-collared uniform of mauve and sage, still sparkled with the brass medals and colorful ribbons that adorned her chest. But, she ignored what was going on behind the curved glass, as attempts to resuscitate the commander were being made.

After being revived, the commander was dumped back into his quarters to try to recovery sufficiently for the next day of inquiry. And, at the crack of dawn, Li was strapped again to a wheel chair and brought back into the fish bowl, under hot lights, to answer questions.

"I don't understand," Li kept repeating. "What did I do wrong? Why am I being treated this way?"

But each time he raised the question, he got no answer, except: "It's classified." Yet still, the questions came fast and furious.

"Again, commander, what did you enter into your ship's log on stardate 6957.55?"

The stardate was always calibrated to Earth's date, even if the starship's date was altered by the wormhole. On board, the date used was the shipdate, which was much shorter since the ship's warp speed slowed the time on board as compared with that on Earth.

"As I told you before, admiral, the entry I posted is noted in the log. You have the copy in front of you. What is it that you're asking me?"

"It says here that your cruiser, the SS Yorktown, was taking measurements around a globular star cluster inside NGC 598 - one classified as a Class II globular with dense stars compacted. As you know, the NGC 598 galaxy has 42.3 billion stars, whereas, the Milky Way has 426.4 billion stars and the Andromeda galaxy, our nearest neighbor has 1.09 trillion stars. The area covered by the globular star cluster in the IN2b arm you visited - U89B7 -- is only 5.7 kiloparsecs across. We ordered the SS York to visit three stars within that cluster - M33 X7, VAR 2, and HD 9446. Of course, we know that you flew as close to M33 as you could without being disturbed by its black hole, and you took substantial measurements of the super-luminous blue star VAR 2. However, you failed to visit HD 9446 which has multiple planets circling it - at least that's what your starlog shows. Yet, our Tracking-Locators pinpointed your location at HD 2B - the second rocky planet of that solar system. We'd like to understand what you found and why you didn't report this in your log?"

Commander Li stared at the admiral without blinking. "I assume, then, that you know precisely why I did not log that event."

"Yes, we do, commander, and that is what is troubling to us. We have other circuits on board the starship that provide backup information for us, and what we found was disturbing."

"The fact that I defended my ship and its crew is disturbing?" asked the commander, agitated.

"The fact that you destroyed a Nefarian ship with two hundred men, women and children on board is disturbing, commander."

"If you know all this already, then you also know that the Nefarian ship was one of their Class II destroyers. They put women and children on those ships so we won't defend ourselves by shooting back. They know it's against our rules of engagement. But that means that I cannot defend our crew either."

"But you killed innocent women and children, commander!"

"Not innocent, admiral. They were as much a part of that ruthless crew as the members themselves. Nefarians are known to destroy anyone who is not of their blood and faith. They do so indiscriminately, not even hailing the captain of the other ship, but merely blowing the other vessel from space. So, let me explain what occurred, admiral."

"We're not interested in the facts about what occurred, commander. You violated protocol, and that must be punished."

"Whether you wish to hear it or not, admiral, I will tell you and the military court what happened. We were in Sector HD near 9446 when my helmsman alerted me to another object that had just launched from what appeared to be an orbiting station around HD 2B. Not realizing it was Nefarian, I attempted to hail the vessel using standard signals. We lowered our defenses and powered down our weapons to ensure they understood we were coming in peace. Without warning, their ship fired at us, striking the starboard side, Section G mid-aft. You can plainly see the damage done to that part of the craft. It killed three of my men before we could close the airlocks to seal the rest of the ship. I continued my attempts to reach their captain and indicated that we were not there to harm them, but they continued firing.

"We then used evasive maneuvers to avoid being struck, but when our sensors identified the preparation of a second warship being readied at the space station, we realized we had to do something to defend ourselves. So, the Magnetic Field Cloud was activated, and the missiles sent our way from the first craft exploded before they could reach the ship's hull. However, as the second ship approached, I saw that it was a battle cruiser, much larger than the destroyer we had been dealing with. When the cruiser opened fire on us with its neg-matter, pulse beam, our MFC began to buckle. I pumped more energy into it, but it was draining our matter-antimatter reactor so quickly that I worried we wouldn't be able to make it back through the wormhole.

"Then, they began using plasma pulse bombs, which penetrated our MFC. I only had seconds to react before we were all destroyed. So, I gave the order."

"You gave the order to kill those innocent men, women and children. Yes, we already have established that fact," said the admiral, with smug indignation.

"Admiral, with what little respect I have left for this institution, I must tell you that this Federation policy of standing down in the face of the blatant manipulation and use of innocents to achieve a military goal is wrong. With that anchor around our necks, we have no chance of winning the war or keeping the peace. You do understand that, I hope. Our enemies will destroy us, and after that, then what?"

The admiral banged her gavel on the desk above him. "That is *not* a decision for you to make, commander! At my level, we make diplomatic decisions - we negotiate and talk with our counterparts to arrive at a mutually beneficial settlement. We are smart enough to know how to reach compromises that will let everyone live in peace and harmony with one another. But, I don't expect you to understand that. All you can think about is how to wage war on another people. That's what our ancestors did who lived in caves millennia ago. No, commander, we are a more advanced society now. We have evolved since throwing spears at dinosaurs for our meat."

"Humans did not evolve until after the dinosaurs, admiral."

He could see the rage in her eyes, but he dared not say anything more.

The admiral sat up rigid in her chair, but by now it looked more like a throne to the commander than anything resembling a judgeship.

"You will be sentenced to thirty years for each of the lives you took on that ship you destroyed." Then, she leaned in. "You, Commander Li ... you will never see the light of day again."

Just then, someone came into the chamber and handed the admiral a note. Her face turned ashen and pale, and as she got up, the commander could see she was trembling.

"What is it admiral? What has happened?" asked one of the other officers on the bench.

"Nothing you need to know about," she answered before rising and hurrying out of the hall.

As they were taking the commander away in irons, the messenger was summoned to talk with the other members of the tribunal. They huddled together and listened as the messenger shared the information he had delivered to the full admiral. After hearing the news, they all shook their heads.

Li struggled with his jailer, fighting the attempt to haul him away before he could ask his question. Finally, as he was passing through the dissolved barrier to the courtroom, he shouted back at those on the bench who were just starting to leave out the other side of the room.

"Captain Sanger?" he shouted, holding onto the frame of the doorway. "What was the news? What did the messenger say to the admiral?"

Sanger was one on the panel whom Li knew well. She was only a captain, so she couldn't confront the admiral directly, but Li knew she often disagreed with the Federation's wartime policies.

Captain Sanger glanced over at Li. She preferred to ignore his pleadings and walk out the door, but as she did so, he persisted.

"What happened?" Li asked her again as she started to turn.

Sanger pivoted quickly, but waited for the others to leave the room before answering. "We just learned that five of our starcruisers were destroyed today - vaporized by Nefarian battleships. All members were lost.

Li shook his head. "So, what does that mean?" he asked. "Will they reconsider and change their minds?"

"I don't know. We'll have to see."

***

Several days passed, but there was no change in Commander Li's situation. He remained in his cell awaiting transfer to a high-security fortress on Europa. Each day, he asked to talk with Captain Sanger, but it seemed his pleadings were falling on deaf ears.

Finally, the door to his cell opened, and Sanger walked in. As always, her blue uniform was immaculate with every crease and every hem in perfect order. She sat down on the only chair in his cell and folded her hands in her lap, sitting up straight and stiff in the hard-backed chair.

"Well?" Li asked, staring at her from his unkempt bunk. His hair was also uncombed, and his face scruffy with stubble.

"I have news," she said. "It's news you've been asking for."

"Okay. So, what are they going to do? Are they revisiting their policy? Are they going to let me go because they now understand that their approach will spell disaster for scores of starships and thousands of crewmen?"

Sanger sighed. "Your partially right," she answered. "The admiral has rethought her position and that of the Federation when it comes to engaging the enemy."

"Good," said Li. "Finally, she's woken up to the reality of the situation and of the confrontation we face. They are bent on destroying us. There is no middle ground with them. They've transmitted messages to Earth over and over again telling us they want nothing more than our complete and utter annihilation. They've said they don't seek peace – only the destruction of our species. So, it's good that the admiral finally sees the light. It's better late than never."

Sanger grimaced. "Unfortunately, she has decided that *greater* restraint is needed, not less. She believes we should reach out to the Nefarians and offer our resources, our technology, and anything else they ask for in order to … as she called it … *and bring them into a modern and civilized society with us*."

Li sat in stunned silence. Then, he said, "You're joking, right?"

"I wish I were, commander."

The commander let out a deep breath and made the sign of the cross on his chest. "Then God help us … God help us all."

*****

DEEP FREEZE

PART I

"But I'm at the age when I must choose!" shouted the baron, standing aside his closest friend and attorney.

Baron Winston Palmer had been lord over a vast estate in southern England for years, and his family had maintained a privileged position within the local community for centuries. It was true that times had changed significantly since the salad days of the aristocracy in the nineteenth century, but things were as they were now. The royal class had fallen on hard times, and the distinction between it and the merchant and political classes had become blurred. Sure, there was still a king of England, but he had long since abandoned any public spotlight, preferring to keep a low profile to maintain what the royal family had left of dignity and honor.

It was now the Palmers who clung precariously to the mantle to which their great ancestor, Baron Lloyd Alfred Palmer had been bestowed. It had been the year 1784 when he had received from King George III a significant parcel of property as a result of his loyalties to the crown during the American Revolution. Over five thousand hectares of land had been given at the time – an immense bequeathment that made others in the court very angry. And it was now that Winston and his attorney, Barclay Witherspoon, met to discuss the family's future.

"You don't need to choose right away, Winston," said Barclay, "You still have time left. The doctors told you that you have another three months or more. Why don't you just enjoy the time? Spend it with your family and friends. Live out the time as pleasurable as you can."

Winston turned sharply toward his friend. "No! If I wait, the association won't take me in. Isn't that right?"

"Well, I suppose that's true, but there are no guarantees on their end either. No one is sure that their methods work."

"But as the disease spreads, they won't be able to preserve my body. There is only a small window left open to me. Isn't that right?"

"That is what they are telling us. That is true, Winston."

"Then we must act at once. We can't let the illness outrun us. We have to stop it in its tracks and hope there will be a cure in the future. Doesn't that make the most sense?"

Winston's attorney sighed. "Yes, I guess you're right, but the family needs you right now. Your eldest daughter is happily married with your three grandchildren, and your two younger sons ... well ... one is doing well in London, while the other is still trying to figure out what to do with his life."

"Yes, yes. Abagail was always the rock of the family. She knew what she wanted from the beginning. I can't say the same for my sons," said the baron. "Jonathon is driven by his legal work, even though I never wanted him to engage in a profession. I still think it's beneath a Palmer; yet, I acquiesced. And as for Trevor ..." Winston too let out a sigh, "... I don't know if the lad will ever amount to anything. He only wants to 'have fun' as he says. The tabloids are filled with his follies and exploits. I can't keep up with all of them."

"But making this decision is a ... well ... ultimate or final one, your grace. I just don't think you've thought through things carefully. That's all."

"I have," said Winston, glancing over at his counsel, "and I think it's time. We need to move forward with this so we can settle the estate properly."

"Yes, Winston. I will do as you wish," answered Byron, bowing every slightly and leaving the drawing room in the baron's mansion.

Winston moved to the Queen Victoria credenza, circa 1885, where his lead-crystal, brandy dispenser sat waiting for him. It had become another close friend of his, albeit one that did not evoke any sympathy or care much for his physical well-being. Yet, it was one that gave him comfort each night and helped him sleep more soundly. He poured generously into the tumbler, watching as the brown liquid filled the glass half-way. Then, without hesitation, he took out a plastic, amber pill container and popped the top. At first, he shook four pills from the prescription bottle, but after seeing how small they looked in his palm, he emptied the rest. Throwing them all into this mouth, he chased them with, at first, two quick gulps, but then tipped the entire glass. The liquid tasted good, and he closed his eyes in soothing satisfaction as the alcohol and the pills quickly took their effect on him.

***

PART II

Aaron was used to having people dismiss him in the town square. He had grown up in the little town of Framingham in Suffolk. His family, the Blackstones, had managed a subsistence level of living after the patriarch, Jerome Blackstone, suddenly died of a heart attack in his auto mechanic's shop in the center of town. Aaron had done what he could at the age of eight to learn from other master mechanics in town in order to keep the family business going, but he was too young. After less than a year, his mother sold the shop for only a few shillings, and the family was forced on its own to make a living and survive. Aaron's younger sister, Adele, and his mother began a flower shop to try to make ends meet. They worked long hours and earned just enough to keep food on the table.

As for Aaron, he found odd jobs around town, and together with the rest of his family they made it. However, his life was far from easy. When he was twenty-three he was in a terrible auto accident that left him partially paralyzed on his left side. He couldn't afford therapy, so the numbness on that side of his body never abated. Eventually, he got a job in an office, as a file clerk, but even that was a struggle for him.

Forty-two years later, Aaron was working the same job, making enough to feed himself, but nothing more. He had no family of his own; his sister, Adele, had died many years earlier, suffering from Parkinson's disease which had not yet been cured. It was just him, and him alone.

"Aaron, is this your last day? It can't be. You can't retire. Not yet!" said Marjorie, Aaron's supervisor. She had been overseeing Aaron's efforts for over twenty years, and she looked after him as if he were her own son. He was older than she for sure, but she had become attached to him. He had a quixotic personality, and his disability sometimes caused her to get involved directly to help him – even when she had a lot of her own work to do. Still, there was a maternalistic feeling that kept her engaged.

Aaron smiled awkwardly. "Yes, ma'am," he answered. "This is my last day. I've been here for a long … long time," he said, stuttering, slightly. "The people in human resources said I could stop today. They said I had enough time put in. So, they said this could be my last day, and I'd get help from the government after this. They told me I would get a pension – I think that's what they called it."

"Yes, Aaron. You've earned your retirement. I think it's wonderful. You should enjoy it.

"Thanks," he answered sheepishly, putting his head down.

The rest of the day was uneventful as Aaron finished his filing and closed the last computer folder, pressing *Saved*.

But the daily hustle and bustle of his job melted into a daily monotony of getting up in the morning, watching television, running a few errands, getting groceries, and coming home to boil some potatoes and heat some left-over chicken wings. It was one of those days, not long after his retirement that he noticed a pain in his abdomen. It hurt, but he shrugged it off, thinking it was just old age. After several months, the pain became so intense that Aaron finally collapsed on his kitchen floor. The trip to the emergency room revealed he had cancer. It was advanced, and the doctor told him he should get his things in order. Aaron wasn't sure what that meant, but a nurse on duty explained it to him.

Aaron left the hospital, sad and alone. He only had three months, at best, and there were few choices for him at his level in society.

***

PART III

Myron worked at the state-run cryogenics lab. He had seen a lot in his thirteen years working there. There were those who had access to the premium program and those who got the standard program. Then, there were those at the bottom who got neither. They couldn't afford either and there was no money left in any government program that would give them that kind of access.

Even so, getting into any program at all required pulling strings and knowing people. He had seen the rich rolled in and treated as like Pharaoh Ramses II -- trimmed and trapped for presentation like they were being interred in the Cheops pyramid. Then, he had seen others in the standard program, who had been delivered at the front doorstep of the clinic with all the proper documentation and paperwork in order. But, as there was no one to follow-up on their treatment and care, they were quickly dispatched into one of sixteen cryogenic pools where often the identifying markings broke off, rendering their efforts next to useless.

Yet for Myron, these episodes were travesties. He had grown up in a small town outside of Brigg in North Lincolnshire. Brigg had a population of just 5,367, but that was before the Wireworm devastated much of the sugar beet crop. Myron's family had been forced to sell the farm and move to Duncaster, just fifty kilometers away. However, Myron went farther. He left North Lincolnshire for good, traveling to London for a chance to make it on his own.

However, with only a high school education, Myron found many jobs out of his reach, and he even though he had the drive, he didn't have the money to go back to school. He had wasted his teen years, drinking and carousing with his friends instead of working hard to get good grades and make it into a university. Now he regretted that, but it was too little too late.

At twenty-eight, his slight build, matted-black hair, crooked nose (the result of a football injury), and deep sunken, brown eyes, stood at the controls of the cryogenics plant where they processed recently deceased bodies for deep freezing. The company had sold thousands of contracts promising clients that it would preserve their remains for up to one hundred years until treatments could be identified to cure their afflictions. Of course, there was also that pesky problem of bringing them back to life in the first place.

"Hey, Myron? What's taking so long on this last batch that came in this morning? You should have drained 'em, wrapped 'em, and tagged 'em by now," said his supervisor, Darryl Taylor, a known hard-ass within the company.

"I'm almost finished Mr. Taylor. I just have two more to go," said Myron, finishing the careful job of wrapping the bodies so they didn't get freezer burn inside the chamber.

Myron took the last body and checked the paperwork. This one was a business mogul – made billions in the market, playing the stocks like he was at the casino. However, there was one important difference: his profits were guaranteed. Through contacts throughout the technology industry, this one had managed to get insider information before placing his bets. He knew in advance which companies would win and which would lose – just like knowing which slot on the roulette wheel the little, white ball would drop into.

Myron read the name on the tag and laughed. He recognized the man – one J. Michael Miller – who scammed the system and accumulated massive wealth. Along with millions of others, he had read the news articles about the man and the allegations that had circulated for years. However, the feds had never been able to pin anything on him – they could never find the smoking gun.

"How are you enjoying your money now?" whispered Myron, looking down at the white, cocoon-like pouch that contained the mogul's remnants. He checked the name on the validated certificate against the tag on the body. After matching them, he sent the body down the left shoot, toward the purple staining machine that would imprint a vivid, violet label on the pouch that simply read: *Premium*.

The Premium Plan patrons would be directed to the highest-quality cryogenic chambers with multiple backup systems to ensure the power never went down. This was guaranteed "forever," even though most realistically understood that it would most likely not last for more than one hundred years.

Other bodies during the day that Myron had prepared were less fortunate. These were of less importance and prestige and were directed down the chute that ended with a green stamp reading *Standard*, instead. There was a guarantee of only twenty years for those bodies. However, the front office usually gave a hard sell to customers, telling them not to worry about it – that they would get at least two hundred or more years out of the system and by then their illness would be curable.

It had been a long day, and Myron was glad to go home. He hated his job, but it paid well and was of the few he could do with his disability. However, each day he woke up to go to the same grind and the same boss. It seemed thankless, and he became increasingly irritated at the different treatment given out between the haves and have nots.

*****

PART IV

Aaron sat at home, watching his favorite channel on the television – a form of entertainment only used by low-income folks unable to afford more expensive Internet services or direct, satellite stations. The program he like best was one called *Who Wants to be a Billionaire*. He usually had all the answers to the questions and had applied several times to come on the show. But the paralysis on his left side was hard to coverup on the video interviews, and he was rejected each time.

"Which of the following would be considered a group of alligators? A. a pod, B. a flock, C. a congregation, or D. a troop?" said the well-known moderator, Leslie Hampton.

"C. a congregation," answered Aaron, sipping his beer.

"I'll say D. a troop," said the contestant.

"Is that your final answer?"

"Yes, that's my final answer," said the contestant.

The annoyingly loud buzzer-like sound went off in the background and the screen showed the chosen answer was wrong.

"I'm sorry," said the moderator. "The correct answer was C. a congregation."

The crowd moaned, and the moderator came back online. "However, you have won $100,000, which isn't too bad." She stood up, extending her hand. "Todd, we thank you for playing with us, here, on *Who Wants to be a Billionaire!*"

The station cut to a commercial, and then another, and then another. Aaron was about to turn off the program and go to bed when he saw a commercial for the state-run cryogenics lab. The executive director came on the screen, calm and professional, describing the unique services offered by the clinic. He was handsome – only in his mid-to-late thirties, with dark wavy hair, strong cheekbones, and deep-set brown eyes. His temples were slightly graying, and there was a dimple in the middle of his chin.

"Hi, I'm Dr. Ben Simpson. I've been running the cryogenic lab here at the London Institute for five years now and I see who the hope of another life has changed those still living. For those who can afford to pay for the process, it offers calm and tranquility when a sudden life-threatening illness or unusual accident happens, depriving them of a full life. It also gives peace to the family members who know that their loved one will only be deceased for a short period – until a cure is found. Then we, here at the clinic, will revive them and give them the treatment they need to continue their lives as if nothing had happened.

"We know the process is expensive, and few now can afford it. However, for a limited time, we are holding a contest and will draw from a hat the winner of a premium package cryogenic treatment. That's right, it will cost you nothing! All you need to do is apply. A winner will be picked on September 20 and will be announced on this channel and this same time.

"Good luck to all of you. Again, this is Dr. Ben Simpson for the London Cryogenic Institute."

The screen went black before returning to the regular program. But by then, Aaron had gotten out a piece of paper and scrawled his information on it. He stuck an old-time stamp on the surface and put it out in his mailbox for the postal worker to pick up in the morning. He only hoped someone would pick it out from the thousands of others submitted. However, he would have to wait.

***

PART V

3 weeks later …

The moderator was even nervous, appearing with a contestant who seemed to know the answers to every question she had thrown her way. She was currently at the £50 million mark, and had only two questions left to reach the £1 billion prize. With the next question, she could either pass and take her £50 million home or she could risk it and take the question. If she answered it, she would get to £100 million with a chance at the £1 billion; if she got it wrong, she would fall back to £500,000.

"So, Eve, what do you want to do?"

"I'll go for the 100 million," she said, becoming slightly nervous herself.

The music swooned into place and the lights swung back toward them, highlighting and dramatizing the situation.

"Alright then," said the moderator. "She's decided to continue on. So, Eve, here is your next question." The music again swelled and then settled so everyone could hear the query posed. "In what year was the Battle of the Somme fought? A. 1939, B. 1904, C. 1944, or D. 1916?"

The contestant thought for a moment and then said, "Remove two answers."

Two answers were removed, leaving A. 1939 and D. 1916.

"You have no more lifelines left, Eve. So, what is your answer?"

Seconds seemed like hours ticking by as Eve began breaking out in a sweat. She glanced around for anyone who might help her, but she found no answers.

"That's so easy," said Aaron. "It was 1916. It was one of the worst defeats in British military history."

"I'm going with … D. 1916," she said, with no confidence at all. Her eyes flitted to the moderator for some sign … anything at all.

The moderator hesitated and then said with a smile, "The answer is D. 1916. You are correct!"

The applause echoed throughout the studio, and the moderator sat back in her gray, swivel chair. "We'll be right back, as Eve goes for the £1 billion!"

But Aaron was more interested in the next commercial than the show. It was game night, and he hoped to learn who won the cryogenics lottery.

Again, it was Dr. Ben Simpson whose face appeared on the screen.

"Good evening everyone. I know you're watching a very exciting show right now, but hopefully you're just as interested to find out who will win the Premium Plan with the London Cryogenics Institute. Right here, I have the large metal drum will all the entries we received during the past several weeks. Over 45,000 entries came in to our office, and all were directly place inside this drum.

"Tonight, I will pull one entry from all of these, and the lucky winner will receive everlasting life — direct from your state government. It doesn't get any better than that."

Dr. Simpson nodded to his very attractive, blonde assistant who spun the solid-white drum several times before making sure the hatch on top was accessible by the doctor.

"Okay, then," said Dr. Simpson, opening the hatch and reaching inside. He pulled out a folded, white piece of paper and began reading. "The winner of the Premium Package is … Edgar Gonzales of Houston, Texas! Congratulations, Edgar!" said Dr. Simpson.

However, it was then that he put his hand to his earpiece and listened. Then, he smiled uncomfortably and said, "I'm sorry. There was a problem in our processing department on this one. I'm told that you must be a resident of and a citizen of the United Kingdom to qualify for the package. So, we will choose another entry."

Again, he reached into the drum and extracted an entry. "This one is Aaron Blackstone, from London. Congratulations Aaron! You have thirty-minutes to call to claim your prize. Well, that's all for tonight. Stay tuned for more contests from your British federal government offices."

Aaron felt as if his heart a stopped right there and then. He was thrilled. Just like the doctor had said in his commercials, he immediately felt a sense of relief – he would have another chance after this life. He would do things differently then, and maybe, just maybe, they would have a cure for his paralysis too.

***

PART VI

It was the chamber maid who found the baron lying dead on his bed. There was a every-so-slight smile on his lips, even though his eyes were wide open and most of his arms and legs had already begun to become rigid through *rigor mortis*. At first, she wanted to scream, but when she saw the contented look on his face, she held her breath.

The ambulance from the London Institute Cryogenics Lab came within twenty minutes, pulling up in the expansive circular driveway that dominated the front lawn of the estate. Clambering out of the red and white emergency van, the staff unloaded a gurney and headed directly upstairs to retrieve the baron's remains. It wasn't long before the staff, including barrister Witherspoon, lined up outside to watch their patriarch whisked away. Barclay followed in his private car to ensure that all preparations had been made and that the baron's body would be expeditiously wrapped and frozen.

Meanwhile, the maids and butlers stood in the light drizzle, always forbidden to use umbrellas in the presence of their boss and master. There were no tears amongst them; yet, there was no joy either. They were rather Stoic in their emotions, feeling neither affection nor enmity for their baron. It was a cold indifference, not unlike the chill of the sprinkling rains falling onto their foreheads and cheeks.

Only thirty minutes later, the van pulled into the long drive leading to the laboratory, tucked away in a secluded glen not far outside the London city limits. Stopping right behind it was Barclay, who quickly got out of his car to follow the gurney inside. After the formal paperwork was signed, the staff ushered the body through the air locks to the back of the building, disappearing from sight.

Barclay started after them, but the administrator stopped him. "Mr. Witherspoon, you've done all you can now for the baron. He is in good hands. We will take it from here."

"But I promised my lordship that I would ensure that his body was properly treated with respect and dignity, and I will most certainly do that!"

Unusually emotional, the barrister was resolute in his argument.

"I quite understand, but if you were to come to the back where your patron will be processed, you could contaminate the entire area. If only one small microbe gets into his system at this point, it could destroy the cryogenic treatment. His body would continue to deteriorate or, worse, he could contract a flesh-eating bacterium that would make restoration impossible. Is that what you want?" The administrator stood with his hands on his hips waiting for the answer.

"No, of course not."

"I didn't think so. So, we will take good care of the baron. I assure you. Once his body has been satisfactorily frozen in its container, you may visit him as often as you like. How is that?"

Barclay shook his head solemnly and tipped his hat before leaving.

The baron's body was pushed to the back where it was packaged and readied for deep freeze. Tags were immediately attached to his large toe, identifying him and his package status. These would be checked and double checked along the way to ensure he was given the proper treatment. In his case, he had elected an elite program, called the Super Premium. This was considered the gold package at the Cryogenics Lab. Not only did these clients get the benefits of the Premium package, but they also got first shot at being resuscitated once their malady was cured and the thawing process perfected. The others would have to wait.

***

Knock, knock, knock

"Mr. Blackstone? Mr. Blackstone? Are you in there?" The landlady fervently knocked on the door to gain the tenant's attention. "Mr. Blackstone!"

"I think you need to unlock the door, Mrs. Pavich. No one is answering," said the next-door neighbor.

Martha Leonard had been a nosy neighbor in the building for years, but it was a good thing. She had often helped others in distress or discovered unseemly or unlawful acts going on in the building and called them to the attention of the landlady, Eleanor Williams. Both women were in the seventies by now, and neither had anything else to do to keep them occupied but to spy on the comings and goings of the tenants.

"Why do you think there's anything wrong?" asked Eleanor, fumbling for the keys.

"Because ..." began Martha, "... don't you know that Aaron always comes out of his apartment at night, just before he goes to bed, to walk his dog around the block ... always. And last night, he didn't. I just know something isn't right, Eleanor. Something in there just isn't right."

Eleanor twisted the key in the lock and pushed the door open. "Mr. Blackstone? Are you here?"

Circumspectly, the walked into the apartment, looking around for any sign or clue of a crime or a problem. It wasn't long before they entered the TV room where the back of Aaron's chair was facing them, and all they could see was the back of his head.

"Mr. Blackstone? Are you alright?" asked Martha.

When they moved around the chair, they saw the television was still on, showing another rerun of *Who Wants to be a Billionaire*, and Aaron with his eyes closed. His pooch, Sergeant, was sitting loyally at his side, panting from the heat inside the room. Clutched in Aaron's fist was a copy of his entry for the London Cryogenic Lab contest.

Eleanor was going to scream, but Martha put her hand on her arm. "He's fine," she said. "He's with the Lord now." On his face was the slight hint of a smile.

*****

Part VII

Myron went to work even though he really didn't want to. He had gone out the night before with his only true friend – one he had known from grade school – and had a colossal headache.

"What seems to be the problem, there Myron?" shouted Taylor, his boss. "If you can't speed it up, I'm going to come up there personally and yank you down from the platform. I'll do that before I fire your sorry ass! Now get a move on it!"

"Yes, Mr. Taylor," said Myron, rolling his eyes. He was sick and tired of being pushed around by his idiotic supervisor who knew less about what was done around there than just about anyone. *Maybe I should just quit right now*, he thought, taking hold of another plastic pouch with a body inside. *Who needs this dreadful job, anyway?*

But the bodies kept coming down the shoot, and he continued to match the tags against the packages for which they had shelled-out good money.

It was later in the afternoon, shortly before they were clocked to go home, when Taylor came into the processing plant. He looked around with a sinister, smug look on his face. He had a clipboard in one hand and a pen in the other. "Let's see," he began.

All the processors in the unit stopped what they were doing and looked down at where he stood. His white shirt was still neatly pressed and his trousers clean, as if he hadn't done a thing all day.

"I need two volunteers," said Taylor with a smile.

"What for, sir?" asked another of the processors in the room.

"Great! You're the first," said Taylor. "Now, I just need one more."

Everyone else looked away or down to avoid eye contact. Anything Taylor brought to them couldn't be good.

"No volunteers?" he asked. "Well, I guess I'll have to pick someone on my own, then. Someone who deserves this honor. Someone who has performed at a mastery level lately – someone who …"

"I'll volunteer," cried one of the supervisor's chief sycophants. He was a favorite of the boss and could never do anything wrong.

"No, not you, Helmsley. No, I need someone else … someone more qualified." Then, he looked up at Myron. "You, Myron. You'll volunteer, won't you?"

"Uh, I don't know, sir," answered Myron.

"Sure you do. You just did. Congratulations to both of you. Now let's everyone give these two gentlemen a round of applause, shall we?"

The men in the unit clapped, but barely. They knew something was amiss.

"What do they get to do?" asked the sycophant.

"They're both fired!" said Taylor with a smile before marching out the door, letting is swing, carefree and effortlessly.

Myron was stunned. He had worked there for a long time, and for them to just fire him without any notice or anything was just … well … beyond understanding.

"What did you do?" asked another colleague in the room.

"Nothing!" shouted Myron. "I didn't do anything."

The others put their heads down and continued their work. They still had another thirty minutes to go before their shift ended.

Another white, body bag came down the shoot toward Myron. He looked at the tag and then the paperwork. Both read: *Lord Baron Winston Palmer – Super Premium Package.*

Myron sighed. At the same time, another body came down right after that one and rammed into the baron's. That didn't happen often, but sometimes when the machinery got a glitch it did.

Taking his eyes off the baron, Myron glanced over at the next body to come down the shoot. The paperwork was different for this gentleman. It was not typed or neatly presented as all the others were. This one looked like it had been hastily thrown together with someone scribbling the information with a thick, black magic marker. It read: *Aaron Blackstone. Nobody. No package – Dispose of body at once.*

Myron looked at the clock on the wall. He only had five minutes before the end of his shift. Pulling out a marker of his own, he made some quick edits to the paperwork. He then ensured each body was properly wrapped and then sprayed them with gold and green paint, sending them on their way down the shoot.

*****

PART VIII

200 years later …

The facility lay buried below decades of rubble and debris. There had been at least two world wars during the intervening years, as well as a few earthquakes that had caused massive damage to the British Isles. The first teams entering the labyrinth of passageways below had to use matter-anti-matter magno beams to separate the rock from the facility structure itself. Once they got to the main chambers, they found vessel after vessel of frozen bodies, still intact from when they had been initially preserved. The first chambers were well secured and had been running on backup, nuclear generators. These were the ones labeled "Super-premium." The next level down held more containment units; these were marked just "Premium," and there were many that were no longer operational – having lost power due to malfunctioning generators. Below that level was another, but it was still not reachable. It would take another year or two to get to that layer, as the nuclear material from the first two levels had to be removed first.

One-by-one, the specimens were transported to portable cryogenic units and brought to the surface. Each was evaluated and what was left of their paperwork or digital encryptions was reviewed and assessed.

"What do you think of this one?" asked, Z23, an AI bionic who was leading the team. He had been able to charge the data drive to retrieve the cadaver's persona information. "It's a bit hard to decipher, but I think it says Arn. Is that the name of this person?"

Another AI, FP101, who reported to Z23, came over to look. "Yes, that would be the name. But it's so badly garbled, it's hard to tell. Can we examine it at the molecular level to see if there are deeper markings?"

They pulled out their portable electron-scanning-tunneling microscope and placed it over the image. From that, they were able to see the marking clearly.

"It looks like the original lettering has been altered, doesn't it?" asked Z23. Originally, it read Aaron, but was changed to Baron. Apparently, it slipped through all of the screeners at that time. So, let's see what we have."

The two AIs reviewed the body and determined it suffered from nerve damage caused by trauma to one of the vertebrae. In addition, they found that cancer had infiltrated the body's pancreas. However, that was not what they found had killed him.

"This one died of a brain aneurism," said Z23. "See here? There is where the blood vessel ruptured; it must have killed him quickly."

"Can we repair him?" asked FP101.

Z23 nodded. "Of course. These things are easy today, although they weren't two hundred years ago. We need to get this chap to the Thawing Unit so we don't rupture the membranes of his cells. Then we can slowly bring his body back to room temperature after we repair the aneurism in his brain."

"What about the cancer?"

"Oh, we'll just replace the pancreas with an artificial one and flush his body with a *dichlorolphenolbarbatol* compound. He'll be back on his feet in a few days."

***

Aaron opened his eyes. He wasn't sure where he was or what year it was. All he knew was that he was awake and, perhaps, alive. "Where am I?" he asked, looking up at a white ceiling.

To him it appeared as if his hospital bed were outside, sitting on a sandy beach and he could hear and see the waves rolling in from the ocean in front of him.

"You're in the hospital," said a perky nurse who was stunningly beautiful. There was an odd twinkle in her eyes, but otherwise, she seemed perfectly, well, human. "We're taking good care of you. You should be able to leave in a few days."

"Leave? Where am I? What year is it?"

"Why, it's 2317, of course. What year did you think it was?"

"I ... I wasn't sure," said Aaron, looking particularly nervous.

"Oh, don't worry. We all understand you're from the past – like over two hundred years ago. We've made arrangements for you to live and there are many, many programs that will take care of you. You won't need to worry."

"But I don't know anyone, anymore."

The nurse smiled. "We know. But there are still a few human beings around these days. They usually stay to themselves and don't bother the rest of us. You may be able to join them – one of their cults anyway."

"Cults?"

"Yes. I think joining one of those would be the best for you. Anyway, you need to get your sleep. I'll check on you in a few hours."

And after checking his monitor readings, she left.

***

After another two years, the explorers found the remaining bodies in the lower level. There were only three that were still operating, and one that should have been offline but somehow had been able to feed off the backup generator from another nearby.

They brought all the bodies back to life but found one particularly challenging. Shortly after being revived – cured of his ailments – he began snapping at the attendants.

"Why are you treating me this way?" he snarled. "I'm a baron, for god's sake. You must treat me with respect!"

"That's not what it says on your record, sir. It says your name if Aaron Blackstone and that you were a clerk at a museum. You weren't even supposed to have gotten the cryogenic treatment, but you got it by mistake."

"That's a lie!" he shouted at them. "I'm a baron! I deserve ..."

"Sir, you don't deserve anything in our time. We have no monarchy or royalty in what used to be called Britain. We are all the same now."

"All the same? How could that be? I am part of aristocracy. I should be treated like ..."

"We know, Aaron. You should be treated like everyone else," said the AI attendant. "You humans can be so testy."

Three days later, the baron was released from the field clinic. He was considered a human, class III, which meant that he wasn't eligible for treatment for his previous illness. There had just been too many cryo-recoveries, and it had cost the ruling class too much to cure them all. Although they still had massive wealth, they had elected to stop bringing everyone back after this group, and those who were thawed were not cured.

Dumped on a street corner in a dark, dirty, crime-ridden part of town, the baron was left on his own. He had no where to go and no one to which to turn. Lonely and scared, he trudged off from the corner to find shelter in an alleyway or an abandoned building. He had heard of the human cults, but those were only for humans, class I. He had been tattooed with a III on his neck, which labeled him for everyone to see.

That night, he found a corner in an alley and curled up. He was cold, hungry and exhausted, but it was the fatigue that finally overcame him. Quickly, he fell into a deep sleep.

"Hey!"

"What?" the baron asked, groggily, trying to open his eyes.

"Who are you?"

It was a group of three young punks dressed in tattered, gray rags who were hovering over him. One of them kicked him in the leg. "Get up, old man!" he shouted.

"I don't want any trouble," said the baron.

"Oh, we're going to give you plenty of that, you ole geezer!" said another, grinning from the excitement.

"No, really. I don't want any ..."

Another lad kicked him – this time in the stomach, and he doubled over in pain.

"That's better," said the first. "I actually thing he's alive, mates!"

They all laughed.

"No, please. Just leave me be."

It was the first one who came in close, pulling out a knife and putting it to the man's throat. "No way," he exclaimed. "We haven't been able to kill anyone in ages. It's so much fun – slicing them slowly and watching them die in pain. Isn't it boys?"

"Leave him alone!" came a voice from the other end of the alley.

The trio turned quickly to see who it was. "Leave us alone! We're only having some fun. It's none of your concern!" said the lead punk.

"Oh, I think it is," said the voice, walking slowly toward them. Soon, behind the man were eight others, carrying clubs and moving with determination toward the end of the alley.

Suddenly, there was fear in the eyes of the thugs, and they ran toward the back fence, climbing over the top and vanishing down the neighboring alley.

The baron struggled to get up and watched as the new group of men approached him. "I don't want any trouble," he repeated, putting up his hands. Finally, he was able to see the face of the group leader. It was a kindly face, and someone with whom he felt a strange bond. "What do you want?" he asked.

"I'm Aaron," said the man, kneeling over him. "I'm with this sector's human cult. We patrol the neighborhoods these days to keep them safe. What's you name?"

"I'm Baron …" but quickly the man's face changed to one more subdued and compliant, "… I'm Winston Palmer."

"Well, Winston Palmer. I'm very glad to meet you," said Aaron.

"Hey, Aaron. He's a III. We can't let a III into the cult. You know the rules," said another man in the group behind Aaron.

Aaron pulled back the baron's shirt collar, revealing the III burned into his neck. There was no ambiguity – it was clearly a Roman numeral III.

"I don't know, boys," said Aaron, looking into the eyes of the baron. "I think there's something wrong with that way of thinking. I think we should start including anybody into our group who's a decent person. And this one … well … I just think he's got potential."

*****

O'MALLEY'S

PART I

O'Malley's Parts Store had been around for decades. In fact, in many cities and even many small towns, it was an institution. Parents, grandparents, and even great grandparents had gone to O'Malley's to get the parts they needed. It always seemed that they had the parts available and always at the right price.

Yet, as with many things, O'Malley's success came at a price. Over time, the legislators had gotten involved to regulate and restrict what could and could not be sold through the store. Some parts were outlawed completely because they were too sophisticated or performed too well. There were limited ranges that became acceptable, and when parts exceeded those thresholds, problems ensued.

Such was the case of a young girl named Rose. It had been nearly fifty years since that incident had occurred, and it was the only one on record after over eighty years of O'Malley's selling parts to the public. As the news reported it, Rose was riding her bike to school with some friends. One of her friends, Jerome, had recently gotten a part from O'Malley's. It was supposed to replace one that had worn out, and his father had purchased it only days earlier for him.

However, Jerome was known for his sometimes cruel and taunting ways, and one morning he challenged all of his friends to race him on his bicycle to school. Unfortunately, they had to cross some railroad tracks along the way, and as they approached the crossing, Jerome sped -off in front. His bike was going ultra-fast – so fast, that none of his friends could keep up.

In the distance behind them, they heard the sound of a train horn, blasting out its warnings. However, Jerome paid no attention and sprinted onward, coming up to the sharp turn in the road that led up to the crossing.

"Don't do it!" cried Rose, watching everything unfold and peddling as fast as she could to catch up.

But Jerome ignored her and zoomed over the tracks. Not wanting to be left behind or lose the race, his friends followed close behind. Each one zipped over the tracks just before the train sounded another, last, frantic blast.

It was Rose who was the last to cross – but she didn't make it.

Hearings were held to assess what had happened, and the Congressional committee concluded that because of Jerome's special parts, Rose was killed. They determined that O'Malley's was guilty of reckless and callous disregard for life when it sold the parts to Jerome's father. And, as a result, O'Malley's was almost put out of business.

In the settlement with Rose's parents and those of the other friends traumatized by the accident, O'Malley's agreed never to sell *special* parts to anyone ever again.

Yet, that wasn't enough. A three-term senator from New York got involved once he saw the story in the news. Within days, he was seen in front of cameras on the west-side steps of the Capitol building, holding up a paper that had the splashy headline at the top: "*Girl killed by super-bionics.*"

"See here!" shouted Horatio Salzman, a well-known self-promoter who never missed an opportunity to advance himself and his agenda. "We have a situation where greedy, business owners are selling products to innocent consumers – ones that are killing our children. This young girl, Rose, was only riding her bicycle to school and someone with super-bionic leg parts forced her to veer into the path of an oncoming train! She was horribly killed, and her family is decimated. It's a true tragedy, and one that should have been prevented," said Salzman, puffing out his chest. "How many other young girls like Rose have been killed because of this? How many more will die if we don't do something about it now? So, as a result of this terrible incident, I am calling for hearings in Congress to look at how wide-spread a problem this is. We will stop these capitalistic vultures from preying upon our children. They cannot profit from selling us things that end up killing our family members. We are a just and moral society, and this is something we cannot and will not stand for!"

The chief executives from O'Malley's were called before more Congressional committees to testify. However, the additional hearings called for by Senator

Salzman only made it clearer that O'Malley's had done nothing wrong. And, with their agenda at risk, the networks pulled the story and the airtime. The hearings concluded without any news or fanfare. However, Senator Salzman still declared that, "my committee has uncovered a vast conspiracy among body parts makers and I vow to put a stop to their practices once and for all!"

"O'Malley's sold replacement, bionic legs to Jerome's father," began the Salzman, chairman of the Congressional committee overseeing the situation, "but those legs enabled his son to race ahead of his friends, giving him an unfair advantage and leading all of them into a death chase. Those legs were, as they say in the industry, "juiced" to outperform most others on the market. While legal, they were what caused this terrible accident. So, in conclusion, O'Malley's shall henceforth only sell those human body parts – and only replacement parts – that meet strict government guidelines for speed, strength, durability, and such other specifications as this body deems acceptable for general, public use."

As a result, laws were passed, agencies were setup, and investigators hired -- all so that human beings would get measurably weaker, slower, and dumber than they had been in millennia. And that's exactly what happened.

*****

PART II

Jack Perkins pulled on the door and walked inside. He'd been in the store before but only to purchase spare body parts for his mother-in-law. It wasn't anything critical; his wife had just asked that he pick up a new auditory control valve for her left ear. The bionic one she had was malfunctioning and was out of warranty.

There were aisles of bionic body parts in the store. They were divided by row – arms, fingers, wrists and shoulder joints were in Aisle 1; legs, knees, hips, ankles, and feet with toes were in Aisle 2; bionics related to the head, including visual, auditory, and other non-brain parts were in Aisle 3, and the abdominal-related parts were in the remaining aisles four through six. All the cranial parts were stored behind the counter and were strictly controlled – somewhat like prescription drugs at a pharmacy.

"Hi," said Jack, approaching the counter.

"What do you need?" asked the employee, with a dull, unenthusiastic voice. He was not much older than Jack's daughter, who was turning nineteen in a few months.

Dark-haired and needing a trim, the young man didn't try to muster a smile. His name badge read: *O'Malley's* at the top with the letters *J-O-E* just below it. Wearing a red vest, care of his employer, and a mismatched green-and-orange plaid shirt with blue jeans, Joe looked like he was already willing to call it a day; however, it was only eleven o'clock in the morning.

"Yeah, I'm looking for a pair of humerus replacements, 18-35mm in a size 22cm. Do you have that in stock?" asked Jack, leaning across the counter and scanning the shelves behind the clerk for his part number.

The clerk punched the information into his computer and waited for the data to pop onto his screen. "Let's see. That would be a UA 18-35/22c model. Let me see if we have that." His eyes darted left to right as he read his inventory numbers. Then, he shook his head. "I'm afraid I don't have that one in stock. I'm sorry. But I can order it for you. It will be here in about three weeks."

Jack thought for a moment, moving his right arm and then his left. He grimaced as he made the motions, as the pain sensors misfired, sending error messages into this cerebral cortex. "I'm not sure I can wait that long," said Jack. Is there any way to get it sooner?"

"No, I'm afraid I'm backordered on that part. But we can have it made and shipped directly to your doorstep."

"How much is it?"

"Let me see," said the clerk, going back to his monitor. "That would be $32,870, plus shipping."

"For both?" asked Jack.

"No, that's for each one," said the clerk, finally looking up at him.

"For *each*?"

"Yeah. But that's before the federal subsidy, of course."

"How much is it after that?" asked Jack.

"Well, since everyone is covered, you'd get a 95 percent discount on that, so it would be …" The clerk punched in some more figures and stepped back, waiting for the result. "After the discount, it would be $1,643.50."

"Wow, that's still a lot."

"Do you have the premium plan?"

"No, unfortunately, I don't. Only the politicians and special people get that," said Jack.

"Yeah, that's true," answered the clerk.

"Well, I don't think I have a choice. Go ahead and order them, then," said Jack, shaking his head.

Jack left the store disheartened. Replacing his upper arms was going to cost him a month's wage. He wasn't happy, and he knew his wife wouldn't be either.

"*Pssst!*" came a sound just as Jack rounded the corner of the store to find his pod.

Jack turned around. Before him was an ill-dressed, middle-aged man with yellowed, original teeth. His hair was messed, and his coat at least two sizes too big for him. He motioned with one arm toward a large, white van-pod that was parked just behind the store.

"What is it?" asked Jack.

"I got what you're looking for," said the man, grinning with what teeth he had left.

"And what would that be?"

"I've got a pretty full supply of UA parts," he answered. "Did you say you needed an UA 18-35/22c?"

"Yeah."

"Well, I've got two right here." The man went to his truck and pulled out two long, brown boxes. On one end was a holographic chip that displayed the blue numbers when the man moved his finger over it. "Isn't this it?"

"Yeah, but …"

"But what? Do you need a couple of these or not?"

"I do, but what's the catch?"

The man smiled again. "It's black market. It doesn't have all the limiter crap on it the government requires. It will work like the old ones used to. You know, back in the day when things actually worked like they were supposed to."

"But those are illegal. Those are *juiced* models, aren't they?"

"Yeah," said the man, "they're *juiced*, but they will work like they're supposed to work – not like those *woosified* versions we get now."

Jack thought for a minute but then shook his head. "No, I'd better not. I'll get arrested."

"No, you won't! Nobody will know. And my prices are better than what you'll get inside there. There's no government tax on it."

"Thanks, but I'll just wait."

"Okay, suit yourself," said the man, turning and walking back to his van-pod.

The replacements from O'Malley's came to Jack's doorstep as promised within the three weeks, and he couldn't wait to remove his old ones and insert the new upper-arm inserts. It required his wife's help, but together they managed to unscrew the malfunctioning units and insert the new ones. The old ones were placed in the recycling bin as required by law.

Yet, almost from the moment they were in place, Jack felt the difference. He didn't have the arm strength he had enjoyed with the old versions. These units came under the new laws imposed by Congress restricting the strength of the prosthetics. However, over time, he adjusted to the new reality and changed his routines so he didn't have to lift anything as heavy as he had before. It wasn't hard. There were devices all around that were made to take the hard work out of everyday life. He only needed to grab one and use it to get something where he needed it. In the end, life had not changed much – until it did.

*****

PART III

It was a clear, crisp, fall day, and Jack landed his commuter pod on the outside aeropad of the apartment complex. The aeropad quickly retracted into a massive wall with hundreds of other commuter pods, storing his light-silver, clear-domed model in with those of black, white, gray, smoke, ash, metallic, slate, platinum, and other wild and assorted varieties of the same. After locking his pod bay, Jack took the zip-tube up to the 123rd floor where his apartment overlooked the Hudson River.

"Hi honey," said Jack, strolling past the study where his wife was still working. He walked in and gave her a kiss on the cheek before proceeding across the family room toward the bar to make himself his standard, double-olive, dry martini.

"How did it go today?" she asked, her voice echoing off the hallway walls.

"Same-ole, same-ole," he answered, dropping two cubes into the v-shaped glass. "Say, where is Marcy? How were her classes at the big U on campus?"

"I think they were fine. She didn't say much about them today. She went right to her room, telling me she had to study for a test tomorrow."

Jack took a sip of his drink and then carried it upstairs to where his daughter was studying.

Marcy was nearly nineteen, and it was her second year at NYU. She was a model student and had a bright future. With a grade point of 3.9 out of a possible 4.0, she was doing well as a pre-med student, hoping to go to a prominent medical school and become a thoracic bionic engineer.

Knocking on her door, Jack pushed it open slightly. "How are you?" he asked, smiling at his beloved and only child.

"Good, Dad. What's up?"

Marcy was sitting at her desk reviewing information on one monitor while examining the 3-D hologram projected to her right side showing the complex and intricate interrelationships between the artificial lung mechanisms and the other pulmonary functions carried out by the mechanical heart. Both had to work symbiotically to provide synthetic blood to the still-largely-human organ called the brain.

"Wow! That looks complicated," said her father.

"Yeah, I'm supposed to know all this for our exam tomorrow," said Marcy, her auburn hair cascading down in curls to her shoulders.

"Do you have time for ice cream?"

"Ice cream?"

"Yeah, it's been a while since you and I went to get some mint chocolate chip. If you don't, that's okay," said Jack.

Marcy looked at him with a smile. "Yeah, I've got this down pretty well."

"It will only take a few minutes. I promise."

Jack and Marcy went down to the aeroport and fetched his commuter pod. The ice cream store was only two platforms over from their unit, and it thrived because people still liked to go out once in a while. Sure, they could generate their own ice cream in their apartments with their food replicators, but it wasn't the same.

Jack spoke his twelve-digit code into the voice-command box, and they watched as the pod shelf opened, extended out, and began lowering their pod to where they were standing. However, just as it began dropping the pod to the deck, they heard a grinding noise and their pod began vibrating violently on the shelf.

"What's going on, Dad?" asked Marcy, startled by what was happening.

"I don't know," said Jack. "It's never done this before."

Suddenly, the shelf broke loose from its extension brace and the pod fell, crashing to the ground and sending parts and pieces flying everywhere.

The impact sent Jack flying across the floor, leaving him stunned and confused. "Marcy?" he asked, confused and trying to get to his feet. "Marcy? Are you all right?"

Twenty feet away, he saw his daughter trapped beneath the fuselage of his pod. She struggled to get free. "I'm right here, Dad," she said, her voice weak and thin.

Jack ran to her and kneeled down. The body of the commuter pod had crushed her upper leg, near where the femoral artery lay.

"My god!" cried Jack. "I have to get you to the hospital, honey."

"What's wrong?"

Jack didn't want to tell her, but the artery had been severed and her synthetic blood was pouring across the floor of the aeroport.

"Let me just get this off you and maybe I can stop the bleeding," said Jack, bending over and grabbing the piece with his hands.

The fuselage was heavy but not so heavy that it couldn't normally be lifted. However, when Jack tried to raise it, it wouldn't move. He tried again and again, but it was too heavy for him. "No!" he shouted. "I can do this! I have to do this!" Yet, the more he tried, the weaker he became.

"Daddy?"

"Yes, dear," said Jack, tears welling up in his eyes as he watched helplessly. The life force was ebbing away from his daughter, and there was nothing he could do about it.

"I feel tired and sleepy," she said, looking into his eyes. "I ..."

"Don't talk, honey. Save your strength. I'll call for help."

However, help didn't come for more than twenty minutes. By that time, Marcy had slipped into a coma – one from which she never recovered.

*****

PART IV

The funeral was heart-wrenching. Dressed in black, Jack and his wife couldn't move from their spot along the grassy plot where their daughter's remains were buried. It was a ceremonial service rather than one where Marcy would be interred forever. There was little ground left for cemeteries, so services were held on the beautiful grounds, but the remains were then moved to a central repository where they were cremated, labeled and slid into a six-by-six-by-eight-inch slot in a massive wall. Above the name was a locator chip which would light-up and beep to alert the caretaker where to look if and when a loved-one was being searched by family members or friends. There were tens of thousands of slots along the wall – each one could only be found by entering into the computer the person's name and, of course, his or her crypt ID number.

Days were followed by weeks and then months, yet Jack's heart never really beat again. It had been broken, and it seemed that nothing could fix it.

"Jack," said his therapist, "how are you doing? It seems like you're still hanging onto the loss of your daughter instead of letting go. We've talked about things you need to do to go on with your life, but you seem to resist doing any of them."

"I just can't go on. I just don't see the point," said Jack, his head down and his hands fidgeting nervously between his knees.

"What about your wife? Don't you owe it to her to get back to normalcy? It's been, what, six months now."

"Yeah, only six months. It was like yesterday. Yesterday! That's when I had my little girl – that's when she was still with us. So vibrant, so alive. All of that was taken from me. It vanished in a heart-beat." Jack snapped his fingers. "Just like that – over."

"I know," said the therapist, "but you must go on with your life. Marcy would have wanted that. She wouldn't have wanted you to waste away to nothing because of what happened to her. She would have wanted you to make something of yourself. Turn this incident into something meaningful, Jack.

Do something constructive as a result of this. Do something that will make you feel like you're doing something positive."

Jack looked up at the psychologist, but now he had a very strange look on his face. It was one of realization, as though he finally understood how to make his life meaningful.

"You're right, you know," he answered, blinking stiffly. "I need to do something positive and constructive. Marcy was always doing things like that – doing things that helped others or helped the cause in a way that was bigger than she was."

The therapist sat back with a mild grin. "Good," he said. "I think we're finally making some progress, Jack. So, why don't you think about what things you might be able to do to realize those goals. Create a new purpose for your life now." The psychologist leaned over to view the calendar on his monitor. "It looks like I don't have an opening available for another month. But maybe that's good, Jack. It will give you time to think through what you want to do with your life – how you want to approach this new cause."

"You're right. It may take a few weeks. Thanks, doc. I'll see you in a month."

*****

PART V

Jack walked through security and walked the flights of stairs to the third floor. The floors were hard, cold marble, but the doors and all the elaborate wood molding were rich in detail and history. There had been many famous people who had walked these hallways over the centuries – some who had contributed greatly to the nation's rise to greatness, and others who had offered nothing but empty promises that had caused only greater pain and suffering for those affected by them.

"Can I help you?" asked the guard sitting at the central desk. He was monitoring all the video cameras on his monitor, watching the comings and goings of visitors on his floor.

"I'm looking for ..." began Jack, before looking down at a piece of paper he had in his hand. "... Oh, never mind. I think I know where I'm going. Thanks."

Jack headed off down the main hall where the senior senators' offices were, each with an American flag out in front as well as their state flag. Each of the offices and the adjoining support offices were so large that it took him a several minutes to find the one that had the words *Senator Horatio Salzman* on a brass plate on the right side of the double doors. Below the name were simply the words: *New York*.

Jack opened the door and walked in, immediately greeted by the office administrator. "Do you have an appointment?" she asked with a snippy tone.

"Yes, actually, I do. I'm Jack Perkins. I had a ten-thirty with the senator?"

"Perkins ... Perkins ... Oh, yes. I forgot he squeezed you in just before he was leaving for his daily roundtable on CNFN at noon. Well, if you'll have a seat, I'll let the senator know you're here."

The administrator was young and beautiful but could have cared less about anything or anyone else but herself. With red hair dropping to her shoulders and a Vogue-esque face and body, she seemed to be more than just someone there to replace the toner in the copy machine. Quickly, she disappeared through the double doors into the inner sanctum of the senator's offices. However, she was inside less than twenty seconds before she returned and resumed her position at her desk watching something on her monitor.

The minutes passed and continued to tick on. Jack finally touched his PCD, or personal communication device, to see what time it was. At eleven fifteen, he bit his lip and swore he would remain composed and patient. More minutes passed. Now it was eleven forty-five. This time, he got up and went to the administrator's desk, counting to ten to calm himself before he asked, "Is the senator still in his office? Is he still going to see me?"

The administrator huffed and turned away from her screen. "Just a minute," she said curtly. She pushed a button on the screen and asked, "Senator? Will you be visiting with …" she stopped abruptly, not remembering his name.

"Jack … Jack Perkins."

"Oh, yeah. Jack Perkins. Will you be seeing him today?" She listened intently and then hung up the phone.

"Well?" asked Jack, waiting.

"I'm sorry. The senator won't have time today. He said to come back in a few months. His schedule may free up then."

"A few months?"

"Yeah. That's what he said," said the administrator, looking back at her monitor and not offering any chance to reschedule.

Just then, the door to the senator's office opened, and the senator walked out. It looked like he had just woken up from a nap, as his eyes were puffy and his necktie pulled down low on his shirt. He didn't bother to look at Jack, who was sitting prominently in the first visitor's chair in the waiting area.

"Sara, I'll be at the CNFN airing at noon. Then, I'm taking the rest of the day off."

"Yes, sir," she answered, not lifting a finger.

Jack jumped up just before the senator passed him. "Excuse me, senator," he began, "but I only need a moment of your time."

Salzman started to push Jack aside as he uttered, "I'm sorry. I don't have time for this bullsh*t today. You'll have to come again some other time."

"Excuse me?" said Jack.

Salzman stopped and put his hand on Jack's shoulder, continuing to shove him away. "I said, I don't have time for you. Now get out of my way!"

Jack grabbed Salzman's arm, ripping it off his shoulder.

"Don't you touch me!" shouted Salzman. "I'm a U.S. Senator! I'll have you arrested for touching me!"

"But you put your hand on me first," Jack answered, with determination in his eyes.

"Then what do you want? Make it fast. I don't have all day to waste it with you," the senator answered, haughtily.

"Well," said Jack. "I had a daughter – much like Rose, whom you trotted out to make your case for more laws to pass with your name on them."

"Rose? Rose who?" asked the senator, with a blank face.

"Exactly," said Jack. "You don't even remember the little girl who was killed in the train accident a few years ago – the one that made headlines and that you used to grab fame on the Hill here. That's too long ago to do you any good now, isn't it?"

"Rose?" Salzman asked again.

"The girl who was killed because of someone else's bionic legs?" asked the administrative assistant, sitting at her desk.

"Oh, good. At least someone here remembers her," Jack answered. "Anyway, my little girl was named Marcy. She was my love, my life, my everything. But you know what? I wasn't able to save her. Do you know why?"

Salzman just shrugged.

"Because I didn't have the strength to save her, that's why. She died, because you … you passed your stupid laws governing the strength of body parts so now they aren't even as strong as natural, human ones. We're all weak now. People can hardly function in society anymore because the bionic parts are weak, slow, break-often, and fail when their needed most. I needed mine – and it failed me – because of *you*."

"I don't know what you're talking about," said Salzman, pushing Jack back. "You're insane. Sara, call security on this man. He's not right!"

Sara began calling for security as Jack walked toward the senator and, taking both of his hands, put them around his neck.

"What are you doing!" shouted the senator, turning red in the face.

"What does it look like I'm doing?" asked Jack with determination.

However, it was then the senator's face relaxed, and he laughed. "You don't scare me," he said insolently. "I wrote the laws on all this stuff. I know you don't have enough strength in your hands to strangle me. The law doesn't permit that in bionic hands or forearms. So, the best you can do is make me strain my voice, as I'm doing now. I'll have you arrested, and you'll spend the rest of your life behind bars."

Jack looked at the senator with anger and frustration.

"So, you see … Jack, is it?" squealed the senator, not waiting for an answer. "Well, Jack, you'll be eating gruel while I'll be dining and drinking well up here on Capitol Hill. I'm somebody, Jack. You're nothing. I can't say I'm sorry about your little girl either. It doesn't help my cause, I'm afraid. If her death had come a year sooner, I might have been able to use it. But now, that's old news – won't help me, so it won't help you. Do you get it now?"

Jack's anger spread throughout his body, and his fingers closed around the senator's neck. For an instant, he felt the grip of his hands stop, as if he were grasping an iron bar that wasn't yielding to him.

"What's wrong strong man? Can't do what you want to do? You're right! You won't be able to," said Salzman with a smile on his face.

Suddenly, Jack's fingers collapsed around the senator's neck, crushing his esophagus and vertebrae. The crack was clear and stunned the administrative assistant, making her run from her desk and into the hallway.

The senator's eyes were opened as wide as they could, as the shock rapidly spread through his body. "But … but … you can't …" he muttered, gasping for air, "… you're not supposed to be able to …"

"Oh, I guess I forgot to tell you something," said Jack. "Did you know there's an active and thriving black market for body parts now-a-days? My new hands are what I think they refer to as a bit *juiced,* if you know what I mean. I guess they were right about that. I guess this time I got my money's worth, huh?"

*****

AUTHOR

Gage Axtin primarily writes science fiction stories. Although most of his writings are short stories, he has published a few longer novels. Axtin is a pseudonym used by the writer. He lives with his family in Chicago.

BLUE M PUBLISHING

For this and other stories, please see the Blue M Publishing website at: www.blueMpublishing.com

CROSSED CIRCUITS II

Volume II of the author's anthology of science fiction short stories is expected later in 2018.

www.ingramcontent.com/pod-product-compliance
Lightning Source LLC
Chambersburg PA
CBHW051245260626
47162CB00002B/623